ROCK BOTTOM

ROCK HARDER BOOK ONE

KAT MIZERA

1

Z*eke*

"Minneapolis—give it up for Onyx Knight!"

The crowd roared, and I threw my guitar strap over my shoulder as I walked out on stage. Tommy was already at his drum set, thumping away on the bass drum to get the adrenaline going.

It was another sold-out crowd tonight, despite the winter storm that was headed this way, and I raised my hands over my head to get the audience clapping in time to Tommy's beat.

"Where the fuck is Carter?" Kellan, my rhythm guitarist, growled in my ear.

I glanced at him questioningly before swinging my gaze toward the wings.

No sign of our wayward bass player, and I gritted my teeth in annoyance. He'd given the term "sex, drugs, and rock and roll" new meaning the last few years, but this kind of shit was getting old. I caught my singer's eye since he was still in the wings, motioning toward where Carter should have been standing by now. Kingston always came out last, so he tended to dawdle, letting the crowd get worked up in anticipation, but he instantly understood that Carter was missing.

He whirled, disappearing from view, and I struck a chord on my guitar.

"How's everybody doin' tonight?" I asked, talking into my stand mic. "Are you ready to party with us?"

The crowd yelled and cheered, and I spotted a woman in the second row lifting her shirt for me. I winked, tossing a pick in her direction before glancing over at the side of the stage again. Just as I was about to panic, I caught sight of Carter. He was zipping up his pants, two blonds still hanging onto him for dear life as he dragged them toward the stage. Kingston said something to him that made him laugh, and he gently handed the two girls off to one of our roadies.

He was such a fucking Romeo, blowing them kisses as he grabbed his bass.

Then he bounded onto the stage like nothing had happened.

"What's up, you Minnesota motherfuckers?" he yelled into his mic.

I caught a glimpse of Kingston rolling his eyes before Tommy counted us off.

"1-2-3-4!"

We launched into the opening licks of one of our bigger hits, "Shotgun Wedding," just as Kingston came running out, the tails of his faux tuxedo coat trailing behind him.

"It's cold outside, ladies," he crooned. "But it's going to get fucking hot in here—who's ready for the Knight?" He danced across the stage as a hot pink bra landed at his feet. Without missing a beat, Kingston scooped it up, wrapped it around his neck and started to sing.

I grinned, moving toward the edge of the stage.

Fucking Carter had almost given me a heart attack.

It was a good thing I loved the unreliable little fuck like a brother.

We'd been friends a long time, going back to high school. We'd had another band back then, and then we'd met Kingston Knight. He was tall, blond, and charismatic, and we hadn't cared if he could sing or not. Then he opened his mouth, magic happened, and Onyx Knight was born. By the time we added Kellan and Tommy, record companies were already sniffing around, and our first album went gold. Five multi-platinum albums later, we were superstars, touring the world and selling out venues five nights a week.

We were rich, successful, and had it all.

At least it felt that way most of the time.

Nights when Carter got so fucked up we had to use a recorded track because he couldn't be trusted to play was a different story.

Luckily, that wasn't tonight.

Despite how late he'd been, he was on point, flirting with girls in the front row, dancing around the stage, and putting on the show people were here to see.

I was still planning to kick his ass later.

"What the hell were you thinking?" I asked him once our third encore was over and we were in our dressing room.

He shrugged, his eyes twinkling as he took a pull from a bottle of Sam Adams. "What can I say? Two beautiful ladies felt the need to suck me off. Could I say no?"

"You could have told them to wait until after," Kingston muttered, shaking his head.

"Come on, all's well that ends well. I got there, didn't I?" He finished his beer and reached for another.

Jesus. We all drank, but Carter practically mainlined the stuff.

"Boys." Our tour manager, Ross Laken, came into the room. "There's a journalist here to interview you. Some college kid named Presley something or other."

"Presley?" Tommy asked, laughing. "Like Elvis?"

Ross shrugged. "Dunno. I just know she's here. Aurora didn't set it up, so I don't think she's with anyone big. Anyone feel like talking to her?"

We all looked at each other.

"Nah." I stood up and yawned. "I'm headed to that resort for the next two days. I'll see you guys in Chicago."

"I'm going back to the hotel," Kingston said, getting up.

"Yeah, not tonight." Kellan waved a hand. "Didi's waiting."

"She cute?" Tommy asked, wiggling his eyebrows.

Ross made a face. "She's okay. One of those fresh-faced girl-next-door types. No makeup, glasses, you know what I mean?"

"Pass." Tommy grabbed his duffel bag. "I'm out."

Carter burped, laughed, and looked around. "You guys are such fucking party poopers."

"You party enough for all of us," Kingston told him. "Next time you're late, you're getting fined."

Carter rolled his eyes. "Yeah, man. Whatever."

I grabbed my bag and walked toward the exit with Ross on my heels.

"Your rental is right outside by the tour bus," he said, handing me a set of keys. "You can drive it to Chicago when you're done with your mini-vacation, and one of the crew will return it for you."

"Thanks." I nodded.

"Your suitcase is in the back too."

"Perfect. You're the best." I headed out, anxious to be on my way.

I was just about to turn down the hallway that would lead to the exit when I saw her. She was tall, with long dark hair and oversized glasses. She looked sad, her eyes widening as she recognized me.

No doubt this was the journalist.

She took a step toward me, but I quickly turned away, picking up speed to avoid contact. I caught a glimpse of her face—filled with disappointment —just before I turned, and a flicker of guilt shot through me.

Dammit.

I felt bad, but I didn't have time for this tonight.

I wasn't in a great mood and exhausted to boot. The last thing I needed was some inexperienced wanna-be journalist asking me how old I was when I'd first started playing guitar. Some days I had the patience for it; this wasn't one of them.

I'd booked two nights at a resort just outside of Minneapolis and was looking forward to having forty-eight hours of downtime. A massage, good food, maybe even a pretty lady to keep me company. Mostly I wanted peace and quiet, though. Not that I didn't love my job. I loved rock and roll, and being the lead guitarist for one of the biggest bands in the world was amazing. The music, shows, fans, interviews, travel, almost all of it. Almost.

This tour had been brutal.

Carter, Kellen, and Tommy had outvoted Kingston and me on using the jet. They thought it would feel more authentic if we got back to our roots and traveled by bus. So I slept on a fucking bunk on a bus a lot of nights, which was a hassle for a big guy like me. Even a bus as expensive as ours had limits, and a man who was six-five and two hundred and fifty pounds was one of those limits.

I'd insisted we sleep at a hotel at least twice a week, but it wasn't enough for my body. It took a lot to stay in touring shape, and sleep was part of that. Of course, fucking Carter never slept. His drug use had ramped up in the last year, and while it hadn't yet impacted his playing, I could see the changes in him. His skin was pale and drawn, he'd lost a lot of weight, and he was always late. Whether it was booze, women, or the drugs, unless someone escorted him, he wasn't on time for anything.

Luckily, it wasn't my job to babysit him.

I got into the waiting SUV, typed the address into the GPS, and put it in gear. I pulled out of the lot and headed for the interstate.

A feeling of peace washed over me the moment the arena was out of sight.

My phone rang and I glanced down, shaking my head.

Mom.

She knew this was the time of night I was getting off stage and she always wanted to hear how it went. We didn't talk every night, and it had been a few days, so I hit the button to accept the call.

"Hey, Ma."

"Hi, honey. How was it?"

"Sold out. Loud. You know how it is."

"What was your final encore?"

I chuckled. "Guess."

"Tempo in Reno?"

"Nope."

"Judgement Call?"

"That was second to last."

"Break Your Promise." She sounded disappointed.

"It's only our biggest hit," I said, laughing.

"Yeah, but I'm bored with that one."

"Luckily, you aren't our target audience."

"Whatever."

"So what's up? How's Grandma?" My father's mother lived with my parents now that she was in her seventies. I'd had a cute little casita built for her on my parents' property and it seemed to be working out for everyone.

"Always in my business," Mom muttered. "But fine."

"Hello, pot. Have you met the kettle?"

"You hush!" She laughed.

"Just sayin'."

"You always take her side," she complained.

"Only when you're wrong."

"So where are you headed?"

"Me, personally? A resort for two nights. The band is heading for Chicago."

"Oh, you're taking a little mental health break?"

"Yeah. Plus, I need to sleep on a real bed. My back is killing me. This leg of the tour is over in May. So there's about six weeks left. Then I'm putting my foot down for Europe."

"Will you come home at all before you head over there?"

"I think there's two weeks between when this leg ends and when we pick up over there. I have some shit to take care of at home anyway."

"Is Nobody's Fool going with you?" My mother was apparently a big fan of our opening act.

"Not to Europe, no. But we may tour with them again in the fall. You can see your buddy, Tyler." Tyler Thompson was their bass player, and he and my mother had become pals. They even followed each other on social media, which cracked me up.

"Well, it'll be good to have you around, even if it's just for a week or two."

"I miss you too, Ma."

"Call me more often, would you?"

"Promise."

"Love you, Zeke."

"Love you too." I disconnected and stared out at the road in front of me.

A storm was coming and it was starting to snow, so I needed to get there already. If I was lucky, the kitchen would still be open.

2

———————

P *resley*

I SHIFTED MY BEAT-UP, ten-year-old Honda into gear and headed for work.

The last twenty-four hours had been frustrating, difficult, and unfair.

Life, I'd begun to realize, was increasingly unfair.

Whether it was my Aunt Meg's multiple sclerosis diagnosis, the leak in the basement of our house, the hours at my job getting cut, or not getting the Onyx Knight interview, I seemed to be on a downward spiral of bad luck. On top of that, I was running late to work because of the weather, and my boss had already warned me I'd been late too many times this winter.

And frankly, I'd run out of excuses.

He didn't care that the tires on my Honda weren't in any condition for snow. Or that Aunt Meg had fallen three times in the last month. Or that I was going to fail my senior project because I hadn't been able to procure the interview I needed to write my final article. Nope. All Mr. Hopkins cared about was me showing up on time and making sure the patrons of his exclusive resort were happy.

I already worked the crappiest shifts because of school. Monday and Tuesday nights, which were typically dead. The occasional Friday day shift, also dead. Once in a blue moon, if someone called out, I got to work a weekend and make real money. Beyond that, I was the new girl, and probably the least attractive compared to the others, so I took what I could get. To be fair, even a Monday night at the resort was better than eight hours at McDonald's, but I could have been making so much more with a few decent shifts.

I pulled into the parking lot a minute before my shift started and ran as fast as I could into the building. I practically skidded into the ladies' locker room, where I secured my things, sliding my feet into the low-heeled pumps we had to wear and stuffing my winter coat into my locker as quickly as possible. I clocked in at seven-oh-one and walked into the bar. Normally, I was a waitress, but on nights like tonight, where the tables were empty and only a handful of patrons lingered, I got to tend bar.

Mr. Hopkins wagged a finger at me as I waved. "I'm watching you, Lee!" For some reason, everyone here had shortened Presley to Lee, and now it had stuck.

I waved at him with a smile. "I know, Mr. H!"

"By the way." He came up behind me. "There's a storm coming. I don't know that you'll be able to drive home in it once your shift is over."

I grimaced. I'd known that was a possibility, but I couldn't miss work. Aside from already being on thin ice, Aunt Meg and I needed the money. "I'll be okay," I told him.

"We're supposed to get a couple of feet. If that happens, you can sleep in the lounge."

"Thank you." I nodded, surprised. There was a rule that forbade us from sleeping in the employee lounge, but I figured the blizzard headed our way was an exception. Otherwise, there wouldn't be anyone to take care of the guests that were here, regardless of the weather.

Humming to myself, I started wiping down the bar. The day shift hadn't done a great job at it, which was typical. Everyone hated working days, and tended to escape the moment they could get away. I didn't mind, though. It kept me busy and that kept Mr. Hopkins off my back. He wasn't bad for a boss, but he seemed to watch me like a hawk.

I was lost in what I was doing, cutting up lime and lemon wedges, when someone cleared their throat. My head snapped up in surprise and I blinked at the guy leaning on the bar.

"Can I get a Guinness on tap, please?" he asked.

I stared for another moment, mesmerized.

He was huge.

Handsome.

Familiar?

Why did he look familiar?

I couldn't put my finger on it, so I quickly nodded and poured him the beer. I put it in front of him on a coaster, with a bowl of pretzels. "Do you want to put it on your room account or start a tab?" I asked.

"Room 1505."

I smiled, nodded, and put the information into the computer.

Why did he look familiar?

I turned back, trying not to stare.

"Would you like a menu?" I asked him.

"Yeah. Thanks."

I handed him one and started humming again, singing under my breath as I went back to cutting lemon wedges.

"Wicked ex," he said.

"Excuse me?" I looked up in confusion.

"The song you were humming. It was 'Wicked X,' right?"

My cheeks suddenly felt a little warm. I hadn't even realized that was the song I'd been humming. "Yeah. I'm a big Nobody's Fool fan."

"It's a good song." He took a pull from his beer.

"One of my favorites. That's a great album. I listen to it all the time."

"You're not alone. They're popular with the fans." He paused. "We've enjoyed having them on tour with us."

I froze.

Oh shit.

That was why he looked familiar.

He was one of the guys in Onyx Knight.

The guitar player who'd blown me off last night.

Now it all made sense.

He obviously didn't recognize me, but that made sense since I'd purposely dressed down last night, not wanting to look like a groupie. I hadn't been wearing makeup or my contact lenses, my hair had been in a ponytail, and I'd been in leggings, an oversized sweater, and boots. That had obviously been a tactical error on my part, but there wasn't anything I could do about it now. I was too embarrassed to remind him I'd been the journalist he'd blown off, and anyway, I didn't want to do anything that might piss him off because I needed a good tip since he would potentially be my only customer tonight.

"How can anyone not enjoy their music?" I asked after a moment. "Lexi's voice is amazing."

He smiled. "It is."

"So what's touring like?" I asked, opting to steer the conversation in another direction. Maybe, if I was careful, I could get enough insight into touring to write the first article of the new online rock magazine I'd created without doing an official interview.

"Exhausting," he said, taking a sip of his beer. "Hours and hours of doing nothing, only to spend an hour on stage."

"But isn't it great seeing so many people at the shows, no matter what time of year or what the weather's like? That has to be a rush."

"It is." He nodded absently. "I'm incredibly lucky and grateful for what I have. But it's been eight years and I'm tired. We tour back-to-back, go into the studio to record, and then go right back on the road. Sometimes it's a hassle."

"How come?" I asked curiously. "Seems to me you're living the dream."

He seemed thoughtful for a minute. "It's complicated. The band is going through... I don't know what to call it. Growing pains? We're at a point of success where we essentially have it all, you know? But now we all have different ideas of what that means."

"Please don't tell me someone wants to do a country album or something!"

He chuckled, and I realized I was enjoying the raspy timber of his voice. "Not hardly, no. We're on the same page with music. Just other shit, like how long to extend the tour, when we're going to record the next album, how to travel from city to city. Some guys like the bus, the rest of us prefer to fly... I know. First world problems."

"Maybe. But I'm sure any business venture worth millions of dollars would have to be at least a little complicated."

He looked up, his eyes meeting mine, and as I stared at him, I realized he had two different colored eyes. One was a bright, aqua blue, and the other a deep, dark brown. It was as intriguing as it was gorgeous, and I wondered how I'd missed this when I'd been researching the members of Onyx Knight.

"Heterochromia," he said, not looking away.

"Excuse me?" I blinked in confusion.

"The condition of having two different colored eyes is called heterochromia. I figured that was the next question."

"Oh. No. I was just thinking how beautiful they are."

"Thank you." We stared at each other a beat longer than necessary.

God, he was hot.

I'd been so focused on getting the interview last night, I hadn't given his looks a second thought. I knew his full name was William Zerkesian—I'd done my homework on everyone in the band before attending the show—but he went by Big Z professionally. I'd wait to see if he told me his name, though. I couldn't imagine his friends and family calling him that.

"Is it genetic?" I asked, curiosity overriding manners.

"They don't know. There are studies that show it is, but it's so sporadic, especially complete heterochromia—which is what I have—so I guess the answer is maybe."

"Does it impact your vision?"

"No. Luckily, it's usually pretty benign when it's not caused by an injury or brought on by another disease. At least that's what the specialists have always told me, and my vision is twenty-twenty."

He'd obviously answered these questions many times before and I was suddenly embarrassed. "I'm sorry. It's none of my business. I was just curious."

"It's okay. I don't mind."

We shared another long, lingering look that made my insides flutter with excitement.

Stop it, I silently chided myself. *He's just making conversation with the bartender. He's not really interested in you as a woman.*

"Are you ready to order?" I asked him, suddenly uncomfortable with the way he looked at me, as if he could see right into my soul. As if he knew me.

"Sure." He closed his menu. "I want the sirloin, baked potato with everything, and the squash."

"How do you want your steak?"

"Is there any way but rare?" he asked, arching a brow.

I chuckled. "You would think not, but I get a lot of requests for a well-done steak."

He shuddered. "Jesus."

I laughed. "Anything else?"

"I'm going to want some of that blackberry cobbler after I'm done."

"You got it." I nodded, typing his order into the computer and grabbing some rolled silverware.

It would be quiet tonight as the storm rolled in, but we had quite a few guests already staying at the resort, so I was hopeful at least a few of them would come down to eat.

"Lee, I'm going to be up in the spa for a little while," Mr. Hopkins said to me. "If you need anything, page me."

"I'm good." I waved him on.

"You don't look like a Lee," Big Z said, cocking his head slightly.

"What should my name be?" I asked playfully. It was on the tip of my tongue to tell him Lee was just a nickname, but I decided against it. I really didn't want to say anything that would trigger his memory about last night. It occurred to me I had the perfect opportunity to ask him for an interview again, but what was the point? The whole band had ignored me after the show, and while there was a chance he would say yes this time, what if he didn't? I couldn't risk pissing him off. If he complained to my manager, I'd get fired, so I had to be careful.

"I don't know... something bright and cheerful. Like you." He squinted slightly as he thought. "Sunny," he said slowly. "Because your smile reminds me of sunshine, even on a dreary day like today."

I flushed, somehow delighted that was his impression of me. "And what should I call you?" I asked.

"My friends call me Zeke."

Zeke. It suited him.

"It's nice to meet you, Zeke."

3

Z*eke*

I DIDN'T USUALLY GET a hard-on for bartenders, but there was something about this one. She really did remind me of sunshine. Bright, sweet, and warm. I wasn't sure what it was about her, but she was easy to talk to. As if we'd known each other much longer than an hour or however long it had been since I got to the bar.

I'd worked out this morning. Then I'd had a great massage, followed by some time in the sauna and the jacuzzi. I'd showered, taken a nap, and then wandered down looking for food. With the storm that was coming in, I wasn't going anywhere, and I'd hoped it would be quiet when I came down to get something to eat. The last thing I'd expected was a hazel-eyed beauty behind the bar that was an odd mixture of flirty and innocent.

She wasn't my type, not at all, but I was enjoying talking to her. Either she hadn't recognized me right away or wasn't impressed by the fact that a rockstar was at her bar, but either way she hadn't acted any different once I'd mentioned being on tour with Nobody's Fool.

A couple of guests wandered in, sitting at the other end of the bar, so I got a nice view of Lee's backside as she got them drinks. She was tall and slender, with dark hair that fell down past her shoulders and long legs. I could picture her flat on her back, legs spread, waiting for me to fuck her.

Was she wild in bed or timid? It was hard to tell just from talking to her. I usually could get a feel for what a woman would be like, but not with Sunny.

It was that innocent part of her.

I could get laid almost any time or place I wanted, but something told me I'd have to work for it with Sunny. She wasn't going to just jump into bed with me, so I had to make a decision on whether or not it was worth the effort of wooing her. I was out of here tomorrow, heading to the show in Chicago, and I'd never see her again. Typically, the answer would be no, but there was something about her.

"Here you go. Bon appetite." She put my meal in front of me with a smile. "Another Guinness?"

"Please." I dug into my steak heartily, glad that something was distracting me from thinking about seducing Sunny.

"Let me know when you're ready for the cobbler," she said, putting down a fresh beer and taking away my empty glass.

"Will do." I took another bite. "You weren't here last night, right?"

"No. I only work a few shifts a week. I'm in college."

"Yeah? What are you studying?"

"My degree is in communication, which means a lot of nothing these days. It's the new English degree."

"Is it?" I cocked my head. "Does that mean you don't know what you want to be when you grow up?"

She laughed. "Pretty much."

"Can I ask how old you are?" That was probably something I needed to know, though I wasn't overly worried since they wouldn't allow her to work behind the bar if she was underage.

"Twenty-two. What about you?"

"I'll be twenty-nine in June."

"Did you always want to be a musician?"

"I want to say yes," I admitted. "But I can't deny that as a little kid I wanted to be an astronaut, fireman, and doctor. All at the same time."

"Same. Not a fireman, but astronaut, doctor, and super model. I think we all have dreams when we're kids."

"By the time I was about fifteen, I knew I wanted to do something with my music. My parents were supportive, but I had to graduate high school and take at least a few classes at the community college."

"Did you go to college?"

"I got my associate's degree," I said, chuckling. "Which also means a whole lot of nothing other than it made my parents happy."

"Sometimes that's important. My dad died when I was a baby, and my mom died when I was fifteen."

"Oh, hell. I'm sorry."

"It's okay. I moved in with my Aunt Meg, my mother's older sister. And even though I miss my mom, Aunt Meg was always in my life, so it wasn't like I had to live with a stranger."

"Are you still close?"

"I still live with her," she replied. "She was diagnosed with MS a few years ago, so she needs me around. And anyway, I couldn't afford to go to college and live on my own."

"When do you graduate?"

Sadness clouded her eyes for a moment, and she looked away. "Hopefully in May. I've missed a lot of classes this semester because Aunt Meg fell a few times, but I think I'll be able to make up the work."

"Sounds like Aunt Meg is lucky to have you."

"I was lucky to have her," she countered. "I was devastated when I lost my mom. Aunt Meg took care of me, but she also let me grieve. She let me take my time going through Mom's things to take what I wanted. She didn't tell me to get on with my life or any of that. Those were rough times." She leaned against the bar, and I was surprised to see a faint smile on her lips. "But it taught me a lot about resilience. Patience. Self-care. And unconditional love. Aunt Meg's husband was killed in Desert Storm. She never remarried, never had kids. Then she stepped into the role of parenting a teenager seamlessly." She cleared her throat. "What about you? Are you close to your family?"

I hesitated. "To a degree? I mean, yeah, I come from a big, close-knit family. Lots of aunts, uncles, and cousins. Everyone's in each other's business all the time. But once I got rich..." My voice trailed. This wasn't the type of thing I talked about. Ever.

"I would guess money changes people," Sunny said softly. "Sometimes it's the person with the money who changes, but other times it's the people around them. I hear a lot of stories like that working here. Most of our clientele is wealthy, and it's hard to believe the things they deal with. Families who expect you to take care of every fifth cousin twice removed you've ever had, along with the neighbors, their high school English teacher, and everyone's pets."

"Not to mention, pay for all the weddings, baptisms, and family vacations," I said dryly.

She wrinkled her nose. "Is it really like that?"

"You know, sometimes I just shake my head. I make a lot, so I don't mind helping out the family. Paying for college, medical emergencies, stuff like that. But when I get a fifty-thousand-dollar bill so my cousin can take his new girlfriend shopping in Paris, it pisses me off. Especially when he doesn't even have a fucking job."

"That happens?" she asked, her eyes wide. "And you allow it?"

"My mother makes it happen when she lends people her credit cards," I admitted. "And that makes it complicated. She grew up dirt poor, so now she thinks it's my job to make sure no one in the family has to experience that."

"But they should at least work, no?" she asked softly.

"You would think so." Our eyes met and she shook her head.

"I'm sorry. That sounds really selfish. Of all of them."

"Sometimes. Other times I feel guilty because my life is pretty damn good so why shouldn't I share the wealth?"

"Except when your bandmates start pushing for a country-western album." There was a teasing glint in her eyes and we both chuckled.

"Don't say that," I rumbled. "Jesus. That's all I need. Carter hears that and he'll run with it."

"Sorry."

The impish little grin on her face told me she wasn't, but that was okay. She made me laugh, something I didn't do much these days. Especially not with women. Unless they were business colleagues or family, I only had one reason to interact with a woman. I wasn't interested in a relationship and wasn't even sure I ever wanted to get married. I'd watched way too many of my friends go down that road, and most of them ended in disaster. My plan was to stay single well into my thirties, and maybe at some point find a woman who was okay with monogamy without legalities.

Someone with long legs who made me laugh without even trying.

"You have a boyfriend, Sunny?"

She blinked, and though it was hard to tell in the bar's dim lighting, I could have sworn her cheeks got red. That was interesting.

"No. I don't... well, I don't have time for that. What about you?"

I shook my head. "Same. Not into guys either."

She rolled her eyes. "Very funny."

"No time for anything serious with me on the road eleven months of the year. Though I do enjoy the company of ladies from time to time."

Yup. She was definitely blushing.

"I'm... um, I'm sure you do." Those long-lashed hazel eyes were staring into mine with a mixture of curiosity and nervousness.

"A good orgasm can fix a lot of things," I said, curious about how embarrassed she was. Was she really as innocent as she seemed, or was it an act she put on while working behind the bar? "Stress, high blood pressure. Hell, it even helps you sleep better."

"I work, go to school, and take care of an elderly relative," she said. "I have no trouble sleeping. I'm usually out the minute my head hits the pillow."

"When do you have fun, Sunny?" I suddenly really wanted to know. I complained about tour buses and travel and uncomfortable mattresses, but I had it easy compared to most people.

"I guess I don't," she said after a long hesitation. "Don't get me wrong, my life isn't bad. I'm just busy. Especially since Aunt Meg's diagnosis. She needs me and what should I say? Oh, no, sorry, you'll have to put yourself to bed. I'm going out with my friends."

"What would she do if you weren't there?" I asked carefully. "What if you'd gone away to school?"

"I probably would have had to come back, but I didn't even consider going away. It's too expensive to go out of state. This way, I can live at home, which saves me a ton in student loans."

"No parties? Sororities? Dances?"

She shook her head. "I'm not exactly the girl all the guys beat down the door to go out with."

I was surprised. "What does that mean? Are you saying guys don't ask you out?"

"Not really, no." She dropped her gaze, almost embarrassed.

Geez, were college guys so immature these days they didn't understand different kinds of beauty? Sunny wasn't necessarily the kind of woman who'd make heads turn when she walked down the street, but she was stunning. Big eyes that reminded me of warm honey were fringed with long lashes that didn't appear fake. She had the cutest dimples when she smiled, and her cupid's bow upper lip made me want to suck on it. Her slim body seemed toned and firm, and in my experience, women with small breasts seemed to be more sensitive in that area. There wasn't any science in that observation, but I'd been with enough women to feel confident about it.

Immature college boys were missing out.

Had she ever been with a real man? Someone a little older and a lot more experienced?

My guess was no.

I could show her so much.

Just thinking about it had me hard as granite behind my jeans.

I really needed to touch her.

Now the only question was whether or not she wanted me to.

4

———————

P *resley*

ZEKE and the middle-aged couple at the other end of the bar were my only customers. Nights this slow usually dragged, but not this one. Tonight, I had this gorgeous, interesting rockstar to keep me company. We talked about music, movies, and even multiple sclerosis. He told me about his many cousins and extended family, while I told him funny stories about Aunt Meg and our cat, Puffy.

When the chef brought out his blackberry cobbler, covered in vanilla bean ice cream with a touch of blackberry liqueur-infused whipped cream, Zeke immediately took a bite.

"This is fucking awesome," he murmured after he swallowed.

"I've never had the cobbler before." The food here was too expensive for me, even with my employee discount, so I rarely got to try any, but I couldn't admit that.

"Here. Try it." He proffered the spoon and my mouth seemed to open before I could stop it. His eyes met mine as I leaned over the bar toward him, and he leaned forward. The way he was looking at me made my insides flutter with excitement. He was only offering dessert, but even someone as inexperienced as I was recognized the desire in his gaze.

Was it possible one of the hottest guitar players in the world wanted me?

Before I could fully digest that information, my lips closed around the spoon, and he pulled it out of my mouth ever so slowly. The rich tangy fruit flavor, coupled with the flaky crust and the sweetness of the whipped cream made me moan with appreciation. Or maybe it was lust. I couldn't discern the difference.

"Awesome, right?" he asked, his voice dropping an octave or so.

"So awesome," I whispered, licking my lips.

"Share it with me."

"I'm not..." The words died on my lips as he held up another bite and I opened for more. "...supposed to," I finished after I'd swallowed.

"There's no one here but us. And I won't tell."

"O-okay." Some whipped cream dripped down my chin but before I could grab a napkin, Zeke reached out and wiped it with his finger. Our eyes locked, he slid the finger into his mouth.

"Mmm. It's even yummier when it has you on it."

I opened my mouth, but nothing came out. What was happening here? Zeke was way out of my league. Not only did I have no experience with rich, famous rockstars, I had no experience with men. Period. Other than a few kisses and dates in high school, I was as innocent as the Virgin Mary. And while I recognized the desire coursing through me, I didn't have a clue what to do about it.

We finished the cobbler in silence, with him looking at me like I was his next meal.

Just the thought of him licking anything on me the way he licked that damn spoon made parts of me come alive that I'd thought were fairly dormant.

I'd been too shy for sex as a teen and too busy to meet someone I liked enough to do it with now.

I'd do it with Zeke, though.

I didn't even care about the interview anymore.

"I'm guessing you could get in a lot of trouble if I kissed you across the bar," he said quietly.

"Y-yes." I swallowed. "But I'll be off soon."

"How soon?"

"I..." I felt the warmth of a flush spread over me. Good grief, what was I doing? "Around eleven, maybe sooner if I can get through clean-up quickly."

"Okay." He wiped his mouth with his napkin. "That's an hour from now. How about another beer?"

"Sure." I hurriedly poured him another Guinness and cleared his plates away.

"Hey, Lee, the kitchen's closed!" The chef called out to me.

"Got it." I waved to let him know I'd heard him.

"How much do you have to clean?" Zeke asked as I started putting things away behind the bar.

"Not a lot. I'll put away the fruit I cut up, juice goes in the fridge, and then I wipe down the bar, counters back here, and all the tables."

"Want some help?"

I shook my head. "I've got it. But you can talk to me while I work."

"Sure. Tell me something about you that no one knows."

I chuckled. "I wouldn't even know where to start. I'm probably too introverted for my own good. At least that's what Aunt Meg tells me. She says I need to take time to enjoy life, that I'm letting it pass me by."

"Your Aunt Meg sounds like a smart woman."

I'd come around the outside of the bar to start wiping down the regular tables. I paused in front of him and rested one elbow on the edge of the bar. "I think maybe I had to grow up too fast when my mom died. Between school and grieving, I didn't have the heart to party. I figured there would be plenty of time for that kind of thing when I got to college, but then Aunt Meg got her diagnosis. And even though the meds are finally starting to work, she falls a lot. That first year, there was so much trial and error figuring out what combination of drugs would help for her different issues, I was always checking on her, making sure she was okay. I was terrified I might lose her too, because she's all the family I have. So, boys and partying and all that were the furthest things from my mind."

"But she's okay now, right?" he asked quietly. "Or at least doing as okay as she can, since there's no cure?"

I nodded. "Yes. She's much better now. Even though she keeps falling. She uses a cane now and we're trying to get a wheelchair for the days she feels weak."

"Then things are better?"

"Yes."

"So maybe you deserve a night of fun. With me." When he looked at me, it was like no one existed but the two of us. And I didn't understand why he had this effect on me when no one else ever had.

I swallowed. "I... I'm probably not what you're used to, Zeke."

"What am I used to?" His eyes never left mine.

"Women with... experience. Who know what you want."

"Oh, I think you know exactly what I want."

"Zeke, I'm..." I couldn't just tell him I was a virgin.

Could I?

"You're what?" He reached out, brushing a strand of my hair off my shoulders before resting his hand on the side of my neck. It was a good thing the couple at the end of the bar had left because I nearly moaned at the warmth of his hand and the electricity that shot through me the moment he made contact with my skin.

"I have to clean up," I whispered, scurrying away.

Just that small touch had sent me into a state of arousal I'd never felt before. I knew about sex, understood the mechanics of it, and had a few girlfriends who'd told me about their experiences. It sounded like something I wanted to try, but someone like Zeke, who'd undoubtedly slept with hundreds, maybe even thousands, of women, wouldn't want to spend the night teaching me the specifics of how to please a man in bed.

Would he?

I wiped down the tables almost furiously, desperate to either talk myself into or out of whatever it was we were doing. I wasn't naïve enough to think he wanted anything beyond sex, but I'd promised myself I would rid myself of my virginity if and when the opportunity presented itself as long as the man was someone I genuinely liked. And I liked Zeke. Much more than I'd thought I would when I'd begun researching the band.

The man I'd been talking to the last few hours was nothing like the enigmatic musician I'd seen on stage last night or the aloof celebrity dodging a journalist I'd run into after the show. No, that was Big Z. This was Zeke, who was someone else entirely. I wasn't sure how I knew that, but I did. Maybe we were both pretending to be someone else. In his case, it was when he performed; in my case, it was when I came to work. Shy, virginal Presley wouldn't get the tips she needed to help Aunt Meg with the bills, so I pretended to be a flirtatious waitress named Lee when I had to.

I was being ridiculous.

Zeke was bored and wanted to get laid, so I had to decide if this was it, the night I'd finally learn what sex was all about.

He was gorgeous, with his long dark brown hair and those two different colored eyes. I could stare at them all night. He was a big guy, probably six or seven inches taller than me, which said something since I was five-ten. He had a strong, masculine jawline and broad shoulders, which I really liked. And his voice. I'd been enjoying his voice quite a bit. The idea of him whispering sweet nothings to me in that deep baritone made my girlie parts clench with excitement.

Did guys whisper sweet nothings when they were inside of you? They did in the romance novels I read, so there had to be an element of truth to it, even if it didn't happen all the time.

"Did I scare you away, Sunny?" His quiet voice behind me made goose flesh break out on my skin and I slowly turned around, tilting up my head to look into his handsome face.

"I'm not scared," I whispered shakily.

"No?" He didn't touch me, even though he could have since he was only a few inches away from me. So close I could feel the heat radiated from his body. His very strong, muscular body.

"I'm cautious," I said, my voice soft but more confident now.

"I won't hurt you, Sunny." He still didn't touch me. "I just want to make us both feel good."

"That's the problem," I muttered.

"That's the *problem*?" He chuckled. "Why is us feeling good a problem?"

"Because I don't know how."

He frowned slightly. "I'm not sure I understand, honey. I like you and I think you like me. I'd like to spend some more time together tonight. More of what we've been doing the past few hours."

"I'd like that too."

"But?" He reached for me, putting one of his big hands on the side of my waist. "It's snowing like crazy out there, so I can't imagine you're going home."

"No."

He waited, watching my face.

"It's embarrassing," I whispered.

"What is? You on your period or something? Because that's what showers are for."

I shook my head. "No." I took a breath and steeled myself, bracing for rejection. "I'm a virgin, Zeke."

5

Z *eke*

A VIRGIN.

Holy shit, she was even more innocent than I'd thought.

And here I was doing my best to seduce her.

You're a bad, bad man, William Zerkesian.

The angel on my shoulder was not pleased with me because he already knew I was going to do this. If sweet, hazel-eyed Sunny wanted me to pop her cherry, who was I to turn her down? She was twenty-two, not some teenager. So, if her only concern was not knowing what to do, I had no issue with that at all. I knew enough for both of us.

"That's not exactly a turnoff," I said after a moment.

"It's not?"

She looked so confused I desperately wanted to touch her, reassure her, let her know her virginity was the furthest thing from a deterrent. I was the first to admit I had enough alpha male in me to like the idea of being the first, the only. Even if it was just for the night.

"What do you drink, Sunny?"

"What?"

"You said you don't party much, but you must drink a little? What's your favorite?"

"Oh. I like Moscato."

"Get a bottle and put it on my tab."

Her eyes widened.

"It's okay. Get whatever you like for you, and if you have a bottle of Macallan back there, I want one of those for me."

She squinted, all shyness suddenly gone. "I didn't picture you a scotch guy," she said. "I would have thought bourbon. Maybe tequila."

"My tequila days are behind me," I said. "I'm too old for that kind of hangover. I'll occasionally take a shot if we're celebrating something, but scotch is for sipping. Relaxing. Winding down."

"Okay." She moved away from me, and I felt the loss, though I'd barely touched her.

Damn, I hadn't been with a virginal college girl in years, but I liked it. Hell, it had been years since I'd been with an innocent woman. The women I usually went for were the opposite of innocent, someone well-matched with me in bed, but someone I could also simply fuck and forget.

She had no way of knowing it, but tonight would probably take me as far out of my comfort zone as it would take her out of hers.

I could only hope it was what we both needed.

She finished wiping down all the counters and tables and then pulled two bottles from behind the bar, handing them to me along with a wine glass and a crystal tumbler, before doing something on the computer.

"I need to get my phone and charger from my locker," she said. "In case Aunt Meg needs me."

"I'll wait for you here."

"Okay." She disappeared into a room down the hall, and I waited for her by the elevators. The place seemed deserted other than a tired-looking receptionist at the front desk. They normally had twenty-four-seven security and a concierge, but tonight the concierge desk was empty and although I figured the security guard was around, he wasn't outside like he normally was. Not that I'd expect him to be. It looked brutal out there and I was glad Sunny wasn't driving home in this.

"You weren't driving home tonight, were you?" I asked her as the elevator ascended to the tenth floor.

"No. I planned to sleep in the employee lounge. Normally we're not allowed to do that, but my boss told me I could. I think he was grateful I even came in. Almost everyone called out."

"I'm glad the chef was here," I admitted.

She smiled. "Blane is always here."

"How is it working here?"

She shrugged. "I like it, but I get the slow shifts, so I'm only here a few times a week. And if the weather's bad, they call me because they know I need the money."

"Couldn't you get a job working somewhere else that would give you more hours?"

"It works out okay because I'm so busy with school and Aunt Meg. I'd struggle if I had to work somewhere four or five days a week. Working two or three nights is enough for now. I'll be done with school in May and then I'll find something better."

I nodded as I unlocked the door to my suite, letting her walk in ahead of me.

"This is nice," she said, putting down her purse and looking around. "I've never been in any of the suites."

"It's comfortable. I've stayed here several times, whenever we come through Minneapolis."

"I must not have been working last year," she said, walking over to the sliding glass doors and pulling open the curtains. "Oh wow… look at all the snow."

I followed slowly, gently wrapping my arms around her from behind and resting my head on top of hers. "It's brutal out there."

"I'm glad I didn't try to drive home." She shivered slightly, and I pulled her closer.

"Me too." For whatever reason, I wasn't in a rush. I wasn't nervous, per se, but it had been a long time since I'd been anyone's first. I was trying to remember exactly what I could or should do to make it decent for her. There probably wasn't anything. In my experience, some girls barely had any discomfort, while others cried and bled and all sorts of nonsense.

Okay, that probably wasn't fair. I knew enough about life—and biology—to know the ones who hadn't enjoyed it usually couldn't help it. Hell, I had a buddy once who told us the story of his high school girlfriend and how they'd tried and tried, and he never got in there. I'd forgotten what it was called, but she'd literally had to go to a doctor to have her cherry medically removed. Hopefully, we wouldn't run into anything like that tonight.

"You want a drink?" I asked, my mouth close to her ear. She leaned back against me, her slight frame shivering against me. "Are you cold, Sunny?"

"Nervous," she admitted.

"Don't be. We're not in a rush, and if you change your mind, that's okay too." I hoped she wouldn't, but at the end of the day, there would be a line of ladies waiting for me tomorrow when I got to Chicago, so it wasn't like I'd be without company. I was many things, but a man who forced himself on women wasn't one of them.

I turned her around, so I could look at her. The more I stared, the prettier she got, and I hadn't had enough to drink for that to be the alcohol talking. She was so warm against me, and she smelled good too. Her hair had a hint of coconut, like a day at the beach, and I closed my eyes as I inhaled. I leaned forward, nuzzling her nose with mine. She wrapped her arms around my waist, rising a little on her tiptoes, and tilted up her head.

Our lips met tentatively. I kept my mouth closed, savoring the feel of her lips, her warmth, and tasted something minty she'd put on when she'd gone to get her purse. Oh, hell, she was sweet. I used the tip of my tongue to trace the seam of her lips, waiting until she gave me the opportunity to slip inside. When her mouth opened for me, I took charge, sliding one hand into the hair at the back of her neck and using the other to cup her round little ass. I was gentler than I wanted to be, but I needed her to get worked up, to not just want to do this, but to need it. Once her body was on board, the rest would be easy. Easier.

I took my time, nipping her plump lower lip in between thrusts of my tongue. She shifted, winding her arms around my neck, kissing me back with interest now. There was nothing tentative about her reactions to what I was doing, and I scooped her up in my arms. I sat on the couch, with her in my lap, and kissed her some more. Over and over, long and hard and deep, until she whimpered and clutched my shoulders. It quickly became obvious she had no idea what she was doing, and it turned me on more than I expected. I finally broke away, looking down at her chest.

"You like this?" I murmured, running a knuckle over one of the hard nipples peeking through her blouse.

"Very much." Her eyes were glassy, lips swollen from the kisses we'd shared. I didn't usually like to kiss this much, but it was different with Sunny.

I didn't know what the hell had come over me.

"I want to see you," I said gruffly. "All of you."

"I..." Suddenly her face fell, and her cheeks burned with embarrassment.

Shit.

She was nervous again. "Don't be afraid, Sunny."

"It's not that." She bit her lip. "I'm... messy."

"Messy?" I frowned, trying to read between the lines. "Like, you need a shower messy? Have your period messy? It's okay to talk about this stuff, especially when you're about to have sex."

"My friend Jodie..." Her voice was barely audible. "She says I'm...hairy. You know, down there."

"Pubic hair?"

She nodded, looking away. "But I've never had any reason to...do anything. Just a little shaving on the sides when I wear a bathing suit, but that's almost never, so..."

"Hair is okay," I said thoughtfully. "But less hair is better."

"I'm sorry."

"No, it's fine." I ran my fingers through her soft hair. "What if I shaved you?"

Her head shot up and she stared.

"This is all about you discovering yourself," I said. "You can say no, but why? I think it'll turn us both on."

"Yes." She nodded. "Yes to everything. I don't care. For once in my life, I want to feel what you're making me feel."

Aw, hell.

I was hard as granite, and now she was going to let me shave her fucking pussy. What insane, sexy madness was this? And how was I going to survive without ruining her?

I gently moved her off my lap and got to my feet, holding out my hand. I was going to do everything she wanted and things I was positive she'd never thought of, but she had to say yes every step of the way.

She put her hand in mine and we padded into the bathroom. Without a word, I started getting undressed, hoping she would follow suit.

To my surprise, she leaned against the counter and simply watched. Her lips were slightly parted as she let her gaze travel the length of my torso. I was commando under my jeans, and she licked her lips when my cock sprang free. Then she slowly pulled her blouse over her head without even unbuttoning it. She slid her skirt and tights off and stood there in a simple white cotton bra and panties. Definitely the plainest underwear I'd ever seen, and all I could think about was buying her a sexy silk set. Maybe something in pink or lavender. A push-up bra to give her small but sensitive breasts a little lift.

She reached back and unhooked her bra, letting it fall away slowly, and this time I was the one licking my lips. Her tits were perfection. Barely a B cup, but perky and round, with dusky nipples that made me want to suck on them.

"Fuck, you're beautiful," I whispered. "Let me see the rest."

She took a deep breath, as if she needed courage, and closed her eyes as she slid off her panties.

She was a lot hairier than anyone I'd been with before, but still absolutely stunning in my eyes. She had a small waist that widened into rounder hips, though all of her was slight. Her legs were long and toned, her stomach flat, and even her feet were pretty. How had no one noticed her? Even covered by clothes that were slightly too big on her, I'd seen the potential, known there was a treasure trove of pleasure waiting for me beneath.

I turned and reached for a towel, spreading it on the countertop.

"Hop up," I told her.

She hesitated so I gently lifted her by the waist. "I won't hurt you. It's probably going to turn you on. Then we'll shower before I take you to bed."

"O-okay."

"You can tell me to stop, you know. We don't have to do this."

"I don't want to stop you." She smiled even as she pulled her lower lip through her teeth. "I want to do it. All of it."

"I don't think you have any idea what's coming, sweetheart."

"Probably not." She leaned back against the mirror and spread her legs.

Yup, that was it for me. There was no going back now unless she changed her mind. And looking at the way she'd just opened herself up for me, it didn't appear she was changing it anytime soon.

I got a razor and shaving cream out of my toiletry bag and mentally drew a deep breath. I'd done it with other women before, but this was different. She was embarrassed by her unkempt lady parts and while it didn't bother me, I wanted to give her a taste of what she'd asked for. In more ways than one.

She was nervous when I knelt between her legs, and I noticed she squeezed her eyes shut. I'd fix that in a few seconds.

I leaned forward and spread her open, just a little, placing a light kiss on her clit. Her eyes popped open, and she gasped, so I ran a gentle hand along one of her thighs.

"Relax. Let me make you feel good."

"Holy shit." Her head fell back and I softly licked a trail up her slit.

She moaned, and though her fists were clenched at her sides, her hips shifted up to meet my next pass. I didn't want her to think her natural body was unattractive, and while I was looking forward to seeing her bare, I also wanted to get her off just the way she was. Hell, I just wanted to get her off. I had no doubt I'd be the first guy to make her come, and I planned to make sure she never forgot it.

I held her thighs apart with my hands and went to town, feasting on her sweetness. I loved how she tasted, all woman with a hint of spice. It only took her a minute or so to discover what she liked and to start moving against me. She sounded amazing, little moans and breathy sighs leaving her as I licked and sucked her delicate folds. Her clit was a hard little point and I teased it with the tip of my tongue.

"Oh, god, yes, that..." She arched up and I slowed down.

I used my fingers to tease her entrance while sucking on her clit. She cried out when I pushed inside, but she clenched around me. She was close now, so I added a second finger and bit lightly on her clit.

Her scream as she gushed all over my face was the hottest thing I'd heard in a very long time.

6

P *resley*

THERE WERE no words to describe my first man-induced orgasm. It felt good when I did it on my own, but with Zeke? I couldn't even think straight. My body hummed with an odd combination of satisfaction and arousal, as if I needed more. He'd done things with his mouth and fingers that had made me blush when I heard my girlfriends talk about them, but I wasn't blushing anymore.

I felt sexy. Strong. Independent.

Beautiful.

Maybe I wasn't, but right now, it felt like I could do anything.

I hadn't even realized Zeke was shaving me until I finally pried my eyes apart. I couldn't see what he was doing, but it didn't matter. I trusted him and wanted him to show me all the things I didn't know.

I'd held on to my virginity simply because I hadn't had time to find someone who fit whatever parameters I'd created in my mind. I'd been waiting for the right time, the right guy, the right situation—and this was all of that. Never in my wildest dreams did I imagine that one of the men whose posters had graced my locker in high school would be my first lover.

"Shower time," Zeke said, getting to his feet and holding out his hands for me.

I stood up and looked down.

Oh, wow. Bare as a baby's bottom. Smooth and white. I hadn't known what to expect, but I liked it.

"It's so sexy," he breathed into my ear. "How do you feel about it?"

"It's nice." I leaned against him and tilted up my head. When he slid his tongue between my lips, I tasted myself on him. It was a heady flavor, tangy and different from anything I'd ever experienced, but having Zeke's arms around me made all the difference. I knew I was playing a dangerous game with my heart, because I had no experience with sex or romance or rockstars or anything I'd been doing in the last five hours or so. All I knew was that I'd never have a chance like this again, so I was willing to risk it.

We stepped under the warm spray together, and he immediately pulled me against him, so my back was against his strong chest. He splayed his hands across my torso, moving them up slowly to cup my breasts. He held them gently, as if they were delicate, and began to stroke my nipples with his thumbs. His lips were pressed against the side of my neck, nibbling and kissing.

"How can you think you're not beautiful?" he whispered, his thumbs rubbing harder over the stiff peaks my nipples had become. "They write songs about women like you... long, cool women."

"I don't think I have a black dress." I chuckled, understanding his reference to the classic rock song performed by the Hollies.

One of his big hands moved between my legs, stroking over the now bare skin.

"You'll feel so much more now," he said. "And when I'm inside of you, you're gonna feel every inch, every stroke..."

If he'd said those things to me last night, I might have died of embarrassment. But not now. I'd undoubtedly be mortified tomorrow, or whenever I went home, but tonight? I had zero fucks to give. Just this once, I deserved to do something that made me feel beautiful, no matter how temporary it might be.

His hands were all over me, touching and squeezing and taunting me right back into arousal. He scraped his teeth along the soft skin behind my ear, making goose bumps break out on my flesh. I tilted my head up, greedy for his mouth, and his lips covered mine. How such a physically imposing man could be so gentle was a mystery to me, and I let myself get lost in this. I forgot about work, school, even my lack of experience, and let him lead me wherever he wanted to go.

We got out of the shower, and he wrapped us in one big towel so our bare torsos were pressed together and the towel covered our backs and sides.

"I love a tall woman," he murmured, kissing me again.

"You have condoms, right?" I asked, momentarily coming back to earth. "I'm not protected."

"I do." He reached across me and into his toiletry bag, where he pulled out a handful.

"Can we get the hard part over with?" I whispered, meeting his eyes.

"We can," he whispered back, stroking my cheek, his eyes never leaving mine.

God, that was my favorite thing he did. Okay, one of my favorite things that he'd done so far, because his lips on my nether regions had been amazing too.

"I'm kinda scared," I admitted as he disposed of the towel, picked me up, and carried me groom-style to the bedroom. He sat me on the bed and crawled over me, his mouth finding mine without giving me a chance to say anything else. His body was huge and strong and gorgeous, covering mine. I loved the weight of him, how it felt to be pressed into the mattress by his sheer bulk while his mouth ravaged mine.

I heard the crinkle of plastic, felt him shift above me and then he was... *Right. There.* I tensed, waiting for the inevitable pain, but all I felt was pressure. Something thick and hard breaching a place that had never been touched by anyone but me, him, and my gynecologist. I gasped as he went deeper, but still, there was only a faint twinge of discomfort.

"How're you doing, baby?" He pressed his forehead to mine, his body completely still.

"Is that...it?" I asked dubiously.

He chuckled. "Not even close, but if you're asking if I'm all the way in, then yes. The worst of it is over for you."

"It didn't hurt," I said in awe. "I thought it would."

"I'm so glad to hear that because now it's going to feel really fucking good," he whispered, moving to suck on my neck. His lips were firm and warm as he gently increased pressure until I knew he would leave a mark. And I loved it. My body was aching for something I couldn't identify, and I shifted beneath him.

Then he moved.

I felt every inch sliding through me, pulling out to the tip before pushing back in.

His movements were slow and deliberate, giving me the opportunity to feel everything, and I softly moaned.

"Oh. Wow. That's..."

"You like it? You okay?"

"I'm wonderful."

"You ready for more?"

"Yes."

He picked up speed, moving faster and harder. My legs opened wider, anxious to feel more of him. I'd thought the first time would be painful and awkward. Instead, I was gearing up for another orgasm, my body surrendering to the sensations starting to overwhelm me. I'd had no idea intercourse would be this powerful, or all-encompassing. Unless it was the man who made it feel like that.

Either way, the feeling of him gliding in and out was heavenly, and when he reached down to cup my ass and raise it up higher, my world splintered. Shockwaves of pleasure rocketed through me with such force I screamed his name, my nails digging into his biceps. He growled and moved faster, finally letting out a roar as he jerked inside of me.

I'd never felt like this before. Breathless and satisfied and *sexy*. No one had ever made me feel beautiful. Not my friends, not any guys I'd ever met, not even Aunt Meg. It didn't matter that this was just sex. One of the biggest rockstars in the world *wanted* me. Whether I could have him for five hours or five days, I loved every second of this.

∼

WE DID it three times before I dozed off, my body completely wrecked by the things he'd done. After the first time, he'd positioned me on my hands and knees and come at me from behind. That had been a different sensation, different pressure, and I'd come again. Round number three had been with me on top and that had been so intense I'd come almost immediately.

He was huge. I didn't have to be experienced to know he was bigger than other guys. I occasionally watched porn, heard stories from my friends, and had done some innocent groping on a handful of dates. None of them had a penis like Zeke's. No wonder his nickname was *Big* Z. I was sore, but in the most delicious way possible, and hoped we would do it at least once more before he left for Chicago and I headed home. He'd created a monster, and it was odd to think in a few hours I might never see him again.

I was nothing if not realistic, though, so I curled into his arms as I tried to sleep. It wasn't easy, with someone so gorgeous in bed with me. How many women had been in my exact position, wondering if the rockstar with the big hands and even bigger... music, would call. Text. Want to see her again. I couldn't be the only one. Part of me wanted to be sad, but I also wanted to enjoy the time I had with him.

Tomorrow, I had to go back to caring for Aunt Meg and figuring out what the hell I was going to do about my final project.

Ugh. I really didn't want to think about that tonight.

"Why aren't you asleep?" he rumbled in a raspy, sleep-addled voice.

"I don't know," I admitted.

Before I knew what was happening, he'd flipped me onto my back and was on top of me. "You want more, my sweet Sunshine?"

I giggled. "Maybe."

"I've created a nympho," he said, pretending to be annoyed. "What am I going to do with you?"

"I'm pretty sure you know the answer to that question." I ran my hands down his warm, chiseled back. He was already hard, his cock resting against my thighs as he lowered his head to kiss me. I felt him sliding through my slickness, pushing inside of me.

"Zeke! Condom!" Even in my haze of lust, I realized he was bare.

"Shit." He immediately pulled out, rolled over and grabbed a condom. He sheathed himself and then was inside me again, both of us moaning from the pleasure. It felt so good, even though my nether regions were sore. The pleasure far outweighed the slight ache, and I arched my hips, taking him deeper.

"You learn fast," he murmured against my mouth, pumping harder into me.

Our bodies moved together easily, everything we'd done the last few hours already second nature. When his lips captured mine, our tongues engaging in a passionate dance, flames all but burst inside of me. I didn't know what I needed, but I had to have it.

"Zeke..." I panted, unsure how to ask for what I wanted. "More... please!"

"God damn, baby. Your pussy was made for my cock." He rocked back, winding up on his haunches. He slid a pillow under my ass, pushing my knees back to my shoulders and then glided into me in one long, firm thrust. My eyes rolled back in my head, the pressure was that intense.

"Oh, fuck."

"That's right. Take it all. Every goddamn inch." He thrust in hard, so deep I wasn't sure I could take more. And yet, I took it all. He went at me repeatedly, heatedly, until we were a sweaty, grunting tangle of limbs and tongues. When my orgasm shot out of me, I felt a rush of liquid, as if I'd peed myself, and while I didn't understand it, Zeke groaned and threw back his head.

"Fuuuck!"

For what seemed like an eternity, neither of us moved. Finally, he pulled out and collapsed next to me.

"Bet you didn't know you were a squirter."

"A what?"

He chuckled before explaining what it was.

"Is that... normal?"

"Well, yeah. And it's hot. I fucking love it." He leaned over and kissed me. "We should get cleaned up. Then I've got to get some sleep."

"Okay." With a smile on my face, I let him carry me into the bathroom. I really needed to wash up and wished I'd brought my glasses with me because I never slept in my contacts. There was no help for it now, though, and I closed my eyes as he pulled me against him in the shower.

In the morning, or in a few hours, I'd slip out and head down to the employee lounge where I could get my things and put on clean clothes. Maybe we could even have brunch before he had to leave.

7

—————

Z *eke*

My ALARM WENT off at nine and I rolled over, expecting to find Sunny's sweet, sexy body there, but even though the sheets were still warm, she was gone. It was too quiet for her to be in the bathroom, and I sat up curiously. Had she really snuck out like a thief in the night? I'd thought sure she would want to have breakfast, talk a little more, maybe even go another round before we had to go. Hell, I wanted to get her number, which made no sense.

I never asked women for their contact info. I barely remembered their names five minutes after we were done fucking, but I'd remember everything about last night for a long time.

She was sweet.

There was no other way to put it.

Her innocence was charming, and when she'd finally lost her inhibitions, it had been a wild night. I'd fucked her in different positions, gone down on her twice, and then taught her how to suck my dick in the shower. If I was honest, I hadn't had such a great night in a long time. The sex was good—fantastic, really—but it was more than that. She hadn't given a shit about my rockstar status, and it had been all about mutual pleasure, respect, and fun.

God knew, I needed more fun in my life.

Sex, drugs, and rock and roll wasn't all it was cracked up to be sometimes. I made a stupid amount of money, but I sacrificed almost everything. Friends, family, relationships, even my health. It took a lot to tour eleven months of the year. I couldn't remember my last real vacation, or the last time I'd hung out with non-musician friends. I had a mansion in Benedict Canyon, and my parents lived there with my grandmother and a handful of staff. I literally had no idea what went on in my own house.

At some point, that had to change.

Maybe spending time with a sweet girl like Sunny could bring some light to my otherwise dark existence. Maybe she could show me how to have fun again. I even felt like writing a song, words rumbling through my brain as I showered, shaved and got dressed. I had a feeling Sunny was downstairs, in that employee lounge, probably looking for clean clothes, or to fix her makeup or something. Women tended to worry about things like runny mascara.

Personally, I thought she was perfect the way she was, but it wouldn't hurt to see her in jeans or something. And I definitely wanted to feed her. I found her beautiful, but her ribcage was painfully obvious when she was naked, and her hip bones protruded more than I thought they should. My family was Armenian, so I'd grown up in an atmosphere where food was plentiful and women had a little meat on their bones. If I thought her slimness was natural, it would've been fine, but my gut told me she didn't eat enough.

I went downstairs, smiling at a handful of employees I passed. The storm had ended but there was a mountain of snow outside, so no one was going anywhere until the plows came. Which meant I had time to find Sunny. Feed her. Fuck her again. My mouth watered at the memory of her squirting all over my cock early this morning. It would be so fucking hot if she did it when I was going down on her.

I remembered the hallway where the employee lounge had been and hesitated outside the door. It was open about a foot, and I heard voices inside. I probably shouldn't go inside if there were other employees, especially women, changing and such.

A man was talking, and it sounded like he was on speaker phone. "Presley, the deadline is right around the corner. Did you get the Onyx Knight interview?"

"I'm working on it."

I froze.

That was Sunny's voice.

Lee. *Presley.*

Wasn't that the name of that journalist the other night?

Son of a bitch.

"Well, work faster. You don't have a lot of time."

"I will. Promise. Look, I have to go."

"Text me later with an update."

"I will."

I wasn't sure which emotion hit me harder: rage or disappointment. I'd thought Sunny—Lee, or Presley, or whatever the hell her name was—was different. Apparently, she was like everyone else who'd just wanted something from me.

Normally, I didn't give a shit, but for some reason this one hurt.

I was still standing there outside the door when she came out, wearing glasses with her hair in a ponytail. And then it all came back.

The shy, awkward girl standing outside the dressing room. I'd only caught a glimpse but now I saw her clear as day.

Sunny was Lee—I'd known that—but Lee was actually Presley.

Fuck.

"Zeke." She stared at me, wide-eyed.

"Are you kidding me right now?" I demanded. "That's what last night was about? You traded your cherry for a goddamn interview?"

"N-no!" She shook her head. "I didn't—"

"I heard you. *Presley*. You said you were working on it."

"But I didn't mean it that way! I just—"

"You know what? I don't even care. You're just like everyone else." I ran a hand through my hair. "But you know what? You've made a grave tactical error. Because you've only got one cherry, sweetheart. What are you going to trade next time?"

Her mouth fell open, her hazel eyes filling with tears. "Zeke, I wasn't—I slept with you because I wanted to."

"Well, that was your second mistake. Because there isn't going to be an interview. Not with me, not with anyone else in my band, and not with any other bands either. I'll make sure of that."

She stared at me, a single tear tricking down her cheek.

Damn, she was good.

I almost felt bad.

Almost.

But just about everyone in my life used me. For money, fame, favors, whatever it was they could get from me. I'd be damned if I let some college journalist do it with her motherfucking virginity. It wasn't that special. And neither was she.

"Zeke, please. Let me explain." Her voice was a shaky whisper.

"I'm pretty sure I know everything I need to know.

With that, I turned on my heel and strode back toward the elevators. I had a plane to catch and a tour to meet up with.

There wasn't a damn thing keeping me in Minnesota.

~

I CAUGHT up to the band at the arena just before soundcheck. I'd drank on the flight to Chicago, in the limo that picked me up at the airport, and had a bottle of Jack Daniels in my hand now.

"Whoa." Kingston gave me an amused look. "I thought you went to that resort to detox and rejuvenate?"

I snorted. "Yeah, well, you know what they say about the best laid plans."

He cocked his head. "You okay?"

"Yup." I grabbed my guitar and strode on stage. I was itching to play, to do something familiar. Something that didn't remind me of freakin' Sunny.

Presley, I reminded myself.

Sunny was fantasy I'd created in my head, about a girl I'd wanted to fuck.

And I'd done that.

It was time to move on.

"You're in a piss poor mood," Kingston said as we headed backstage. Sometimes we went back to the hotel between soundcheck and the show; other times, we just hung out. Tonight, it seemed like we were going to hang out.

"Remember that journalist who wanted an interview in Minneapolis?" I asked.

He nodded, cocking his head slightly as he waited for me to answer.

"Turned out she was the bartender at the resort."

He arched his brows. "And?"

"Did you fuck her?" Tommy asked, leaning over the back of the couch we'd just settled on.

I reached up and smacked him in the forehead. "Let me tell the story, man."

He chuckled. "By all means."

"Did you give her the interview?" Kellan asked, making a face.

"Would you fuckers let me tell you without interrupting?" I snapped.

Kingston laughed. "This ought to be good."

"So, what happened?" Carter turned a chair backwards and straddled it, seemingly interested.

"I didn't recognize her," I admitted. "She looked totally different behind the bar, all made up and shit. There was no one else there, so we talked while I ate and then while she cleaned up."

"*Then* you fucked her?" Kellan prodded impatiently.

I rolled my eyes. "Yeah, but that's not the story. Get this: In the morning, I overheard her on the phone with her editor or whoever. He was on speakerphone and asked if she'd gotten the interview. She said she was working on it. So the whole thing was a set-up."

"I don't see the problem here," Carter said slowly. "If you'd done the interview the other night, chances are you wouldn't have slept with her. This way, she got her interview and you got laid. What're you mad about?"

"I didn't give her the interview!" I said, scowling at him. "Jesus, she fucking lied to me."

"How is that different from every other chick you sleep with on tour?" Carter asked. "Don't they tell us whatever we want to hear so they can spend the night?"

It was a good thing he was like a brother to me, because sometimes I wanted to smack him.

"It's different because I'd already said no. Then, when we ran into each other again, since I didn't recognize her right away, but she knew who I was, she purposely hid not just her identity, but what she wanted."

"She couldn't have known you were going to be at the bar where she works," Kingston said. "It was a coincidence, right?"

I hesitated. It couldn't have been anything more than a coincidence since I always checked in under an assumed name. Everything was paid for by my business manager, so I didn't have to deal with credit cards or anything. The only exception was when I rented a car, but Presley hadn't been there for that.

"Let me get this straight. You got laid *and* you didn't have to give an interview," Kellan said, laughing when I didn't respond right away. "Sounds like win-win to me."

So why didn't it feel that way?

I felt betrayed.

Pissed off.

Hurt.

Not that I'd admit any of that to these fuckers.

"I don't like being played," I said. "If she'd come clean when I first walked into the bar, I probably would have done it. But the way she went about it doesn't sit right with me." Who traded their virginity for an interview? As annoyed as I was, though, it seemed wrong to tell them it had been her first time.

Kingston nodded. "So did she ever ask you for the interview?"

"Nah. I didn't let it get that far after I heard what she said on the phone. I told her she wouldn't be getting an Onyx Knight interview anytime soon. Or any other band, for that matter."

"Jesus, she really got under your skin," Kingston said, eyeing me.

"The music biz is already brutal for women," Carter said, once again sounding like the voice of reason. "It's hard for them to muddle through, you know? With male journalists, they can just come on the road with us, hang out, party, get laid. But if a woman does it, she's unprofessional. A groupie. A *slut*. You didn't have to threaten her for doing the kind of thing we do almost every night. Now I kinda wish I'd talked to her." He scratched his chin.

"Well, I can tell you where she works if you still want to." I got up, annoyed that my friends didn't understand my frustration.

I didn't know what was wrong with me, but it was nothing my bottle of Jack and a couple of groupies wouldn't fix. Talking wouldn't get the sweet taste of sunshine out of my system, but I was confident alcohol and women would. If not, I'd just keep trying until I partied Sunny right out of my memory.

8

———————

P *resley*

IT WAS late afternoon when I got home. Aunt Meg had all the lights on in the living room, as well as the front porch light, and something smelled good in the kitchen. She looked up when I walked in, and a smile spread across her face.

"Hi! How was your—hey, what's wrong?"

I took one look at her sweet face and the emotions I'd been holding back all day came pouring out as I burst into tears.

"Oh my." Aunt Meg hurried over to me, wiping her hands on her apron. "Sweetie, what happened? Are you okay?"

I let her wrap me in a hug, even though I was nearly a foot taller than her. "I screwed up, Aunt Meg. I screwed up so bad."

"It can't be that bad," she whispered, stroking my hair. "Come on. Let's go sit down."

I grabbed a tissue as I followed her into the living room and sank onto the well-worn couch.

"Tell me what happened, sweetheart." Her blue eyes were filled with concern.

I told her everything that had happened last night. She already knew about the failed interview from two nights ago, and she clicked her tongue sympathetically as I told the story. Her eyes widened when I admitted I'd spent the night with him, and then she grimaced when I got to the part about him overhearing my conversation with my college advisor.

It wasn't until I got to the part where I'd gotten fired that she'd gotten upset.

"That's completely unprofessional!" she said. "You went in with a big storm coming because no one else wanted to. If you hadn't spent the night with Zeke, you would've been on a couch in the lounge. They owe you, the bastards."

"He said I behaved in an unbecoming manner," I whispered, mortified just thinking about how Mr. Hopkins had spoken to me. "Or something like that."

"I'd like to call your boss and give him a piece of my mind!"

"It won't matter," I said miserably. "I'm so sorry, Aunt Meg. I know we need the money. But I'll find something else. Maybe at the mall..." My voice trailed. I was so tired and heartbroken and disappointed in myself. I'd screwed up everything. My chance to ever see Zeke again, the Onyx Knight interview, and my job. Aside from that, I only had a day to write a story that was the final part of my senior project. If I didn't do it, and get a passing grade, I wouldn't graduate.

"It's going to be all right," she said, reaching for my hand. "I'm so sorry things turned out the way they did last night. I know you've waited a long time to be intimate with someone. I wish it hadn't ended the way it did for you."

I sighed, swiping at my eyes in frustration. "He was so mad. And instead of making him listen to me, I just stood there like an idiot. I'm upset with him, but I'm madder at myself for not taking a stand and making him listen to me."

"It's hard to be strong in a situation like that. Especially when you've never experienced it before."

"And what's worse is that he wasn't just mad; he was disappointed too. I could see it in his eyes."

She shook her head. "Oh, sweetie, I'm so sorry. We all make mistakes, though. Don't be too hard on yourself."

"I didn't know what to do. I wanted to tell him who I was, but I was afraid. We clicked, the moment he sat down at the bar, and we were having such a nice conversation. He was flirting with me—no one ever flirts with me. He made me feel beautiful. We had a connection I'd never felt with anyone else, and I didn't want to ruin it. If I'd told him who I was, he would've probably thought the only reason I was talking to him was because I still wanted the interview and that wasn't it at all."

"You were in a tough spot."

"Not to mention, if I said something about the interview and he got angry about it, he could've had me fired." I paused to blow my nose. "Of course, he wound up doing that anyway."

"Did he report you to management?"

"I don't think so, but someone heard us arguing in the hallway, told my boss, and he called me into his office to tell me my behavior was unacceptable. Like I'm the only employee who ever slept with a guest." I threw myself back against the cushions with a huff. "What am I going to do, Aunt Meg? I have less than twenty-four hours to finish my senior project. The online magazine is done except for the cover story, but that's the biggest part of it. It was supposed to be Onyx Knight. I was so sure I'd get the interview once I got backstage... now I have nothing but a bunch of fluff articles and album reviews. No meaty content. The way it is now, not only am I going to fail the class, but I won't graduate either."

"Nonsense. Let's go have some dinner. While we're eating, we can put our heads together and potentially come up with a plan."

"Okay." I wasn't sure what else to do, so I got up and followed her to the kitchen.

"What about your friend Sam's band?" she asked as she put a thick slice of meatloaf on my plate. "The one who got you backstage."

My friend Sam worked at the arena as part of the in-house security team. We'd had a couple of classes together and he'd offered to sneak me backstage in exchange for featuring his band in the e-zine at some later date. I'd quickly agreed, so confident I'd be able to talk someone in the band into letting me interview them. I'd put all my eggs in one basket, and now I was screwed.

"Sam's band is local," I said, resting my chin in my hand and toying with the food Aunt Meg put in front of me. "I don't know if Professor Russell will even consider letting me feature a local band. The whole point of the exercise is to push your limits professionally. He told me from the get-go he didn't think I could get an interview with Onyx Knight. Dammit, what am I going to do?"

"It's too late to ask permission," she said softly. "All you can do now is take control and do the story. Dig into the trials and tribulations of trying to make it in today's music business. Ask him for details about the worst gig they've ever had or a time when they didn't get paid. Stuff that will make people think. Even if it's not what you'd originally planned, don't give up. Show them you can pivot and still create something wonderful and interesting."

"I'll call him as soon as we eat," I said, trying to wrap my head around what she'd said. It wasn't the story I wanted, but it was the one that was potentially available to me. Right now. And I didn't have time to be picky.

"Cheer up," Aunt Meg said, winking. "There's cherry pie for dessert.

I smiled in spite of the churning in my stomach.

I honestly didn't know what I would do without her.

SAM CAME THROUGH LIKE A CHAMP, and though it wasn't the kind of interview I'd been hoping for, it was a lot of fun. The guys in his band, Crimson Edge, were happy to talk, and I got tons of anecdotes about everything from them struggling to find rehearsal space to the summer tour they'd done using Sam's mom's minivan to drive across the country, to a gig where the audience threw dildos at them.

I spent the next two days transcribing the four hours of recordings I had and then writing the story. Aunt Meg edited it for me, and an hour before I had to make my website live, I uploaded the final article. The band had given me a few PR photos I could use, and I'd taken a handful with my phone, so I'd done the best I could with what I had. Professor Russell would be disappointed, I know that, but as long as I passed, I didn't care what grade he gave me.

Once it was done, I stared at the screen of my computer for a long time.

I was exhausted. I hadn't slept much the night I'd spent with Zeke, and I hadn't slept at all last night. My body was dragging, but my brain was still on high alert, worried and stressed and trying to navigate a plethora of emotions. I hadn't had time to process what Zeke and I had done. Not really. Between getting fired and scrambling to finish my project, I'd been in survival mode.

And now I was in recovery mode.

I had to sleep and tomorrow I had to find another job.

Aunt Meg's disability check wasn't enough for us to live on, so I didn't have a choice but to work. Two or three days a week at the resort had been plenty, but if I worked elsewhere, I'd have to get weekend shifts to make similar money. There were lots of restaurants near the mall, so that was where I'd start looking.

I needed to find something quickly, because I had bills to pay, and Aunt Meg didn't have anything extra to give me. Not even as a loan. Her medications cost a fortune, and I didn't mind helping out because she was finally starting to feel better. I couldn't remember the last time she'd been able to cook full meals, but she'd done it the last two nights like she had when I was younger. It felt good to see her moving around again, doing things she enjoyed, like cooking and scrapbooking. So, I'd do whatever I had to for her to be able to continue buying her meds.

There would be plenty of time to think about Zeke and the things we'd done together—not to mention how badly I'd screwed everything up—but not until I had a job. Everything else had to wait.

I was going to get a good night's sleep and first thing tomorrow, I would walk into every decent restaurant in the area. By the end of the week, I intended to have a new job. Maybe even for the weekend. I'd have to train anywhere that hired me, so the sooner I started, the better.

"Are you still up?" Aunt Meg stood in the doorway of my bedroom.

I glanced up at her. "Yeah. The e-zine just went live. Now I'm trying to wind down enough to sleep."

"You look ready to collapse. Shall I make you some chamomile tea to help you relax?"

"I can do it, Aunt Meg." I started to get up, but she waved me back down.

"Don't be silly. You've spent a lot of time taking care of me the last year or so. Let me return the favor while I'm feeling good."

"You've been taking care of me since Mom died," I said softly.

She shook her head. "We've been taking care of each other. And that's what family does, right? We're here for each other."

"I love you, Aunt Meg."

"And I love you, darling. Now put on your PJs and I'll be back in a few with your tea."

No matter how tough things were, I was lucky to have someone like Aunt Meg in my life.

9

———————

Z *eke*

AFTER CHICAGO, we hit the road hard. Almost no days off for the next few weeks, playing to sold out crowds every night and partying until dawn. I hadn't allowed myself to let loose like this in a long time, but Carter was nothing if not consistent, and once he figured out I was in a funk he'd made it his life's mission to bring me out of it.

It was like putting a band-aid on a severed jugular vein.

The harder I partied, the more aggravated I got. I'd even snapped at my guitar tech last night, which almost never happened. He was as good and professional as they got, worth every dime I paid him to not just keep my equipment in top form but to anticipate what I needed before I needed it. And last night I'd lost it over a pick. I was particular about what I used, and normally I didn't use them at all. For the few songs I did, I liked specific ones, and they were different for each song. Roddy had put out a few of each but I'd stupidly thrown the one I needed next into the crowd. Instead of just sucking it up—it wasn't that big of a deal—I'd lost my temper afterward, telling him he'd left me unprepared.

This morning I'd ordered him a case of his favorite scotch whisky and had it delivered to the venue where we were playing. I owed him more than scotch as an apology, but I was still too hungover for that. I'd deal with the verbal shit later.

Stepping over the sleeping bodies all over the suite Carter and I had reserved for the party last night, I grabbed my things and slipped out, going back to my own room. I changed into shorts and a tank top, forced my feet into sneakers, and then headed down to the hotel gym. I didn't like using hotel facilities because I got recognized too often, but I desperately needed to sweat out the toxins I'd been putting in my body. I also needed to drink about a gallon of water, but I settled for picking up a couple of liters at the hotel convenience store.

Kingston was on the treadmill when I got there, and he lifted his chin in acknowledgement as I got on the one next to him.

"Long night?" he asked, grinning.

"Somethin' like that."

"You work whatever it is out of your system?"

"Fuck if I know."

"This about the reporter?"

I grunted in response, picking up speed. I needed to warm up, but I also needed to sweat. Until my muscles burned and my stomach was threatening to revolt. Whether or not it would work I had no idea, but something had to give because I hadn't been myself since leaving Minnesota. I could fake it with the best of them. I just didn't want to.

"You want to talk?" Kingston asked, jogging beside me.

"Nothin' to talk about."

"Come on. I know you better than that."

Kingston had become my best friend over the last couple of years. The whole band was fairly close, but while Carter and I had been growing apart, Kingston and I had found a lot more in common than music. And he was easy to talk to. Even when I didn't want to talk.

"I thought she was different," I said under my breath.

"Ah. *She*. The reporter who got under your skin and then stabbed you in the dick."

I grunted at his crude analogy. "Something like that."

"What are you going to do?"

"There's nothing to do."

"She must've been something. I haven't seen you party this hard in years. Except for the needles, you're giving Carter a run for his money."

I glanced at him in surprise, forgetting all about Presley. This was news about Carter. I hadn't seen him using the hard stuff lately, so I was caught off-guard. He'd been in rehab a few years ago to kick the habit, and I'd thought he was only drinking and doing the occasional line of coke. "You serious? He's using H again?"

Heroin was scary stuff.

I was no angel, but needles weren't my favorite even in a medical setting, so the idea of shooting up for fun was beyond me. I avoided heroin like the fucking plague.

"I haven't seen it," he acknowledged, "but Pete did and told me."

Pete Simms was Kellan's guitar tech.

"Are we doing another intervention?"

"I don't know." He stared straight ahead. "But I'm worried."

"Fuck." I worried about Carter too. We were only a year apart, and he was older, but he was like the fun-loving little brother you wanted around until he broke something. Then you just wanted to call your mom and tell her to take him home. Except we were all the mom in this analogy, and there was nowhere to send Carter if we wanted to keep touring.

"But we're not supposed to be talking about Carter," he said. "I want to know what's up with you."

"I'm tired, man," I said quietly, deciding to talk about the bigger situation that had been going on much longer than the Presley situation. "I love touring, playing music with you guys, but we haven't had any real time off in years. If you think about it, we've been doing this for eight years and we've been going full steam ahead almost the whole time. At some point, something's got to give."

Kingston blew out a breath. "It's hard to figure out a time to take a break. The tour dates, album sales, merch, it's all just one big, interconnected business machine that keeps snowballing. Every time we try to pull back, some other thing happens to push us into the thick of things."

"It's bullshit, King. How much money do we need?"

"I dunno." He glanced at me, and our eyes locked for a beat.

"Is this you or is this management?" I asked finally.

"It's both. I feel like we should ride the success wave as long as we can. We won't be on top forever."

"Why not?" I countered. "The Stones, Crue, Metallica—they've been at it for decades. Isn't longevity the plan?"

"It is, but there are no guarantees in life."

"Of course not. But we're established. All bands have the odd album that flops, it's gonna happen, but the live shows? That's our golden ticket. Every single night is sold out. If you ask me, that won't change. And frankly, I think people will be even more desperate to come to shows if we stop touring for a while."

"That what you want?" Kingston asked. "You need a break that badly?"

"I really fucking do." I picked up my pace and Kingston matched my strides. I was six-five to his six-one, but he was leaner and faster than me in general. My bulk held me back sometimes, though I could bench press him if I had to.

"We're locked in until fall."

"I know."

"Let's have a band meeting. We can talk it out."

"Carter and Tommy are going to say no fuckin' way. Kellan will see which way the tide is running, and he'll follow whichever group he thinks will get him what he wants."

"Let me talk to Aurora and see if I can get Tommy alone," Kingston said. "If you're burning out, and Carter's fallen off the wagon, it's probably time to cut back."

I merely nodded.

I'd heard this before but wouldn't believe it until I saw it happen.

It wasn't that Kingston was lying. There were five men with five distinct personalities in this band, and there was usually a majority when we made these kinds of decisions. How we moved forward would depend on who decided what. And most of the time, that was anyone's guess.

We rolled into Kansas City at dawn on a Friday, and I immediately caught a cab to the Hilton. I was so done with the fucking tour bus, it wasn't even funny. I'd already announced that I wasn't going anywhere in Europe unless we were flying. Period. If they insisted on a bus, they'd have to tour without me. To my surprise, everyone but Carter had been on board, and he'd eventually caved too. I had a feeling everyone was burning out; I was just the only one willing to admit it.

When my phone rang at nine-thirty and I saw my business manager's name on the screen, I hesitated. We talked every couple of months to discuss investments, my spending, any unexpected bills that came along, things like that. I was dog tired and desperately wanted a nap, so I wasn't in the mood, but I figured it was better to get it over with. Otherwise, I'd have to call him later.

"Hey, Bruno."

"Hey, Zeke."

"What's up?"

"Same shit, different day. You know how it is."

I chuckled. "I do."

"So, listen. There's been some spending I think you need to know about."

"I haven't bought much of anything," I said in confusion.

"I know. I'm talking about your mom."

I sighed. This wasn't going to be good.

"What'd she buy now?" I asked warily.

"Three new Mercedes. At least, she's trying to. Along with the insurance and extended warranties. The dealership called me yesterday."

"Three?" I demanded, incredulously.

"Yup. One for your dad, one for someone named Willie Frost, and one for Roman Stepanian."

I huffed out a breath of irritation. Willie was my mother's deadbeat brother-in-law—the husband of her deceased sister—and Roman was my cousin. He was my mother's brother's son. He was thirty-two, claimed he was a mechanic, though I'd never seen him work on a car, and had recently gotten married. I knew this because although I hadn't been invited to the wedding, my mother had gifted him and his wife five thousand dollars.

"There's also a nine-thousand-dollar bill from Macy's and—"

"Nine grand?" I demanded. "Jesus fucking Christ. How many shoes and purses does she need?"

"Oh, my friend, you ain't heard nothin' yet. Fifteen grand at the Coach store and another six at Neiman-Marcus."

"Turn off the fucking Amex," I hissed, irritation washing over me like a blanket of red-hot fire ants. My parents were generally amazing and had been the most supportive people a musician like me could have wanted when I told them I was going to play music for a living. I didn't mind supporting them, and I was extremely generous, but this was ridiculous. I didn't know what was happening with my mom, but I was going to find out.

"You sure?" he asked quietly. We'd done this once before and my mother had cried. It had been a whole ordeal, but I didn't have the patience for this kind of shit anymore. Especially when I was looking to take some time off. I couldn't afford to do that, though, if my family was planning to spend my money as fast as I made it.

"Absolutely. And my dad's card gets turned off at five grand."

"Your dad never uses it."

"I know. But once Mom figures out she's cut off, she'll try to use his and that's not happening."

"What do I say when she calls?"

"She won't be calling. I'll take care of this today. I have to go. Thanks for the head's up."

"So… you want me to pay all of these bills?"

"That's a big no. Pay the department store shit, but the cars? Fuck that. Tell them no."

"Your mom will probably stroke out."

"Believe me, I know, but this is out of control. I'll call you back once I've talked to her."

"You might want to have a couple of drinks first."

"Tell me about it."

I disconnected and stared at the phone.

Fuck. This was going to suck.

My mom would argue and cajole. Once she realized I was serious, she would cry. Her final tactic would be to hang up and freeze me out. Then, after she made my dad insane for a few days, he would call and beg me to change my mind. That wouldn't happen this time, though. And I had to make sure she knew that. Just because I made tens of millions of dollars every year didn't mean I always would. Or that she could spend it like it was hers.

If I wasn't careful, there wouldn't be anything left by the time I had the chance to enjoy it. And there wasn't much I enjoyed in my life these days.

10

P*resley*

WORKING five days a week was exhausting. The money was decent, but it felt like I never slept enough. It had only been a few weeks, and I was dragging. I'd been waiting tables for four years, so it wasn't like I couldn't do the job, but this restaurant by the mall was always slammed. No breaks, no time to grab a drink, nothing but running from one table to the next.

Today I was meeting with my advisor about graduation and his email hadn't sounded like he had good news, which made my stomach churn with anxiety. By the time I got to his office, I felt like I might lose my breakfast, and I paused outside the door to take a few deep breaths.

I'd done a great job on my final project, no matter what he said. I was proud of the work I'd done, even if I hadn't managed to snag an interview with the hottest rock band in the world. I had to keep that in mind as I knocked on his door and walked into his office.

"Hi, Dr. Russell."

"Good afternoon, Presley. Have a seat." He took off his reading glasses and looked at me.

"Based on your tone of voice, I'm guessing you don't have good news for me," I said quietly.

He sighed. "I do not."

Fuck.

"Are you failing me?" I asked, my heart sinking.

"Although you did excellent work on your e-zine, the content isn't what we agreed upon." He sifted through some papers on his desk. "Your design and the technical part of the project was top-notch, but I can't in good conscience give you a pass on that alone."

"Well, if half the project was perfect, and the other half was a fail, wouldn't that be a C?" I asked.

"It's not that simple, Presley. You chose the *project* track, and the agreement was that you would push the boundaries and accomplish something you wouldn't normally be able to do as a college student. The whole point was for those of you who went that direction to be treated like employees, instead of students. If you recall, I tried to talk you out of the music magazine idea, but you insisted you could do it."

"I *did* do it," I said quietly.

"You did. But not the way we agreed it would be done. Frankly, it wasn't what I expected from you, Presley. You've always been a stellar student. This project fell flat. If that interview had been your assignment at a real magazine, your editor could very well have fired you."

"I spent eight months creating the website, the content—even getting legitimate advertising! And you're going to fail me because the guys in Onyx Knight decided to be jerks and blow me off? How is that fair?"

"Did someone tell you that life would be fair? In the music industry, no less?" He sighed, putting his glasses back on. "Look, I have a compromise for you." He ruffled some more papers around on his desk until he found the one he was looking for.

I was already exhausted and nauseated, and now my chest tightened as I waited to hear if there was anything I could do to graduate.

"Re-take the class this summer and find another band to interview. Maybe not quite at the level of Onyx Knight, but if you can get a band with some level of success—instead of a local band—I'll pass you and you can graduate."

I stared at him, trying to understand why he was being such a hard ass about this. He knew how much I'd struggled since Aunt Meg's diagnosis. How she couldn't work anymore because of it. How I was already drowning in student loans since I hadn't qualified for any scholarships. He knew damn well I couldn't afford another semester of classes. Not to mention that I needed to start working full-time as soon as possible.

"I can't afford another semester," I whispered, hating the tears that filled my eyes. "Aunt Meg's meds cost a fortune and her disability only goes so far."

"I'm sorry, Presley. I truly am. If it was just up to me, I could make an exception, but there's a whole committee. You opted for the project track."

"So that's it? You're failing me, so I can't graduate, and I can only get my degree if I come back over the summer, *and* somehow find another big band to write about?"

"Unless you want to change your entire project, but then you'd need to come back for a full semester in the fall."

I opened my mouth, but a wave of nausea hit me that was strong enough to make my stomach roll.

"Presley?"

"I'm sorry. I'm not feeling great. Excuse me."

I barely got out of the room before I heaved into the nearest garbage can. Dammit.

I was so embarrassed and humiliated it was making me physically ill.

"Presley? Are you okay?"

I tried to breathe in through my nose, out through my mouth. "I'll be fine." I spoke through gritted teeth, praying I wouldn't vomit in front of him.

"Can I call someone—"

"No! I'm fine." I dug a tissue out of my purse and wiped my mouth before making a beeline for the nearest bathroom.

SOMETHING SMELLED GOOD, but Aunt Meg wasn't in the kitchen or the living room when I got home, and I momentarily forgot about my miserable meeting and unsettled stomach. Her car had been in the driveway, so I hurried up the stairs to her room.

"Aunt Meg?"

"In here, honey."

"Are you oaky?" I stood in the doorway of her bedroom worriedly.

"Just feeling weak today," she said. "But come tell me about your meeting."

I sighed, perching on the edge of her mattress. "He failed me."

"Bastard." Her blue eyes glittered with annoyance. Her body may have been falling apart, but her spirit was as feisty as ever.

"He said I can re-take that part of the class in the summer if I can find another band to interview."

"Oh." Her face brightened. "That's good news."

I gave her a look. "Aunt Meg. Where will I get the money? I already have student loans up the butt. I don't want to take out more. Not to mention, I have to start working full-time."

"But you worked so hard for your degree. We can get by another few months."

My shoulders slumped, and I felt a fresh wave of tears coming on.

What the hell was wrong with me? I never cried like this.

"It's going to be okay." Aunt Meg sat up. "And get this." She held up her phone. "Remember that video my friend Ginnie and I did for the Insta-whatever?"

"It's called InstaPixel," I said, laughing. She'd only recently discovered that there were social media platforms beyond Facebook. She'd started watching videos on InstaPixel, which was the newest one that had taken the world by storm, and she and her friend had posted something on there last week. I'd been so caught up in learning my new job I hadn't paid that much attention.

"Well, it got 8000 views." She paused. "Ginnie said that means it went viral."

I wrinkled my nose. "I wouldn't say that's viral. Viral is more like a hundred thousand. But 8K is really good." I pulled out my phone and opened the app. "What's your handle?"

"Eye-Lights with Aunt Meg." Her eyes twinkled.

"Eye-Lights?" I asked, as I typed it in.

"Ginnie buys all these so-called miracle creams and potions. You know the ones, where they promise to temporarily make all your wrinkles and shit go away? And then she doesn't use them. So we had a few glasses of wine that night and decided to video ourselves trying them out. We chose four of them, and we each did two, one on each half of our faces. And one of the four worked!"

"Really?" I found the video and played it.

Aunt Meg was a lot of fun, especially after a few glasses of wine. She giggled and told the most cringe-worthy jokes, but they were so bad you couldn't help but laugh. Ginnie didn't have a good persona for this kind of thing, but Aunt Meg killed it. With her infectious laughter, combined with the intelligent way she talked about her aging skin and the changes she was undergoing with the MS, she was incredibly engaging. No wonder it had gotten so many views.

"And today," she continued when the video ended, "someone left me one of those private messages, offering to send me a sample of their cream if I would do it in a video. I don't know if it's a scam or not, but it's kind of fun, right?"

"Let me see." She handed me her phone and I checked out the messages. Sure enough, a new skincare company called SkinWrecked, had contacted her, offering to send her samples if she would do videos talking about them.

"It looks legit," I said. "As long as they don't ask for any money, I don't see the harm."

"Ginnie's going to die," she said, shaking her head.

"I hope not," I quipped, getting up.

"Let's eat," she said. "I cooked earlier and then came up for a little nap. Now I'm feeling better so we can warm up the lasagna and have dinner."

"Okay." I held out a hand to help her as she carefully got to her feet.

"And you'll see. We'll figure out what to do about your project."

"Dr. Russell warned me I was taking a big risk," I admitted. "But I honestly thought I could do it. I was so sure if Sam got me backstage, I could get someone in the band to talk to me. Even ten minutes worth of an interview would've been enough to write the cover story."

"The story you wrote was really good," she said. "You got two more advertisers after it came out. And you're getting visits to the site every day."

"Like forty or fifty," I mumbled. "That's not very impressive. And a lot of those hits are probably the same people coming back every day looking for new content. When they don't find it, they're going to get bored."

"So add new content." She quirked a brow at me.

"It's not that easy," I said. "And besides, now that I won't be graduating, I don't know if I want to keep it up."

"Now you listen to me." She put her hands on her hips as we got to the bottom of the stairs. "You put a ton of heart, not to mention time, into that website. You absolutely need to continue it."

"Aunt Meg. It's hosted on the school's server. Once the semester is over, they'll take it down and I can't afford to pay for web hosting right now."

"Of course we can." She squeezed my arm. "How much can it cost?"

"I don't know. I'd have to buy a domain name and then the server..." I let out a heavy sigh. "It's a lot, Meg."

"I follow a bunch of book bloggers who host websites, and I'm sure they don't all spend a ton of money. There has to be an inexpensive way to do it."

I grabbed two potholders and pulled the lasagna out of the oven. "This is still warm."

"Then let's eat. And you can Google inexpensive website hosting or whatever it's called."

"Okay." I smiled, shaking my head. She was like a dog with a bone once she got something in her head. It was one of the things I loved about her, but I didn't know what I would do going forward. Right now, it felt like the rug had been pulled out from under me. I'd been so sure I'd graduate next month.

I looked down at the piece of lasagna Aunt Meg had just put in front of me and my stomach rolled.

The next thing I knew I was puking my guts out into the trash can.

11

————————

Z^{eke}

VEGAS WAS ALWAYS a great city to play in. The fans loved us, the venue had amazing acoustics, and we were playing three nights, which meant I could sleep in the same hotel room and not have to be on the fucking bus. It also meant my parents, sister, and brother-in-law were coming to one of the shows, which should prove interesting. It was only a four-hour drive for them, so they were coming up Saturday morning, would see the show Saturday night, and probably drive home Sunday. Unless they decided to stay for Sunday night's show as well.

My mother and I hadn't spoken since I'd cut off her credit cards, and as I'd expected, she was making my dad's life miserable. However, he was on my side this time, and he'd told me to do what I needed to do. At least someone in my family understood my frustration. My sister had called to plead my mother's case, but I'd nipped that in the bud when I reminded her that Mom hadn't bought her a Mercedes.

That was the irony of it all.

Mom seemed to think my brother and sister, Stepan and Marina, should earn things the old-fashioned way for some reason. It was all the distant relatives she wanted to help. Cousins, aunts, uncles, and even a handful of family members back in Armenia—people she'd never even met in person. I honestly didn't understand it, and at least until we saw each other in person,

I didn't have enough brain power to try anymore. If she wanted to talk this weekend, I'd be willing to listen, but enough was enough.

"Have you seen Carter?" Pete asked me as Nobody's Fool played their encore. Once they got off stage we would start warming up, stretching and jogging in place to get the blood flowing. I usually played a few riffs, to get myself in the right mind set.

I rolled my eyes. "Seriously?"

"I haven't seen him since soundcheck," he said, his dark eyes narrowed with concern. It was loud, so I was half-listening and half reading his lips. "He took off with some groupie and she looked... rough."

"Rough?" I questioned.

"Rough. Like, drug dealer rough."

"Fuck." I looked around for Kingston and motioned him over. "We might have a problem."

"What kind of problem?" He looked from me to Pete.

"Carter may be AWOL," I said.

"King!" Tommy let out a whistle to get our attention. We all turned, and he made a "come here" motion with his hands.

"What's up?" I asked as we joined him.

"We have a problem."

"Didn't I just say that?" I muttered, following him down to the dressing room. He opened the door and there was Carter, butt naked, sprawled on the floor, and fast asleep.

"I couldn't wake him up," Tommy said. "He's breathing, but he's out cold."

"Get some cold water," I said to Pete, who hurried over to the hospitality table. He tossed me a bottle, and I unscrewed the top, leaning over and emptying it on Carter's face. Carter turned his head from side to side, coughed a little, and then batted his hands, as if trying to stop the water.

"Wh-what's hap-ing?" he asked, his speech slurred.

"We have a show!" Kingston snapped. "What did you take?"

"Ughhh." Carter's eyes closed again.

"Fuck, he can't play like this," Tommy said, his face tight with worry.

"Go find Tyler," I said to Kingston. "Ask him if he can fill in if we can't get Carter going."

Kingston didn't hesitate because Nobody's Fool's last song had just ended, which meant they might be headed out any minute now. They were based in Vegas, so they would be sleeping in their respective homes tonight. In fact, this was the end of the tour for them, so ending it in Vegas had been perfect and I didn't know what their plans were. We were headed to Europe in two weeks, but we hadn't been able to work out the timing to take Nobody's Fool with us.

"Where's Ross?" I asked, looking around. "We can't leave Carter alone, but we need to get on stage soon."

"I'll find him." Tommy took off and I knelt next to Carter, putting a gentle hand on his shoulder. I was annoyed as fuck, but I worried about him too. This had happened before, and I'd thought we'd gotten past it. Obviously, we all needed to pay more attention. Yes, he was a grown man, but he was a rich one who was tempted every fucking day.

Last time this had happened, we'd hidden the issues from the public, but maybe it was time to put it out there. We had great fans in general. They brought us gifts, homemade food, invited us to their homes and businesses, sent us wonderful fan mail. Sure, there was the occasional dickhead, but that happened in every walk of life. So maybe if we made it clear that Carter was struggling, people would stop trying to party with him.

Or maybe not.

Maybe I was living in a goddamn fantasy world where people cared about each other.

"Hey, what's going on?" Tyler and Kingston came into the room, and Tyler's gaze fell on Carter. "Jesus fuck. Does he need a doctor?"

"Tommy went to get Ross," I said.

"How much of our set do you know?" Kingston asked him.

Tyler wobbled his hand from side to side. "Maybe forty percent? But I can fake it. It's not my first day playing bass."

I managed to grin up at him. "No, it's not."

Before Nobody's Fool, Tyler had been the bass player for a band called Pretty Harts. They'd been the sweethearts of the hard rock world before us. We'd been rising to fame around the time they'd been winding down, as their lead guitarist, Casey Hart, fell in love with and married an eastern European king. Now she was a queen with a bunch of kids and responsibilities, and Tyler—along with Pretty Harts' drummer, Bash—had formed a new band.

"Oh, fuck me loud." Ross stood in the doorway shaking his head. "God dammit, Carter."

❧

THANKFULLY, Tyler filled in for us with no problem and Carter just needed to sleep it off. The band, however, called a meeting the next day once Carter had woken up, showered, and eaten. He was contrite today, not looking any of us in the eye as he tried to explain.

"I screwed up," he said. "I was drunk off my ass and when she—"

"Who's she?" I asked, interrupting.

"Tori. I see her whenever we're in Vegas. She never used to be into the hard stuff." He scratched his head. "I guess that's changed. She shot me up before I even realized what was happening. I swear, guys. It was a one off."

"Not true, man." Pete spoke up. He'd made us sign something this morning, protecting his job, because he knew Carter would be furious when he ratted him out. Whether or not he'd be pissed enough to fire him, we couldn't be sure, but Pete had a family back in Oklahoma, so he wasn't taking the chance, and I understood that.

"Come on." Carter gave him a look. "It happened one other time but—"

"Three other times." Pete folded his arms across his chest. He was a big guy in his forties. He'd been a bass tech for a long time and was one of the best in the business, so he wasn't messing around.

"What are you, my fucking mom?" Carter snapped, all signs of remorseful Carter disintegrating and replaced by petulant, addicted Carter.

"It's his job to make sure you're on stage when you have to be," Ross interjected. "And he didn't say a word until last night. Carter, do you not realize how much money we lose if you can't play and we have to refund a full house of tickets?"

Carter rolled his eyes. "Tyler stepped in. It was fine. And anyway, it never happened before. I'm on top of this."

"It's happened more than once before," Kingston said. "Remember Houston a few years back? And then Buffalo last summer?"

Carter didn't respond.

"You're not on top of shit," I muttered. "Look, I love you, man. You're my bro. But you know as well as I do this goes beyond the band. H can kill you. Is the high worth it?"

"Seems to me all it did was make you piss your pants and pass out," Tommy added. "How is that a good high?"

Carter sighed, rubbing his eyes. "Look, I'm sorry. Okay? Like I said, I fuck up sometimes. I'm not perfect like you fuckers."

"Don't do that," Kingston said, shaking his head. "It's not cool."

"What do you want from me? I'm an addict!" Carter threw up his hands.

"You can get sober," I said quietly. "You did it before."

"There's nothing to do on tour," he protested. "We spend twenty-three hours a day chasing the high of being on stage for an hour."

"Seventy-five minutes," Kellan corrected him blandly.

We played a sixty-minute set and then another fifteen minutes or so with our encores. Two songs for the first, and one for the second. Once in a while, we added a third and played covers if we had special guests that would perform with us. We tried to give our fans their money's worth, but that wasn't the point now.

"I said I was sorry."

"We want you to go back to rehab for the two weeks between the end of the North American tour and the start of Europe," Ross said. "Otherwise, we're finding a replacement."

"*What?!*" Carter shot out of his seat. "You can't fucking replace me."

"We can." Ross motioned to a stack of papers on the table. "It says so in the contract. I can read it out loud if you want. If you recall, it was one of the things you asked us to do after you got sober last time."

Carter threw his coffee cup across the room, breathing hard and watching as it shattered, and the dark liquid ran down the wall.

None of us moved.

This was classic addict behavior.

We were expecting him to freak out.

Two weeks in rehab wasn't nearly enough time, but it would hopefully be the kickstart he needed to get us through the summer. Then we'd work on sending him back for an extended stint. Short-term, we didn't have a lot of options. Legally, we could replace him in Europe, but it wouldn't be the same. Carter was magic on the bass—he was a big part of our sound and fans loved him. When he was healthy and performing at the top of his game, he was both a talented musician and an enigmatic performer. When he wasn't, it was a nightmare.

"This is bullshit." Carter glared at us. "This is the first time I screwed up in a really long fucking time. I'm not some kid you get to order around."

"You *asked* us to do this," I reminded him. "It's not like babysitting you is fun."

"Then don't fucking do it."

"If we hadn't been, the show last night would've been canceled and we would've been out a few hundred K," Ross said.

"Fuck you." Carter headed for the door, but Kellan got there first, blocking his path.

"Don't make this into a full-blown intervention," Kellan said quietly. "If we have to call your lawyer, you know it'll be ugly."

"Leave him out of it," Carter snapped.

"Then go sit down."

The two of them eyed each other as long seconds ticked by.

Finally, it was Carter who backed down.

"Where are you sending me?" he asked, resting his forearms on his thighs. It was like the fight had magically drained out of him and now he was just tired. "Malibu?"

"That's where you were last time. You liked it there."

"Food was good," he agreed.

"So you'll go?" Ross asked.

"Doesn't look like I have a choice." He shrugged.

"Hey, you could always talk to my mother about her spending instead," I said, trying to lighten the mood.

He grimaced, since he knew all about my current issues with my mother.

"No thanks. I'll stick to rehab." He gave me a half-hearted thumb's up, and I prayed we were doing the right thing. It didn't feel like it, but nothing felt right anymore. Not in a long time, but especially not since Minneapolis.

12

———

P *resley*

No no no no.

I stared at the pregnancy test in horror.

This couldn't be happening.

It had been exactly five weeks since I'd slept with Zeke.

Two weeks since I'd started feeling queasy.

And now this.

I had two more tests to take but I would have to wait.

Okay, no.

What the hell was I thinking? I couldn't wait until morning.

I'd probably have an anxiety attack by then.

I quickly peed on the other two tests and left them on the counter before hurrying to Aunt Meg's room. I trusted her with everything, and she was probably the only person who'd be able to get me through this. At the very least, I needed her advice because this was the last thing either of us needed.

"Aunt Meg?" I knocked lightly on her door before opening it a few inches. "Are you awake? I need to talk to you."

She looked up from the book she was reading and then slowly closed it.

"Come on in. What's wrong?" She knew me so well.

Without thinking, I thrust the positive pregnancy test in her direction.

The one with the blue letters flashing the word "pregnant" like an angry beacon bringing a message of despair.

"Oh, my." Aunt Meg's eyes widened for a moment. Then she met my eyes. "How reliable are these types of tests? I've never used one."

"I'm waiting for two more tests, different brands, but they're supposedly fairly accurate." My voice sounded funny to my own ears.

"Okay, breathe. You look like you're about to pass out." She swung her legs over the side of her bed with surprising dexterity and moved to sit on the edge of the mattress with me. "This was with Zeke, yes?"

"There's never been anyone else," I replied in a harsh whisper, my eyes flooding with tears. "Oh my god. What am I going to do?"

"You have to get in touch with him." She paused. "Unless you just want to terminate and be done?"

I buried my face in my hands. I had no idea what I might do. The thought of ending the pregnancy, and making the whole thing go away, was appealing. But another part of me wasn't sure. Would I regret it? Would I be a good mom? Did I even know how to be a mom? I had a thousand questions and no answers.

"You don't have to decide tonight," Aunt Meg said softly. "Let's go look at the other two tests. Tomorrow, you go see the doctor."

"We were careful!" I whispered. "He always used a condom and—" My breath stalled in my lungs as my blood turned to ice. "Oh shit."

"What?"

"There was a moment... it was literally seconds. It was early in the morning. He started to..." I had no issue talking to Aunt Meg about most things but giving her the details of the sex I'd had with Zeke bordered on embarrassing. "It was literally just a second or so. He wasn't even all the way in when we realized it and he stopped to put on a condom."

"You know that a man doesn't have to ejaculate, right? The pre-ejaculate, that clear liquid that comes out when he's aroused? That's the same thing."

"Dammit." I closed my eyes.

This was my nightmare.

One of the reasons I'd avoided sex.

I had no business getting pregnant at this stage of my life. I was basically a college dropout since I wasn't going to graduate, was waiting tables to survive, with no idea what the future held. Aunt Meg and I were barely scraping by. How the hell could we afford a baby?

The two other tests were positive as well, and Aunt Meg and I sat up half the night discussing options.

"You didn't do this by yourself," Aunt Meg pointed out. "You have to tell him what happened and find out what he wants to do."

"He wants to never talk to me again," I said miserably. "That's what he wants."

"Too bad. It was his fault he didn't put the condom on right away."

"I don't have any way to get in touch with him."

"Find out his record company or who the band's management is. Then you call and leave messages. If you have to tell them you're pregnant, do it."

"Why is all this awful stuff happening to me?" I asked, using a tissue to dab my eyes. I'd cried so much tonight I didn't know how there were any tears left.

"Sometimes God, the universe, fate—whatever force you believe in—has plans we can't possibly know about until later."

"Was it God's plan for you to be alone after Jeremy died?" I asked softly, referring to her late husband.

"I don't know," she said, sliding an arm around my shoulders. "But maybe if he'd lived, and we'd had kids of our own, I wouldn't have been in a place where I could have taken care of you when your mom died. Maybe helping raise you was what I was supposed to do instead."

"I'd be grumpy about that if I were you," I sniffled. "Trading the man you loved for a hormonal teenager."

She chuckled. "There was no *trade*. Jeremy was going to die that day regardless. You weren't even born yet. And no matter how much I miss him, I wouldn't trade the relationship I have with you for anything."

I got weepy all over again. "I love you, Aunt Meg."

"I love you too. And whatever you decide about this baby, I'll always have your back. If you keep it and Zeke doesn't want to be in its life, then we'll figure it out. Just like we always do."

"Do you think it's possible he's really that heartless?" I whispered.

"I don't know him, so it's hard to say."

Well, one way or another, we would find out because deep down, I already knew I was keeping this baby.

I'D LEFT four messages for Zeke at his management company, and I hadn't heard a peep from him. The woman who answered the phone had sighed heavily the last time I'd called, saying she'd pass on the message, but there hadn't been a word. Part of me couldn't believe he would be this callous, but one call per week over the course of four weeks meant he probably wanted nothing to do with me. Or his child.

I was due in mid-December and the morning sickness had been kicking my ass. I'd called out of work more in the last month than I had in the last four years total, and I had a bad feeling I was going to get fired if I did it again. Of course, I wouldn't be able to carry big, heavy trays for much longer either, so I'd already started looking for something else. The issue was, who would hire someone who was already ten weeks pregnant?

Panic had set in, and I'd geared myself up to make the fifth call on Monday. I wouldn't hang up until I talked to someone in charge. It seemed ridiculous that they wouldn't even address the issue.

"Ms. Figueroa? This is Aurora Bentley. I'm Onyx Knight's manager. I understand you've been calling repeatedly to reach Big Z."

"Yes." I tried to keep my voice steady. "We, uh, had an accident when we were together in March. I really need to talk to him."

"Ms. Figueroa." The way she said my name sounded like she was saying something vile.

As if *I* were vile.

And I was mortified.

"Do you know how many women call here trying to reach someone in the band?" she continued. "If we took every phone call to the band, they would never do anything else."

"It's not like I'm lying," I hissed through clenched teeth. "He'll know for sure in about six months."

"Then, in about six months, when you've taken a DNA test and hired an attorney, have him or her contact us."

"But—" I began.

"Please don't call here again. Big Z isn't interested in you. You know that night you spent with him was just sex, right?"

I didn't know how to respond to that.

I was fully aware our night together hadn't meant anything more to him than sex, but it didn't make it any easier to hear it from a stranger.

"You're that aspiring journalist from Minnesota, yes?" she continued when I didn't say anything.

Oh, god.

She knew who I was. Which meant she'd told Zeke that I'd called, and he'd told her he didn't want to talk to me.

"Y-yes."

I felt like a total idiot.

"A word of advice, woman to woman, from someone who's worked in this industry a long time. A fake pregnancy is not the way to get in with any band. Whether you want an interview, an autograph, or a job. Think about that. And next time, I highly recommend *not* sleeping with someone you want to interview. Take care, Ms. Figueroa."

And with that, she hung up.

I stared at the phone in my hand for a long time before putting it down.

He didn't want to talk to me.

He didn't believe I was pregnant even though he had to remember that moment when he'd been bare inside me.

Didn't he?

The tiny sliver of hope I'd been holding on to disappeared in a cloud of imaginary smoke. I slid beneath the covers of my bed and wrapped my arms around my body pillow, letting the ever-present tears fall unchecked. I'd known he wouldn't want any type of relationship with me, but I'd been sure he would care that he had a child coming into the world.

But he didn't.

And it was devastating.

At the end of the day, I would be okay. One way or another, I'd find a way to take care of my baby and support all of us, even if I had to work three jobs. I just had to get past the hurt first.

It currently felt like the whole world was against me, from Zeke to Dr. Russell to that Aurora Bentley woman, and it was the most painful thing I'd ever gone through. It felt like I'd been bruised and battered, right down to my soul, but I would prove to all of them that I was tougher than they thought. They'd knocked me down, but I'd get up again. As many times as I had to.

It was going to take every ounce of strength I had, and things would probably get a lot worse before they got better, but I didn't have any choice but to push forward. Aunt Meg and the baby growing inside of me needed me.

Hell, I needed me.

To hold my head high and do the right thing for myself and for my baby.

The *only* option was for me to push forward.

One step, one day, one obstacle at a time.

13

P *resley*
One Year Later...

It was late when I got home from my shift at the restaurant. I'd only been working at this place for a month, but I was finally feeling like myself again. Well, I was getting there. My body might never recover from pregnancy, but it was a lot better. It had been four months since I'd given birth to a beautiful baby boy, who was the light of my life. He'd come into the world right on his due date and made his entrance after just forty-five minutes of pushing. Aunt Meg had been there to hold my hand and cut the cord, and I'd made her cry when I told her I was naming him after her late husband.

Jeremy William Zerkesian.

There hadn't been a chance in hell I wasn't giving him his father's name.

The further along I'd gotten in my pregnancy, the angrier I'd been.

At myself, because I was partially responsible, but mostly at Zeke.

We'd had this accident together, and being a rich, famous rockstar didn't give him a free pass to walk away just because he didn't like me. Our son deserved a father, and I deserved the financial support he could provide. I didn't need anything for myself, but I constantly needed things for the baby. Getting to him was another matter. That had proven to be more difficult than I'd anticipated, and short of going to the media, I'd been dragging my feet on calling the management company again.

I didn't want my life to turn into a circus, which was exactly what would happen if I went to the press. Sure, Zeke would hear about it, and if he saw my face, he'd know it was possible I was telling the truth. But at what cost? And what if he decided Jeremy was better off with him? The very thought turned my blood cold.

"You awake, Aunt Meg?" I asked softly as I let myself in. The only light in the room came from the soft glow of the TV, and Aunt Meg was on the couch feeding the baby.

"Of course." She looked up with a tired smile.

"How was he tonight?"

"Better. He slept from seven until about fifteen minutes ago."

It was almost three in the morning, so six hours and change wasn't too bad. I'd hoped he would be sleeping through the night by now, but we hadn't been that lucky.

"Hi, baby boy. Did you miss Mommy?" I leaned over and brushed a kiss across the top of his head. He had a full head of soft, silky dark curls and always smelled so good.

He stared up at me with his blue and brown eyes—heterochromia was definitely genetic in this case—and hiccupped.

"Why don't you go back to bed?" I suggested to Aunt Meg, reaching for the baby. "I can take over."

"I don't sleep much these days," she said. "And anyway, I have to show you something."

"Everything okay?" I asked, settling onto the couch next to her and giving Jeremy the bottle.

She picked up her phone and held it out. "Maybe I'm reading this wrong. Does this say my last post has nearly fifty thousand views?"

I took her phone from her with my free hand and scanned her latest post on InstaPixel. Sure enough, she'd had quite the blowup in views and comments. She'd continued making videos for her page, simply called Eye-Lights with Aunt Meg, and had started getting dozens of makeup samples in the mail every month. It seemed lots of skincare and makeup companies liked what she was doing, and though it hadn't turned into anything that could be considered a full-time job, she'd started making a little money from the a few advertisers. God knew we needed it.

"Fifty thousand..." I mused. "What was so different about this post?"

"I'm not sure, but I started looking at the comments and then I saw that this Lexi Rousseau person has half a million followers and—"

"Wait, did you say Lexi Rousseau?" I asked, staring at her.

"Yes. Why?"

"You know who she is, right? She's the lead singer of that band I love—Nobody's Fool."

"Oh." Aunt Meg's eyes rounded, and she took back her phone, immediately typing into it. "Here's her comment: 'I love your skincare routine, Aunt Meg! And I'm ordering a bottle of No-Glo right now. It looks amazing. Thanks for doing what you do—it sure makes it easier to see a regular person using it first.' And then she put some hearts."

"Wow. That's huge, Aunt Meg. She's a big deal."

"Is she?"

"Yeah. Her band's new album just went platinum."

"Oh." Aunt Meg looked thoughtful. "So she's a pretty big rockstar?"

"Absolutely. Nobody's Fool is hot. And she used to be with an all-girl band called Special Kay years ago too."

Aunt Meg smiled. "This is our chance for you to get your magazine up and running again."

I sighed. "That ship has sailed."

"No, it hasn't. You still get the occasional message from someone asking who you'll interview next. You need to do it. Those early interviews you did, when you were pregnant, were wonderful. Thought-provoking, insightful, and brutally honest. People loved them. If you can get someone like Lexi to talk to you, the magazine will take off. Then you can tell Dr. Russell to go pound rocks."

I stifled a giggle. "I think it's too late, and anyway, I don't have the money to re-take the class, so what's the point?"

"Doing something you enjoy that could potentially become a full-time job? Look at me. If I had the energy to do makeup tutorials regularly, I'd be making money at it. This influencer stuff is real."

"Yeah, but mine is an online magazine. It's totally different."

"But what if it wasn't? What if you combined the two? Get the magazine going with your articles and writing, but then promote it with videos and stuff? Start with Sam. He's been a good friend to you. I bet he'd let you record a rehearsal or do an updated interview where you do edits highlighting the fun stuff and—"

"Aunt Meg." I shook my head. "I'm tired. Between work and the baby, I don't have the energy, not to mention the creativity, for any of that."

"I know the last year has been hard, but it's time to start living life again. Your mother refused to do anything but work and raise you. She died miserable and alone—" She held up a hand when I started to protest. "She was your mom, and she was wonderful. She was. But she was also my sister, so I knew her as a woman, and she was lonely. Tired. Sad. After your dad died, she let it break her. I'm not going to let you do that. Fuck Zeke. Fuck Onyx Knight. You don't need them personally or professionally. You can do this. Hell, you can do anything you set your mind to."

"But Jeremy has to be my priority," I whispered.

"Of course. But he can't become the *only* thing in your life. You have me to help with the baby. It's harder now because he's one hundred percent helpless, but that will change before you know it. Soon he'll be crawling, then walking and talking and feeding himself. A year from now, you'll be in a different place in life."

"Yeah, twice as tired from chasing him around and making sure he doesn't kill himself."

"I'm taking out a home equity loan," she said quietly. "And we're going to use the money for an attorney. Once Zeke starts paying his share—and he *will*, or I'll go public—our lives will get much easier. We'll be able to afford daycare, so you can have a break and potentially get a better job. With the baby in daycare all day, I'll have the time to build my Eye-Lights page. We'll also be able to afford diapers and formula, so we're not spending all day Sunday clipping coupons and menu-planning."

"Aunt Meg!" I stared at her. "You can't take out a loan."

"I can and I will. I called the bank today."

"You don't have a job. How will they guarantee you'll pay it back?"

"It's only ten thousand dollars. And I have equity in the house since I don't have a mortgage anymore. If I don't pay it back, they can take it."

"But it's all you have." I protested.

"Zeke has to pony up," she said. "I know you're dreading a legal battle and you're afraid he'll take Jeremy from you, but that won't happen. He's a touring musician. With a wild reputation. His bass player has been in rehab twice in the last year—what kind of environment is that for a child? No judge will grant him full custody." Aunt Meg had been keeping up with Zeke and the band, and while I'd found it amusing before, it was suddenly important.

"He has a family that can help."

"Yes, but if Zeke's *family* is going to raise the baby, then he's better off with his mother."

"People with money can twist the facts, make me look like some kind of whore or something."

"Nonsense." She wagged her finger at me. "It's time, Presley. I know you were embarrassed when you tried to reach him and his manager talked to you like some kind of gold digger, but Jeremy is here now and he needs not just the money his father can provide, but an actual father. Like it or not, that's Zeke."

I closed my eyes.

She was right.

I'd had this same argument with myself a million times over the last few months.

It had been easy to fall back on the fact that Onyx Knights' management would only talk to a lawyer, and I couldn't afford one, but it was time to pull up my big-girl panties. Jeremy did need a father. And we needed money. It was as simple as that. I couldn't imagine Zeke wanting full custody, no matter how much he hated me, but there was always a chance.

I hadn't wanted to become a mother at this stage of my life, but now that I was one, I'd disappear and move to a remote island in the South Pacific before I let anyone take him from me.

"Let me try the management company one more time," I said finally. "Maybe now that there is an actual baby that I can take for a DNA test, they'll listen."

Aunt Meg scowled. "Maybe. And we have one other option as well."

"Which is?"

"Lexi Rousseau."

I frowned. "We don't want to get her involved." I paused. "Do we?"

"Desperate times, desperate measures. She seems like a nice girl. I bet she would help."

"You don't even know her!" I said, laughing. "Just because she likes your videos doesn't mean she's nice."

She rolled her eyes. "What twenty-something, famous rockstar watches a sixty-year-old woman's videos? She has to be nice, or she'd be watching all those supermodel videos. The ones with the big butts."

I snorted with laughter. "You're killing me, Aunt Meg."

"I let you wallow in self-pity and disappointment and embarrassment for a lot longer than I should have. It's natural and to be expected. But those days are done. It's time for you to get up and start living again. End of discussion."

"I'm not fifteen anymore," I said dryly, amused at her ferociousness.

"If you were fifteen, this would have already been handled." She put a gentle hand on my shoulder. "Trust me, Presley. I've been around the block a few times. Zeke has to man up and do the right thing. You have to swallow your fear and think about how much it impacted you, not having a father. Do you want that for Jeremy?"

I swallowed, a wave of emotion washing over me.

I didn't even remember my dad, which made me sad. I absolutely didn't want that for my son. I just wished the current situation wasn't so complicated.

14

Z *eke*

BEING home in L.A. had been nice at first, but it had been a few months now, and I was done. Done listening to my mother whine about how I've ruined her life. Done with the constant family that came to visit. Done with one-night stands and late-night parties. Just fucking done. Carter had gone back to rehab late last fall and six weeks turned into eight, which then turned into twelve. He'd gotten out, went straight to his dealer to get high, and turned around and went back in.

It was now April, and he was out. Sober and pissed off at the world. Mostly at me because I'd been the one who'd forced the intervention in the first place. We'd done a handful of festival gigs in South America while he'd been inside, and he was furious about it. We were heading into the studio to record a new album next week and he was annoyed about that too, since he said the studio was "boring" and after five months in rehab he wanted to go out on the road.

The last few days had been hell, but I hoped tonight would be better because we were playing a charity gig in Vegas with Nobody's Fool and an up-and-coming band called Fighting Sunshine. It would be Carter's first gig in a long time, so we figured it might be rough. It was only ten songs, so shorter than our usual sets, and I was down for anything that got me out of L.A.

I was a prickly son of a bitch sometimes, and never more so than when I got what I wanted, only to find out it wasn't what I wanted at all. Going home had sucked. Not being on tour sucked. I was bored, lonely, and drinking too much. I hadn't reinstated my mother's credit cards, and we fought about it regularly. Dad couldn't stand to listen to it, so he left the house early and didn't come back until dark, leaving me to deal with her unless I had somewhere to be. It wasn't like I could kick her out. So, it had been months of arguing and bickering and tears, with me almost giving in a dozen times. I'd stood my ground, though.

She'd not only broken my trust, but she'd never apologized. Never admitted she'd done anything wrong. And it hurt. Because I'd given my immediate family anything and everything they'd ever wanted up until last spring. Hell, they lived in my house free of charge. They didn't even pay for food. And I was fine with that. I was just done being taken advantage of. Maybe I was being a hard ass—my sister thought so—but at this point, I would have sold my fucking soul for an apology. Was that too much to ask?

"Z!"

We'd just come off stage after our soundcheck, and I looked to see who was calling my name.

"Hey, Lexi." I smiled at Nobody's Fool's lead singer. She was a stunning blond who had pipes like no other woman in rock and roll. She was also sweet and funny. All of us had lusted after her when we'd first brought them on tour, until it became abundantly clear she was wholeheartedly in love with her pro hockey player husband. But we were pretty good friends, so I was surprised at the dark look in her eyes as she approached me.

"I really expected better of you," she said quietly.

"Excuse me?" I had no idea what she was talking about.

"I know the band has had a dozen or more paternity suits over the years, but this wasn't some groupie. She was a nice girl. A *virgin*. You had to know, after what happened between you, she wouldn't make something like that up."

There had only been one virgin in my life in many, many years, so she could only be talking about one person. The same woman I'd jerked off thinking about for months. The same woman I'd written a motherfucking song for our new album about. The only one-night stand I'd never been able to forget.

But I still didn't understand what she was talking about.

"Lex, I've had my mother yelling at me daily for the last few months, so I'm going to need you to check your tone and start at the beginning."

She scowled. "Unlike the other women in your life, you don't get to tell me what kind of tone to have. Especially when I know the story and what a dick you were."

I blinked.

Lexi was genuinely pissed.

"I mean, even if you wanted nothing to do with the mom, what about the kid? It's your son, Zeke. I've seen him. How could you just decide you weren't going to acknowledge him without even getting a DNA test?"

I stared at her, trying to decide if she was messing with me. "Okay, I don't care what tone you use, but what the fuck are you talking about?"

She moved closer to me, dropping her voice since we'd attracted the attention of the staff and crew that were milling around. "Don't be coy. I'm talking about Presley and your night together in Minnesota last March. I've talked to her on the phone. I've seen pictures of the baby. Your son's name is Jeremy, by the way."

My son.

A weird feeling twisted through my gut.

I distinctly remembered that moment when I'd slid inside of her bare. The way it felt when her warm, wet pussy had tightened around me. Welcoming and hot. It had only been a few seconds before both of us realized what I'd done, and I'd quickly pulled out, but it was the only time I'd gone without a condom in years. Not since my last steady girlfriend, which was more than five years ago already. So, there was no chance I didn't remember that moment.

I'd briefly considered the possibility of pregnancy, but Jesus. It hadn't been more than two or three seconds. Literally. What were the chances?

One hundred percent, apparently.

I was having a hard time wrapping my head around all of this, but my gut told me Presley wouldn't lie. Not when I'd been such a dick to her just before leaving the resort. And definitely not when she knew I would demand a paternity test.

Fuck.

"Then why the fuck didn't she reach out?" I demanded.

"She did. To management. They essentially told her to fuck off."

My heart sank.

Double fuck.

Management meant Aurora, our band's manager.

The same woman I'd been casually fucking the last few months.

I had a feeling my life was about go from bad to worse.

~

I STARED at the phone number Lexi had given me for a long time. I needed to call Presley, but I didn't know what to say or how to even get some kind of dialogue started. According to Lexi, she'd reached out to management multiple times. They'd told her not to call back until she had a lawyer, something I knew Presley almost certainly couldn't afford. Now my son was four months old, and this was the first I was hearing about him.

Instead of calling her, though, I called my lawyer. I gave him specific instructions for setting up a DNA test somewhere close to where Presley lived, making sure we took care of the costs. Even if it turned out the kid wasn't mine—and somehow, I doubted that—it wasn't like the lab fees were a big deal for me.

I'd just gotten off the phone with him when Aurora let herself into my hotel room. She had a key since she'd been planning to stay with me while we were in town.

"Hey, handsome." She put down a couple of shopping bags and sauntered over to me. "I bought you a surprise."

"Oh, yeah?" I eyed her, gently moving her arms when she tried to wrap them around my neck.

"What's wrong?" she asked immediately. "Something happen at soundcheck?"

"Nope." I'd come back to the room even though we had to play soon. Calling my lawyer had been a priority and I still needed to get myself together before performing because news about having a son had hit me hard. I'd need to find out the results before I did anything else, but my gut rarely steered me wrong, and I was almost positive it was true.

"You're scaring me, Zeke. What's wrong?"

"Tell me about Presley," I said quietly.

She looked genuinely confused for a moment. "Who?"

"Presley Figueroa."

It took a beat, but I knew the moment the name clicked because her face morphed into a professional mask of nothingness. "The young woman who called the office incessantly, trying to get your number?"

"Yes. That's the one."

"What about her? I told her if she wanted to bring a paternity suit again you, to hire a lawyer. That was what? A year ago? More? She obviously didn't."

"That wasn't your call," I said, sounding a lot calmer than I felt.

"Of course it was!" She rolled her eyes. "Do you know how many calls like that we get every week?"

"Kingston has had half a dozen paternity suits, not a single one of them panned out, and yet you brought every one of them to him. Every. Single. One. Why not this one?"

"She was some aspiring journalist! I thought she was pissed about not getting the interview. Ross told me you guys blew her off, so I figured—"

"*Ross* knew about this?" I stared down at her angrily, feeling betrayed all over again.

"Well, yes. I needed to see if there was any chance—"

"Fuck, Aurora!" I threw up my hands. "He's almost definitely my kid! I'm waiting for results of the test, but you had no goddamn right to send her away without at least giving me the message. We had a condom malfunction, which is why I believe her even without the test. So if you'd told me, I could have handled the situation. Instead, now you've left me vulnerable. What if she'd gone public? Went to the press and put it out on social media? Not all press is good press. Not when it makes me look like a motherfucking deadbeat!"

She'd taken a step back, taking a more apologetic stance now. "I'm sorry, Zeke. I honestly had no idea you'd actually met her. When Ross told me the band blew her off, I wrote it off as the ploy of a desperate young woman. I wasn't going to bother you with it."

"I should fire your ass," I hissed.

"Zeke, what are you talking about?" For the first time, she looked scared, and I'd probably regret this in the morning, but I couldn't seem to help myself.

"In fact, I'm done with you. After the show tonight, we're having a band meeting and voting on it. You need to pack your shit and be gone by the time I get back." I grabbed my wallet and room key and headed for the door.

"Zeke, wait! Please!" She grabbed my arm, tugging lightly even though she wouldn't be able to budge me if I didn't want her to.

"Aurora, I'm too pissed off to have a conversation right now."

"I know. And I'm truly sorry. Let me make it up to you. Just tell me how."

"There isn't a goddamn thing you can do to give me back the four months I've missed of my son's life."

"You don't even know if he's yours!" she snapped.

"He has my eyes." I pulled out my phone and showed her the picture Lexi had texted me.

Her face paled as she stared at it. "Oh, fuck, Zeke."

"Yeah. Band meeting tonight after the show. Someone will text you the time and place." With that, I pulled my arm out of her grasp and stalked out of the room.

I didn't know where I was going, but I had to keep moving so I wouldn't explode.

15

Z*eke*

IT WAS a risk to walk through the hotel casino, but we were playing here at The Charleston Hotel, so it was the easiest thing for me to do. I didn't even have my all access pass—I'd left it in the room in my haste to get the hell out of there—but it wasn't like the staff and crew didn't know me. I kept my head down to ensure I didn't make eye contact with anyone and arrived at the venue in confusion. We usually got here with either the equipment or through some private side door, so I had no idea where to go.

Jesus, I really was nothing but a spoiled rockstar who couldn't function without Ross or one of the roadies to tell me where to go.

That had to change.

Annoyed, I yanked out my phone and called Kingston.

"Hey, where'd you go?" he said by way of greeting.

"I had to check on something, and now I don't know how to get backstage. I'm in the hallway that goes back there, but all the doors are locked."

Kingston was quiet for a minute. "Uh, hang on. Let me ask Ross."

Okay, good. He didn't know either. Now I felt a tiny bit less like a diva.

A couple of minutes later, Ross stuck his head out of a door, and I headed in his direction.

"Lost, little boy?" he asked as I followed him.

"Maybe a little." I didn't say anything for a minute, but I couldn't let it go. Everything was still too raw. "Hey, Ross?"

"Yeah?" He glanced over at me.

"You ever feel the need to keep something major from me again, you're gone."

"Wh-what?" He stopped walking and stared at me. "What are you talking about, Z?"

"I'm talking about a potential paternity suit. You telling Aurora that we blew off that journalist in Minneapolis last year, knowing why she was asking, and then not thinking about coming to me?"

His mouth fell open. "Are you serious right now?"

I held up a hand. "I'm not going to argue with you. I just want to make sure we're clear. It's not your job to protect me from life. From a dozen fans swarming me backstage after a show? Sure. But the big stuff? Stuff that goes beyond what we do professionally? I don't care if you have to come to me every other day to tell me I might've knocked someone up. If there's a question, a thought, a rumor—you come to me. You understand?"

"I..." He looked shaken but then took a breath. "You're right. I apologize. She made it sound like it was bullshit."

"You know damn well she and I hook up sometimes. I have a feeling there was some jealousy involved there, and part of your job—if you decide you want to keep it because hers is on the line—is to make sure I don't get blindsided. Ever. This isn't just a business. This is supposed to be a family. We've already got a problem child in the band, so I don't have the energy to be caught with my pants down."

"Understood. You have my word."

"Thanks."

We started to walk again. Neither of us spoke for a few minutes, but then he said, "So, is there a kid?"

"There is a kid. We don't have DNA yet, but there was a condom issue, so I'm pretty confident he's mine."

"It's a boy."

I nodded.

"Jesus. Have you talked to her? The mom?"

"Her name is Presley. And no. Not yet. I'm waiting for the results. I was kind of a dick last time I saw her, so I'm guessing it's going to be a stressful conversation."

"What's his name?"

"Jeremy." I was about to yank out my phone to show him the picture but decided against it. I didn't know for sure yet. There was still a possibility that this was all a mistake.

Yeah, right.

Even the voices in my head knew better.

"What are you going to do about it?"

"I don't know. I'm hoping we can come to an agreement without lawyers, but I'm going to support him. Them. She's only twenty-two—well, I guess twenty-three now? Turning twenty-three soon? I don't know when her birthday is."

"Young."

I nodded, wishing I could make this sick feeling in the pit of my stomach go away. It wasn't because I was afraid that Jeremy was mine. In a way, the moment I'd seen that sweet little face in the photo, I'd already accepted that he was. The problem was that I'd treated Presley badly, and though I'd never admit it to anyone else, I'd thought about her a lot. I didn't have a lot of regrets in my life, but the way I'd lashed out at Presley the morning after we'd been together was one of the few. She hadn't done anything to warrant my behavior.

Looking back, I hadn't even given her the chance to explain. I'd been annoyed with my mother, worried about Carter, and stressed about the tour. Instead of taking care of business, I'd taken out all my frustrations on the only person who'd had the misfortune of making a mistake.

She hadn't asked me for anything, much less an interview. Hell, as far as I was concerned, she'd done all the giving because making love with her had been sweeter than sweet and hotter than hell. No doubt she should've found a time to tell me who she was. We'd had a connection and talked for hours. At some point in the evening, she should've come clean. It wouldn't have changed anything, but for whatever reason, she hadn't. I could only hope that once we talked again, we could sort it out and move on. If nothing else, we needed to get past it for Jeremy's sake.

If he was my son, there was no chance whatsoever I wouldn't be in his life.

My lawyer forwarded me the results of the expedited DNA test three days later.

It was a 99.99 percent match.

He was mine.

I had a son.

Holy shit.

Just like that, after a simple phone call, I was a father.

Reality was jarring, despite having already known it on some level.

But now came the hard part. I had to talk to Presley. I needed to see her, but first I had to talk to her. Showing up at her house, even though I'd gotten her address, would probably scare her, which was the last thing I wanted.

Only a handful of people knew what was going on, and my lawyer was the only other person who knew that the results had come back. I hadn't even told my parents. Somehow, I'd been putting off telling anyone until I knew for sure. Now it all came crashing down, guilt and worry and frustration taking root.

What if Presley hated me and didn't want me to see the baby?

What if I sucked as a dad?

What if she only wanted money?

I stopped myself from going down the road. I'd already jumped to conclusions once before and I needed to keep that in mind. I couldn't afford to be angry or resentful or any of the other negative emotions that plagued me. There was an innocent child involved now, so I had to man the fuck up and call Presley.

I typed in the numbers and closed my eyes as I waited for her to answer.

"Hello?"

Her voice was warm but guarded, as if she knew who it was.

"Presley. Hello. It's me. Zeke."

Silence.

"Are you there?"

"Y-yes. How did you get my number?"

"You gave it to the attorney. Didn't you?"

"Oh. Yes. I guess I did."

God, this was awkward. *As fuck.*

But this was Aurora's doing, so I had to be the bigger person here and try to make it at least a little bit easier.

"Listen, we have a lot to talk about. I was wondering if I could come to see you."

Another silence.

"Presley? I know I was a jerk that morning after..." Crap, how was I supposed to refer to that? The morning after I popped your cherry? The morning after we made a baby? "I'd really like to talk in person. Meet the... meet Jeremy. Please."

"Okay." Her voice was soft. Unsure. *Nervous.*

She was afraid of me.

At the very least, she was afraid of what I might do.

"I can be there tomorrow, if that's okay?"

"I'm working a double tomorrow. Can you, um, it would be better if you came the next day."

I wanted to protest, but that would have been selfish. I needed to make an effort here because Aurora had handled things badly. There was no doubt I could be a prick when I wanted to, and I'd been exactly that when I'd last seen Presley, but I never would have turned my back on her if I'd known she was pregnant. That wasn't the man I was, and I needed her to know that.

So I would wait an extra day.

"All right. That's fine. I'll see you then."

"Okay."

"Presley?"

"Yes?"

"Everything is going to be okay. I want you to know that. I'd like to be there for both of you, and I'm sorry about the way Aurora handled things."

"Okay."

She was killing me with these one-word answers. But I probably deserved it. Once we were in the same room, I'd find a way to show her I wasn't always a jerk.

"See you soon." I disconnected and let out a breath I hadn't realized I was holding. A metaphor for all the fucking stress in my life. I desperately needed release, but I didn't know what kind. The last thing I wanted was sex, and I was never, ever sleeping with Aurora again.

Kingston had warned me it was a bad idea, but she was attractive in more ways than one. Older, didn't have or want kids, had the band's best interests at heart—usually—and had a busy career that kept her from being too clingy. We'd hooked up on and off over the years, but she'd had a serious boyfriend for a couple of years. Then suddenly she was single again and I'd been desperate for a distraction from everything going on. I'd never imagined she was keeping something so big from me.

The band had voted against me when I'd asked them to consider firing her. They had a point because while it wouldn't be difficult to find someone else to represent us, it would be complicated as fuck to break the contract. Then whoever it was had to get up to speed on all the irons we had in the fire, which were a lot, so practicality had won out. We'd sat her down, though, and laid out very detailed parameters about the things she could handle and things she couldn't.

We'd also had a team meeting with the entire crew and support staff.

Though we didn't talk about the specifics, we'd been clear that anything to do with our personal lives needed to go through us, even if they thought it was bullshit. If someone showed up backstage saying they knew us, the roadies and security needed to let us know. Ultimately, we needed to be able to make the decisions.

Hopefully, these types of rules would keep something like this from ever happening again.

16

P *resley*

I'D FANTASIZED about the day Zeke would meet his son, but now that it was here, I was a nervous wreck. I changed clothes three times, put on makeup, took it off again, and finally opted to leave my face bare. I didn't really care what he thought of my looks and just wanted to get this over with. He'd sounded contrite on the phone, like he really was sorry about the way things had gone down, but I wasn't sure I believed him. He'd never given me any reason to trust him.

"You look pale as a ghost," Aunt Meg chided me when I came downstairs. "And what are you wearing?"

I looked down. "Jeans? What should I wear? A cocktail dress?"

She shook her head. "You look like someone life has beaten down. Is that what you want him to see?"

"I don't care what he sees," I said quietly. "All I care about is making sure he's good to our son."

"I guess we're about to find out," she murmured as the doorbell rang.

Nervousness shot through me with such force it made me lightheaded. Fuck, why was this so hard? I walked to the door and unlocked it, slowly pulling it open.

And there he was.

He looked... amazing.

Dammit.

Big and strong and gorgeous.

Still.

Just like the last time I'd seen him.

He was holding two big shopping bags and a teddy bear the size of a small horse.

"Hi." His eyes met mine and neither of us spoke for a moment.

"Come on in," I said at last. The last thing I needed to do was look into his eyes and think about the last time we'd been in the same room together.

"Thanks." He seemed huge in our tiny house, his shoulders almost as wide as the small foyer.

Aunt Meg was standing a few feet away, leaning on her cane.

"Hello. I'm Margaret Forrester, Presley's aunt."

"William Zerkesian. But please call me Zeke." They shook hands and I just stood there watching, as if he were any other guest.

"And you can call me Aunt Meg."

They smiled at each other.

"I brought some things for the baby," Zeke said, turning to me. "I wasn't sure what you needed, but I figured developmental toys would be okay and you can give me a list going forward."

"That's very thoughtful," Aunt Meg answered for me, digging into one of the bags.

"Can I see him?" Zeke asked when no one spoke.

"He's asleep," I responded. "But he'll be up soon. I didn't want to wake him in case you were late."

"Okay, sure." He looked almost as nervous as I felt, and we stared at each other.

"Would you like to sit down?" Aunt Meg offered.

"Thanks." He lowered himself onto the couch, but I couldn't bring myself to sit next to him. Mostly, I wanted to run from the room. I was feeling so many disparate emotions right now, torn between wanting to smack him and kiss him. I didn't understand it because all I wanted was to do right by my son. I couldn't afford to be attracted to his father. Not again.

"Can I get you something to drink?" Aunt Meg asked him, making me want to roll my eyes.

"No, I'm okay. Thank you." Zeke looked from Aunt Meg to me and then sighed. "Look, I know this is weird, but it doesn't have to be."

"It doesn't have to be?" I asked incredulously. "How could it be anything *but* weird?"

"I know. But I don't know how to fix that."

"Why don't you just tell me what you plan to do," I said. "Then you can meet Jeremy and be on your way."

He frowned. "Presley, I don't know what you think is going to happen, but I'm not just going to meet him. I plan to be a part of his life."

I lifted my chin. "I'll fight you if you try to get custody. I'm a good mom. So, no matter what your fancy lawyers and managers and whatnot try to say, I'll—"

"Jesus, Presley, stop." He stood up and walked over to me so we were face to face. "That's not what this is. Of course, I'm not going to take him from you. But I won't allow you to keep him from me either. The only way this works is if we co-parent him."

"I'm in Minnesota and you're either in California or on tour. How is that going to work?"

"I don't know yet," he said, showing the first signs of annoyance. "I just got here. We haven't had a chance to talk or figure things out, and I haven't even seen him yet!"

"Okay, let's not get upset," Aunt Meg said quickly. "Presley, you've been through a lot, but let's at least hear him out. And Zeke, I know you only just found out, but we've been going through this for over a year, so it's a bit more raw for us. Especially Presley."

"I understand that," he said slowly. "And I can't apologize enough for the way our management team handled everything."

I'd never been more grateful to hear Jeremy cry, and I practically ran up the stairs. I didn't understand why having Zeke here in the house was so hard, but I'd felt like I couldn't breathe since he'd arrived. He'd been nothing but polite, but I was on edge, ready to explode any moment. A year's worth of pent-up anger, frustration, and fear were roiling inside of me, a veritable explosive ready to blow.

"Hi, baby boy. Mommy's here. Shhh." I soothed my son as I picked him up, even though in some ways it felt like I was desperately trying to soothe myself. There were no words to express how afraid I was. Jeremy deserved to have his father in his life, but it scared me.

"You're good with him."

Zeke's voice made my body tense, and I instinctively clutched Jeremy closer to my chest.

"He's beautiful, Presley." Zeke was behind me now, running one big knuckle across the baby's cheek. Jeremy looked up at him curiously, showing no signs of fear or anxiety.

Thank god.

Babies tended to be intuitive, and Jeremy liked almost everyone. But the creepy guy hitting on me at the supermarket? Nope. He'd howled like a banshee. My boss at the restaurant who leered at me almost every day? Jeremy had thrown up on him one time when Aunt Meg had brought him in to have lunch while I'd been working. So, I trusted my baby's intuition more than my own.

"Do you think he'd let me hold him?" Zeke asked softly.

"Probably. He only screams if he doesn't like someone. Otherwise, he's mostly curious and happy. He'll pull your hair, though." I finally turned to look at him.

"That's okay." He held out his arms.

Handing our baby to him was much, much harder than I'd imagined.

I knew he wouldn't hurt him. That wasn't it at all.

I just wasn't ready to let go. To share him. To share something so intimate with Zeke. Not again. I'd trusted him once and that had been a mistake. Trusting him with my baby was almost more than I could stand. But I had no choice.

"I'll be careful," he said, apparently noting my hesitation.

"I know. I just... I don't trust you," I blurted. "Not with me and certainly not with him."

Zeke let his arms drop, and there was no mistaking the hurt in his eyes. "I'm doing my best to make it up to you," he said. "What do you want, Presley? Money? Another apology? What's it going to take?"

I laughed, but it was humorless.

"Money so Jeremy has everything he needs? Absolutely. But apologies are just words. I need you to prove to me you're going to be in his life and actually care about him. If you just send a check every month, that's fine too, but I need to know. I have to be prepared so I can protect him. So he's not waiting at the door for the dad who never shows up. I don't want my son to be at his baseball game, constantly staring out toward the stands, to see if Dad will make it this time. That can't be his life. I refuse."

"I'm not going anywhere," he said gruffly, his eyes filled with sincerity. "Yes, I'll be on tour again soon. Ish. We don't have a date yet. But I've already said we have to build breaks in. We're not going balls to the wall anymore. You can fly out and visit. Or I'll fly here. I won't just write a check every month. And there will be extended breaks between tours. We've already talked about it."

I stared up at him, willing myself to stay skeptical, to keep him at arm's length. I had to. Jeremy would be fine, I'd make sure of that, but if I let Zeke get too close, he could destroy me. There was a pull there, a magnetism I didn't understand, and it hadn't faded in the year we'd been apart. If anything, it was stronger. Standing here with our baby in my arms, in my bedroom, was the most intimate thing I'd ever experienced.

"Please, can I hold him?"

I averted my gaze when I nodded, lightly pressing my lips to the top of Jeremy's soft head as I handed him to Zeke.

"Hey, big guy." Zeke gently took him from me, expertly cradling him against his shoulder.

"Not your first time holding a baby," I noted.

He smiled. "My sister has two kids. And remember, I have ten thousand cousins, many of whom have kids. There are something like forty-eight of the second cousins or whatever your first cousin's kids are called."

"Second cousin once removed?" I wrinkled my nose. "I don't have any cousins so I'm not sure."

"God, Presley, he's perfect." Zeke was staring at the baby in his arms with awe, the look on his face melting my frozen soul just a tiny bit.

"He is." Tears stung my eyes and I fumbled for my phone. I might not like Zeke's presence, but I needed Jeremy to have a record of the first time he met his father. The first time his father held him.

God, I was such a fucking sap.

Zeke didn't smile as I snapped pictures, keeping his eyes on his son.

Jeremy started to squirm, looking for me.

"Is he done with me?" Zeke asked, a patient smile on his face.

"No. He's just hungry. You want to carry him downstairs? You can hold him while I make his bottle."

"Can I watch?"

"You want to watch me make a bottle?"

He nodded. "I'll need to know how, I guess. I mean, I should know, right?"

"I suppose so." I walked ahead of him, hoping to hide whatever he might potentially see in my eyes. More fear. Guilt. Attraction.

Good grief, I wasn't supposed to be thinking about *that*. Not even when we were in my semi-dark bedroom. Not ever again, I chided myself.

Hell, as far as I was concerned, I didn't want to ever have sex again. Not if it meant another nine months of torture. I loved Jeremy, but pregnancy had sucked. Big time. So my interest in sex, even with the hottest man I'd ever met, was less than zero. If there was a negative to indicate my interest in sex, I would use that.

"Do you think you and I could go somewhere?" Zeke asked as I made Jeremy's bottle. "So we can talk."

"Go somewhere?" I glanced over my shoulder in confusion. "Can't we talk here?"

"Well, sure, but I'd like a chance for us to reconnect. Get to know each other again, you know? I hate how we left things and I'd like to fix that."

I turned and slowly lifted my gaze to his.

"Zeke, I'm not sure what you think will happen here, but this is about the baby. There is no connection between us, beyond him. We won't be friends or fuck buddies or anything else. The only thing we're going to share is Jeremy."

17

Z *eke*

I HADN'T HAD any expectations when I made the trip to Minnesota, but I hadn't considered that she was still angry with me. I'd figured I'd apologize, we'd talk things out, sort out how we wanted to handle this co-parenting thing, and then I'd potentially invite her—and her aunt—to L.A. to meet my family. Because like it or not, that's what we were now. Instead, she was icy-cold. This wasn't the sweet, shy Sunny I remembered.

From her perspective, I'd abandoned her. I totally understood that, but the venomous way she'd said the words "fuck buddies," told me she was still royally pissed. And I wasn't sure what to do about it. I'd apologized and was doing my best to be respectful of her boundaries, but the anger coming from her was difficult to navigate.

"Presley, look, this is definitely awkward. But it doesn't have to be."

She narrowed her gaze. "It doesn't have to be? Well, of course not. Not for you. You weren't alone and pregnant, suffering through nine months of morning sickness while trying to work so Aunt Meg wouldn't have to give up her medication. It wasn't your body that got huge and uncomfortable. You didn't push a nearly ten-pound baby out of your ass and then spend months healing. You weren't the one trying to figure out how everyone was going to eat when my milk didn't come in so I couldn't breastfeed and had to start buying formula we couldn't afford. So, no, I'm sure this isn't awkward for *you* at all."

I winced.

It would undoubtedly take a lot more than a verbal apology and a nice deposit into her bank account to fix things between us. I'd hoped we could start over, be friends, maybe find that same connection we'd had at the resort that night. That didn't appear to be the case, so it was time to pivot.

"I'm sorry about all that," I said patiently, bouncing Jeremy since he seemed to be getting more and more eager for his bottle. "But no matter how much I want to, I can't go back in time and change those things. All I can do is try to be better going forward."

"Great." Her voice was laced with sarcasm as she handed me the bottle. "Do you want to feed him?"

"Uh, yeah. Thanks."

She brushed past me as she headed into the living room, and it was like a jolt of electricity shot through me. Geez, the madder she got the hornier I got.

We settled in the living room, and she put a burp cloth over the baby.

"He spits up a lot," was all she said.

I nodded, watching as my son closed his mouth around the nipple, sucking greedily. He was a big boy who felt solid in my arms, and when he blinked up at me, watching me as I watched him, the resemblance between us was uncanny. He was just an infant, but not only did he share my different colored eyes, his eyes were the same shape. And from what I could tell, his mouth resembled mine too. The jury was still out on his nose, but his full head of dark hair reminded me a lot of the pictures I'd seen of myself at this age.

My mother would be beside herself when she found out she had a grandson. Hell, the family would undoubtedly be in an uproar. I could expect to have non-stop company if I could convince Presley to bring the baby out to L.A. for a visit. Although, it didn't seem like she would be on board for that anytime soon.

Aunt Meg had disappeared, so I figured this was as close to alone as we were going to get.

"Do you want to tell me about... everything?" I asked after a moment.

"Everything?" She quirked a brow.

"It might help to get it off your chest."

Oh, boy, that was definitely not the right thing to say because her eyes had narrowed, and she looked like she wanted to hit me.

"All I mean is that—"

"I know what you mean," she cut in. "You want me to tell you the whole sad story so you can apologize and maybe assuage your guilt. But I have no desire to relive the last year. Other than having Jeremy."

"Fine." I would have to switch tactics because being patient wasn't working. "Let's talk financial support. I'm going to start a trust fund for him, so no matter what happens to me—personally, financially, professionally—he'll always be covered."

"Okay."

"And then I'd like to do something to ease your current financial burden. Tell me what you need. Will fifty thousand cover the last year?"

She blinked, obviously startled.

Thank god I finally had her attention. And not in a bad way.

"Fifty... thousand?"

"Yeah. I'll have to talk to my accountant to figure out the best way to give you that money without tax implications for you, but if we can't, I'll just pay whatever taxes you're responsible for. But that's back pay. Going forward, I'd like to make sure you're comfortable."

"I... the biggest thing would be for you to pay for daycare so I can get a regular job and not have to wait tables every weekend."

I frowned. I had no business telling her what to do, but I didn't want Jeremy going to daycare full time.

"Aunt Meg isn't able to care for him?" I asked softly. I remembered her telling me about her struggles with MS.

"She's better, but she still falls sometimes. When I absolutely have to leave him with her during the day, we use that bassinet over there." She motioned with her head. "It rolls. So she doesn't carry him more than a few feet. At night, he usually sleeps the whole time I'm at work, but if he does wake up, she brings bottles upstairs and it's only a couple of feet from the crib to the bed."

Damn. This had been so much harder than I'd thought. I knew they'd struggled, but I hadn't realized how much. And I also didn't understand why she was waiting tables instead of working a regular job now. I had so many fucking questions, but I had to tread carefully.

"I can pay for daycare. I can also pay for you to stay home and take care of him. There are lots of remote jobs out there. What if you looked for something like that? You have a degree now, right? So—"

"You really have no clue, do you?" she asked, jumping to her feet and starting to pace. "You walked out of the Pullman Resort without looking back and never gave a second thought to what you did to me."

"Actually, I—" I began.

"Shut up." She glared at me. "Did you know you got me fired?"

Crap. I'd had no idea.

"I didn't say anything—" I tried again.

"I said to shut up." She had her hands on her hips, and though her voice was low, there was no mistaking the malice in her words. "Someone overheard you yelling at me and told my boss. He fired me for using my proximity to a guest to get an interview for my little school project." Her chest was rising and falling rapidly as she continued, bitterness now overshadowing her anger. "And because I didn't get the interview, I failed my final project. So I didn't graduate or get my degree."

Fuck me loud. What had I done?

"I had twenty-four-seven morning sickness the entire nine months, so I could only work part-time, and by my fifth month, I couldn't wait tables anymore. All I could do was hostess, which pays nine dollars an hour. Working twenty hours a week, you do the math. Aunt Meg's meds alone are over a thousand dollars a month. Her disability checks barely cover the utilities and taxes on the house, and barely any of her meds are covered. If I don't work, we don't eat. And for a lot of my pregnancy, she didn't eat because she wanted me to be healthy for the baby." Tears squeezed out of her eyes. "I'll be paying off the hospital bill until I'm ninety. Do you know how much delivering a baby costs when you don't have insurance?"

"I'll pay for it," I said, my chest tight with emotion.

"Good. You should. And we need a new roof."

"Okay." At this point, I'd essentially sign over my royalty checks if it would get her to stop crying.

"You ruined my entire life," she hissed. "And I don't know how we can move forward, not even for Jeremy."

"Presley." I desperately wanted to reach for her, but she'd taken a step back.

"You can stay with the baby as long as you like. I'll send Aunt Meg down in case you need anything, but I can't talk to you right now. I'm still too angry and the pain is too raw. I'm sorry." She turned and practically ran up the stairs. A moment later I heard her door slam.

This wasn't how I'd thought things would go, and I hated that meeting my son was being overshadowed by how much I'd hurt his mother. Even if we weren't going to be a couple, I didn't want there to be this kind of animosity. And I never, ever wanted Jeremy to know how I'd treated her. With the exception of losing my temper that morning after we slept together, nothing else that had happened was my fault, but if I was honest, none of the other things would have happened if I hadn't lost my temper.

Because I'd been planning to see her again.

I'd liked her and had been intrigued enough to want to get to know her. There was no way to know if it would have led to anything, but the physical attraction I felt for her was still there. She'd gone out of her way to look drab and plain, and the irony was that it made her that much more attractive to me. The glasses, the ponytail, even the faded jeans. It all added up to the sweet but currently furious ray of sunshine who'd rocked my world just over a year ago.

And somehow, I had to make this right.

"She's not handling things well," Aunt Meg said as she came down the stairs.

"I'm so fucking sorry," I muttered. "I don't know what to do. I had no idea she'd gotten fired, or that she hadn't graduated…"

"It's been a hard year," she said, sitting across from me in what looked like a well-used recliner. "She could have gone to summer school, but not only was she out of money, she lost her job and was so sick during her pregnancy."

"What do I do?" I asked quietly. "How can I fix this?"

"I don't know that you can," she admitted. "But you owe her an interview. And interviews with all your famous friends. And then you can pay for her to retake that last class, after she's gotten her e-zine up and running."

"Done." Fuck, that was the easiest fix ever. "What else?"

"She probably won't want to do an interview with you," she continued. "But someone else in your band. I was thinking about Carter. Would he be willing to talk about his addiction issues?"

I hesitated. "I can't speak to whether or not he'll talk about that particular subject, but I'll make sure she can talk to anyone in the band she wants. Carter's still in recovery, though, so that's not something we can mess with if he's not willing."

"Of course not. That much I understand." She seemed thoughtful.

"Presley said something about needing a new roof?"

"Oh. Yes. But that's not your responsibility. If you can pay off the hospital bill, that would certainly ease our burden."

"Absolutely." I paused. "Does she have student loans?"

"She's deferred payment for now, but yes, she does. About thirty-five thousand dollars."

"Can you send me the info? I'll have my accountant just pay it. I don't want her to worry."

"Thank you, Zeke. I'm very grateful. And Presley is too. But you hurt her. In so many ways. There were a lot of dark days during her pregnancy."

"I want to make it up to her," I said.

"Then I hope you're a patient man."

I hoped so too.

18

P *resley*

Zeke stayed in town for five days, coming over first thing in the morning and not leaving until late. I had to work the second day he was in town, and he hung out at the house with Aunt Meg and Jeremy. While I was grateful that she had support, it left me feeling completely out of sorts. I hated everything about our current situation because part of me just wanted to stay mad, brood, continue to hate him. I was also a little jealous of how quickly he was bonding with Jeremy. The moment he walked in the door, Jeremy wanted to be picked up.

He seemed to enjoy the sound of his daddy's deep voice and tugged at his hair non-stop. No matter what they were doing, whether it was watching baseball on TV or if Zeke was giving him a bottle, Jeremy was relaxed and happy. As if Zeke had always been here. It wasn't like I'd been the one waking up with him at all hours of the night or anything.

It was ridiculous to feel this way, and the intellectual part of me understood that. Emotionally, however, I was a mess. I'd convinced myself what kind of person Zeke was, but the man who'd been with us the last few days was nothing like the Zeke I'd created in my mind. This Zeke was kind, thoughtful, and helpful. Much like the man I'd slept with. He bought enough groceries, diapers, and formula to feed half the babies in

Minneapolis. He'd already gotten a roofer to come and give him an estimate, so the work was scheduled to start in two weeks.

And that was when he dropped a bombshell on us.

"I'd like you to come to L.A. while they're doing the roof," he said on his last night in town. He'd taken Aunt Meg and me out to a fancy steakhouse for dinner, having paid one of our neighbors to watch Jeremy. I'd never left him with anyone but Aunt Meg before, so I kept checking my phone and texting Denise to make sure everything was okay. I was admittedly distracted, so I was only half paying attention when he made the offer.

"What?" I looked at him in confusion.

"The house is going to be loud and messy," he said. "What better time is there for you to get away and come meet my family? I know they'll be eager to meet all of you, so the timing is perfect."

"Perfect for whom?" I asked, irritated all over again. "I can't just take time off from my job."

"I'll pay for everything, including any bills that wouldn't get paid because you missed work," he said easily.

"Not everything is about money, dammit." I slammed my hand down on the table and then dropped my head, taking a breath. "I'm sorry. I shouldn't have raised my voice, but I can't just drop everything whenever you want to see your son. That doesn't work for me."

"Why not?" he demanded. His voice was low, but his eyes flashed with irritation. "I can afford to take care of you and help you get back on your feet. Help Meg with her medication. Make sure the baby has everything. Fix up the house. I can do those things for you, to make your life better. All I want in return is to spend time with my son. I don't even want to separate you—I'm happy to bring all of you to me in California. Why is that a bad thing?"

"Because we aren't *family*," I said harshly. "And frankly, the thought of meeting your family is embarrassing as hell. How are you planning to intro-duce me? This is the bimbo I fucked in Minneapolis last year who got knocked up?"

"*Presley*." Aunt Meg looked shocked, and I was momentarily ashamed.

Even if I thought those types of things, there was no reason to say them in front of her. I didn't care what Zeke thought, but I never wanted Aunt Meg to be uncomfortable.

"Okay, wait." Zeke was shaking his head. "Is that what you think? Is that what you think I think?"

"I don't really give a shit what you think, but to bring my aunt into a situation where your family will know who I am to you? Never going to happen."

"Who, exactly, do you think you are to me?" he asked slowly, his gaze narrowing.

"The unfortunate one-night stand that made me your baby mama."

"There was *nothing* unfortunate about that night," he growled.

We glared at each other until I couldn't take it anymore.

"No?" I leaned back in my chair, somehow still itching for a fight. I wanted to scream and yell, and I wanted him to fight back. I wanted him to be as mean to me as I was being to him, just like he'd done the morning after our night together. I'd never felt like this before and the pressure inside of me was about to boil over. "Give me a break. I was nothing but another groupie, falling for your rockstar charms. You wouldn't even let me explain what happened the next morning. I wasn't even a human being to you, just another person in your life who you automatically assumed wanted something."

"I was upset when I heard you on the phone," he said. "We'd spent hours talking and it never occurred to you to tell me who you were? Yeah, that made me question your motives. But you weren't just another groupie. That's ridiculous. You weren't a groupie at all."

"Technically I was. Onyx Knight was one of my favorite bands." Not anymore, but semantics probably weren't important right now.

"That has nothing to do with anything," he said, spreading his hands. "What do you want from me, Presley?"

"I want you to go home to California and leave me alone," I said. "You can come see Jeremy anytime you like, but we're not going to become a family. We're not meeting your family. And we're not coming to California. Not now, not ever."

I was being childish, but there was so much hurt inside of me, I was a thousand percent sure I would say or do something even worse if I didn't get away from him immediately.

"I'm sorry, I have to go." I got up, grabbed my purse, and walked out of the restaurant.

Yup. I was immature, hormonal, and probably a whole bunch of other adjectives, but I couldn't be bothered to care.

I needed to get as far away from Zeke as possible.

The only good news was that now I could afford to get an Uber to take me home.

∾

I DIDN'T SEE Zeke again before he left the following day. He came to say goodbye to Jeremy and Aunt Meg, but I stayed in my room until he was gone. A little while later, Aunt Meg knocked on my door, peeking her head in.

"Do you have a minute?"

"I guess." I sighed heavily since I figured I was about to get a well-deserved lecture.

She came and sat on the edge of my mattress, reaching for one of my hands. "Do you want to tell me what's going on in your head?"

"I can't be around him," I whispered. "I just can't. Every time I see him, I remember the way he humiliated me at work. The way I felt when Aurora dressed me down on the phone, reminding me what an unprofessional journalist I was. The shame I felt when she told me that they got phone calls like mine every single week. The pain when I realized that Zeke didn't want anything to do with me or the baby."

"But most of that wasn't true," she said. "Aurora never told Zeke about your calls. She essentially lied. Zeke came the moment he found out. That has to count for something."

"We don't know that for sure," I said. "The fact of the matter is, deep down I think he did do all of those things, hoping the situation would go away. It wasn't until Lexi got involved that he had no choice but to do the right thing."

Aunt Meg frowned. "I don't agree with that. I think Zeke is being very sincere."

I shrugged. "Well, we'll never know for sure, and I can't help feeling the way I feel."

"You're entitled to your feelings, yes, but at what cost? The only person you're hurting is yourself. Zeke is a kind, thoughtful man. He's already done so much for us and it sounds like he intends to do more."

"Because money means nothing to him! He could set up a dozen baby mamas all over the country. For all we know, he already has."

"Okay, I think you're being a drama queen," she said, her eyes finding mine. "You know I will always love you, and always have your back, but you need to think long and hard about the way you're behaving. Jeremy isn't going anywhere, so Zeke will be in our lives no matter what. Forgiveness could go a long way toward healing."

"So he destroyed my life, hurt me more than anything else ever has, and now he gets to come back, throwing around money, and that makes everything okay?"

"He's done a lot more than throw money around. Think about all the ways he tried to show you he's sorry while he was here. You don't have to like him, but I truly believe you need to forgive him. And yourself."

"Myself? I didn't do anything!"

"Didn't you?" She cocked her head. "You had a trashy one-night stand with a rockstar and got yourself pregnant. Didn't graduate college. Lost two jobs. Made a mess of your future. You're quite the loser."

Her words stung and it took a moment for me to realize she was only making a point. But she was right. Those were all issues I'd been struggling with. Feelings of failure, insecurity, guilt. And shame. So much shame. It didn't come from a place of morality—this wasn't about religion or the idea you had to be married to have sex or a baby—but I'd become everything I'd never wanted to be.

A college dropout.

A single mother.

A somewhat unemployable dredge of society, even if it was only due to circumstances beyond my control.

Broke. Struggling. Tired.

I was twenty-three but it felt like I'd lived a hundred years, almost all of them bad.

I hadn't lived up to the standards I'd set for myself, and it was disgraceful. In my head anyway.

While I blamed myself for allowing it to get to this point, I blamed Zeke more. He'd started the ball rolling on my fall from grace by knocking me up and getting me fired. From there, everything had gone downhill. Having him show back up in my life, ready to buy my forgiveness, had somehow made it worse. I wanted him to suffer the way I had. I wanted him to be as miserable as I was.

I might not say that out loud, but I'd absolutely admitted it to myself.

"I'm no expert, but I also think there's a touch of post-partum depression going on," Aunt Meg said after a few minutes of silence. "Maybe you should talk to someone now that we've got the money."

"Maybe." I dropped my gaze. "I'm sorry I've been such a pain in the ass."

"You have nothing to be sorry for. All I want is for you to be happy again."

"I don't even know how."

"Like I said, forgiveness goes a long way."

"He hurt me so much," I whispered miserably. "He broke my heart and my spirit. And now that he's being so nice and helpful, it's that much worse because it makes me feel like for someone as wonderful as he is to be that awful to me, it must have been because I'm not worthy."

"Oh, honey." She leaned over and wrapped her arms around me. "You know that's not true."

"I don't know anything," I whispered. "Except how he makes me feel. Good, bad, and everything in between, and it's terrible."

"Because deep down you still feel something for him."

And that little piece of insight made me hate myself even more.

19

Z *eke*

I GOT HOME from Minneapolis late but couldn't sleep. The last five days had changed almost everything I thought I knew about myself. Jeremy had become an integral part of my life, and leaving had been torture. Being there and seeing how much Presley hated me had been hard too. I'd had no idea how much our night together had impacted her life, and there had to be a way to show her I never would have left her to deal with it on her own. Yes, I'd been pissed when I heard her on the phone that morning, but I wasn't such a heartless ass that I would've gotten a young woman fired.

A good journalist did what she had to do to get a story, and while in retrospect it turned out that hadn't been the case, she still had to eat. I'd known about Aunt Meg and her MS, so as angry as I was, I wouldn't have said anything to management. And I sure as fuck wouldn't have let her struggle while pregnant with my kid.

That was Aurora's fault, and I got pissed off at *her* all over again. Of course, being mad wouldn't fix anything. I had to man the fuck up and make things right with Presley.

I just didn't know how I would do that from a couple of thousand miles away.

Somehow, I had to convince her to come to California.

And I needed help to do it.

I poured a couple of fingers of scotch and let the liquid burn its way down my throat. Then I sank into a chair and moodily stared at the now dark gas fireplace.

My mother had turned this empty room in my house into a library, with walls of floor-to-ceiling bookshelves, a gorgeous fireplace built into the wall, and pricey lighting. There were Persian rugs and expensive but comfortable seating, and it had turned into my favorite room in the house. I'd given her shit about it at the time, but now I really liked it in here. I liked writing music when I was here too, and I was suddenly inspired.

I dug around in a cabinet by the wall until I found a yellow pad and a pen and started to scribble lyrics that had been nagging me for days.

Innocent love
Innocent soul.
Innocent heart.
That was the one.
Hard to damage.
Damaging.
Damaging touch.
There it was.
Innocent heart, damaging touch, I need to hold you...
Oh, hell.

This was going to be about my sunshine. The Sunny I'd spent the night with, not the furious Presley who hated my guts. Every word pouring out of me was for her. That sweet, innocent girl whose life I'd made a mess of.

For the next forty minutes or so, I drank scotch and wrote a song, scribbling the lyrics faster than I could stop them. I wished I had my guitar, but I was too lazy to go get one. Besides, I didn't want to make noise because everyone was asleep.

I wasn't sure if this would be a ballad or something faster, but a melody was taking root in my brain as well, and I itched to call Carter. Back when we were getting started, he and I wrote together like this all the time. Not so much anymore.

Innocent heart
Damaging touch
I need to hold you
Too damn much
You're not the one
Who stole my heart
But something's been there

Right from the start.

Take me home, all the way
Take me hard, let me stay
I feel your need, deep inside
Show me, baby, you can't hide
You can't hide, not from me
Even when I'm in misery.
You can't hide, I'm here to stay
Don't push me, baby, we're not going away.

"Zeke?" My mother's soft voice startled me, and I dropped my pen.

"Hey, Ma. Did I wake you?"

"I heard the garage door open and close, but then I didn't hear you go upstairs. I wanted to make sure you're okay." She came toward me in a light blue satin robe, her dark hair piled up in a messy bun. She somehow looked younger, softer like this, and I was suddenly exhausted.

Fighting with her, with Presley, with my band was starting to catch up to me. I needed some relief in just one aspect of my life.

"What's wrong, Zeke?" she asked, sitting in the chair next to mine.

"So many things, Ma. So many fucking things."

"Do you want to talk?"

"Probably." I got up to refill my drink. "Want some brandy?"

"Yes. Thank you."

I poured myself another generous serving and then a couple of fingers of brandy for her.

"What's going on?"

I dug my phone out of my pocket and pulled up one of the zillion pictures I now had of Jeremy. The one I wanted was of the two of us, very clearly showing the matching colors of our eyes. I stared at it for a moment, unable to hide my smile, and then handed her the phone.

Her sharp intake of breath told me she knew exactly who he was to me, and she brought a hand to her chest.

"Zeke? Who is this? Where is he? It's a he, yes?"

"Yes. His name is Jeremy William Zerkesian. He lives with his mother in Minneapolis."

"I don't…" Her eyes snapped to mine. "Why wouldn't you tell us? Even with the way things have been between the two of us, this is my grandson!"

"Believe me, Ma, I didn't hide him on purpose. I only just found out about him. That's where I've been the last week or so."

"His mother hid him from you?" she demanded incredulously.

"No. She tried to get ahold of me, but Aurora…" I took a breath and told her the whole sordid story, not leaving out anything.

"I never liked her," she muttered, shaking her head. "I warned you she was using you. Aurora has never had the band's best interests at heart, only her own. And certainly not yours individually."

"It was just sex between us, Ma."

"Was it that good?" she asked, wrinkling her nose. "Couldn't you find good sex with someone who wasn't out to hurt you?"

"Well, let's not exaggerate. She's not out to *hurt* me. She just has her own agenda, which is making sure the band continues to make a lot of money so her fifteen percent adds up."

She scoffed. "Ridiculous. You should fire her."

"I tried. Band wasn't on board."

"I'm going to have a talk with Carter," she muttered.

"Ma, Aurora isn't the point here."

"Of course not. This young woman, Presley. What is she like? Is she pretty? Do you like her?"

"I do. More than I wanted to admit, even to myself. But she fuckin' hates me now." I took another long drink before finding some pictures of Presley to show her.

"You have to bring them here!" she said abruptly, after scrolling through them. "I have to meet my grandson."

Leave it to my mother to make it all about her.

"I tried. She wants nothing to do with me other than money. And I don't mean that the way it sounds. It's not like she asked for anything beyond some things for the baby, and to pay the hospital bill. She's not trying to keep him from me either, but she refuses to come here or spend time with me. I didn't even see her this morning. She stayed in her room until I left."

"So she still has feelings for you," my mother mused.

I snorted. "Yeah. Feelings of hate. Distrust. Anger."

She laughed. "All the women you've been with, and you still don't really know anything about them outside of the bedroom."

"What does that mean?"

"If she truly hated you, it wouldn't bother her to be around you at all. She would be worried about her child, anxious to make sure he was okay around this person she didn't like and would most likely be doing every-thing in her power to make you want to leave. Instead, she hid. The only reason she would do that is because she has feelings she'd been trying to conceal."

I hadn't thought of that, but I wasn't sure I believed it.

"Her aunt was with us, so she knew Jeremy was safe, even though I don't think she's worried about me hurting him." I paused. "At least, I hope not."

"What are you going to do?"

"I don't know. She's also embarrassed."

"Embarrassed?" She cocked her head. "About what?"

"The fact that she was nothing but a one-night stand. She said some-thing about how humiliating it would be to meet you, knowing that *you* know the details of how she got pregnant."

"I wouldn't say I know the details," Mom said. "But that's silly. You had sex. Big deal. Everyone is having sex these days. And why wouldn't she want to spend time with my famous, handsome son?"

"Because of me, she didn't graduate," I muttered. "Fuck. I don't know what to do or how to get her to forgive me."

"Interesting feeling now that the shoe is on the other foot, eh?" Her eyes met mine.

"Ma, this isn't about us. I have bigger problems right now."

"I know. But it doesn't change reality."

"You want me to say I forgive you? Fine. I forgive you for spending my money like it was your own and making me feel bad in my own house. Happy?"

She pursed her lips. "This is definitely not the time for this conversation."

"No, it's not."

"Well, as for Presley, it's going to take time and patience. And probably a lot of money."

"I don't give a damn about the money. She can have anything she wants." Words like that had never come out of my mouth before and my mother didn't miss a thing.

"Oh, I see. Now you don't care about money, but when I spend it, you're worried about going broke."

"I thought we weren't going to talk about this now?"

"Well, maybe we have to."

"Mom, this is my child we're talking about. My son. Whose mother and great-aunt have been skipping meals to make sure he has what he needs."

She had the grace to look ashamed. "Oh, Christ. I had no idea it was that bad, Zeke."

"Hence why I said I don't care about the money. I just want them to be okay."

"Ah. So you care about her, not just the baby."

I rolled my eyes. "Duh. She's my kid's mother."

"That's all?"

I hadn't blushed in probably twenty years, but I was almost positive I was blushing now. What the hell was wrong with me?

"Well, that's my answer."

"Don't, Ma."

"Must be hard, realizing for the first time in your life you actually have to work for something."

I stared at her. "What are you talking about? You think making Onyx Knight the biggest band in the world was easy?"

She shrugged. "A little. Sure, you had to play and tour and write and practice, but at the end of the day? Easy. Your first album took off. Your first tour was a success. Radio stations and music journalists loved you. You guys didn't spend a decade struggling before you had your first hit. It all happened quick. Now you'll have to work harder than you ever have in your life if you want Presley and Jeremy to be a part of it. Are you up for it?"

I stared at her. "I don't think I have a choice. I already love my son and want to be with him night and day."

"And his mother?"

"We spent one night together. I like her. I want to make this up to her. But I don't really know her."

"Well, at least now you know what the first step is."

I frowned. "I do?"

She shook her head. "Yes, my love. The first step is getting to know her."

"How can I do that if I'm here and she's there? And I can't go there because we go back in the studio tomorrow. I could delay it a day or two, a week, but beyond that, I have to be here."

"Okay, then I amend my statement. Your first step is convincing her to come to L.A. for a visit."

Great.

The first step was the one that seemed insurmountable.

How the hell could I convince Presley of anything, much less to come for a visit?

20

―――――――

P *resley*

AFTER ZEKE LEFT, the house seemed empty and quiet. Jeremy was fussier than normal, and I didn't know what to do with myself. Having some money now—Zeke had left a thousand dollars in cash on the kitchen counter— made everything feel different. From what Aunt Meg said, all the bills were paid, including the huge hospital bill we'd been making payments on. We'd have a new roof in a few weeks, the pantry was stocked, Jeremy had enough diapers and wipes to last until he was potty trained, and there was meat in the freezer.

I was still struggling with a plethora of emotions related to my situation with Zeke, but anyone who said money didn't buy happiness had obviously never been dirt poor. I felt lighter in general, and at work, the normal dread that always filled my chest loosened a little. It was easier to laugh with my co-workers, and I even stayed after one night to have a few drinks, something I'd never been able to do before.

Whether I wanted to admit it or not, having Zeke back in my life made things easier. I wasn't sure if I would ever be able to trust him, but Aunt Meg was right that hanging on to the hurt and anger didn't impact anyone but me. I had to find a way to get past it, no matter how difficult it was. It wouldn't just be better for me, but it had to be better for Jeremy in the long run. I didn't want him to grow up seeing his parents at odds every time they were in the same room together.

I was still mulling things over in my mind when I got home from work late on Saturday night. I'd closed, so it was after two, and I was hoping Jeremy would let me get some sleep since I had to work again tomorrow night. Well, technically, tonight, since it was already tomorrow.

I'd just gotten the key in the front door when I heard Jeremy screaming.

Boy, he was really in a mood.

Poor Aunt Meg.

I was chuckling to myself as I stepped inside and closed the door behind me.

"Rough night, huh?" I called out.

There was no answer and I frowned as I stepped into the room. Jeremy was in his rolling bassinet, arms flailing as he cried.

"Hey, buddy, where's your Auntie?" I looked around, suddenly worried. Aunt Meg would have never let him cry like this if she could help it.

Oh no.

Dread filled me as I considered the fact that she could have fallen again.

"Meg! Aunt Meg!" There was no answer and I rushed into the kitchen, holding Jeremy against my chest as I simultaneously tried to soothe him.

She was on the floor, sitting at an awkward angle with her back against the cabinets, as if she'd slid down.

"Oh, god." I dropped to my knees, using one hand to find a pulse.

"Heart," she whispered, her eyes barely opening.

"Fuck." I yanked my phone out of my back pocket and called 9-1-1, all the while talking to her, trying to keep her awake.

"Baby okay?" she asked in a shaky voice.

"He's fine," I said, trying to quell the panic that was starting to overwhelm me. I didn't know what to do. Aspirin? Something else? The 9-1-1 dispatcher said help was on the way, but it seemed like it was taking forever.

"I'm going to make him a bottle," I told her. "Help is coming."

She nodded and I quickly made two bottles, thinking ahead to accompanying her to the hospital. There was no way I was letting Meg go alone, and obviously I wasn't able to leave Jeremy at home.

"You okay, Auntie?" I asked her as I grabbed Jeremy's diaper bag from the counter.

She didn't respond and I knelt beside her again. "Please, Meg. You're all I have. Don't give up."

"I'm not." Her voice was barely discernible but at least she was conscious and lucid.

I jumped at the knock on the door, running to answer it.

Then there was chaos as paramedics came in, assessing Aunt Meg, getting her on a stretcher and asking me a million questions I didn't have the answers to.

"What hospital are you taking her to?" I asked.

They gave me the information and I finished packing Jeremy's bag on autopilot. Diapers, wipes, the extra bottle, a change of clothes, a couple of toys to keep him occupied in case we were there a long time.

Please, please, please, I thought to myself. Don't let it be something bad.

Other than a handful of friends, Aunt Meg and Jeremy were all I had. I'd already lost my parents, and the idea of losing her was unfathomable. I couldn't—*wouldn't*—accept it.

IT WAS A LONG NIGHT. Thankfully, after the bottle I'd given him at home, a diaper change, and then the ride in the car to the hospital, he'd fallen asleep and was still asleep. It was nearly seven in the morning, and here in this noisy emergency room, secure in his stroller, he slept longer than he ever had at home.

A doctor had seen Meg hours ago and confirmed that she'd had a heart attack. How bad it was and whether or not she would be okay was still up in the air. They were waiting for a cardiologist to see her, and they would decide from there. She was in serious condition, but stable for now, and there was nothing for me to do but wait. And it was driving me insane.

I'd called Denise a little while ago, and she was on her way to pick Jeremy up. She'd lived next door to Aunt Meg even longer than I'd lived there, and they were good friends. I'd always been busy with school and work, so I didn't know her that well, but if Aunt Meg trusted her to watch him that other time, then I had no choice now. The hospital was no place for the baby, and I couldn't focus on Aunt Meg if I was busy with him.

"Good morning." A man in a white coat and glasses came in. "I'm Dr. Shanahan."

"Doctor." I quickly got up. "I'm Margaret's niece, Presley. How is she doing?"

"Well, there's good news and bad news." He smiled at me before glancing at Aunt Meg. "You were very lucky, Mrs. Forrester. The heart attack was mild, but you have some blockages. I'd like to do surgery to put in some stents."

"What does that mean?" I asked worriedly.

He gave us a somewhat detailed explanation of what happened when the arteries in the heart had blockages, how the stents would open them up, and some other information that made my head spin. What it boiled down to was that the stents would help keep blood flowing from her heart to the rest of her body, and that was the most important thing. It sounded like a routine procedure, and he promised she would be good as new, maybe even better, in no time.

"How soon can you do it?" Aunt Meg asked.

"I'm putting you on the schedule for tomorrow." The doctor gave us some more basic information before leaving, and I sighed in relief.

"It's going to be okay," I said, reaching for her hand. "Can you tell me what happened? I was scared to death when I found you on the floor like that."

"I'm so sorry, sweetie." She met my gaze. "I didn't mean to scare you."

"Don't worry about me. Just tell me what happened?"

"I felt off," she said slowly. "I wasn't sure what was wrong, but I just felt odd. Something had been going on all night, so instead of taking the baby upstairs, I put him down in the bassinet. I had a feeling it might not be a good idea to carry him up the stairs. Around one-thirty I was dozing on the couch and felt a weird pain in my chest. It wasn't sharp, but it was enough to wake me. I got up and went to the bathroom and by then Jeremy was stirring. I figured I'd make his bottle while I was up, but the moment I got into the kitchen I knew something was really wrong. Before I could think about grabbing my phone, everything kind of went blurry and all I could do was slide down. I didn't want to fall and hit my head or something."

"Oh, Aunt Meg."

"And I figured you'd be home any minute."

"I hate that happened," I whispered. "I wish I'd been there."

She met my gaze but gently shook her head. "It's okay. Now, you've had a long night. You should take the baby home."

"Denise is coming to get him."

"There's nothing you can do for me here. I'm just going to sleep."

"I don't want to leave you."

"I know." She smiled and squeezed my hand. "You're a good girl, Presley. If I couldn't have a daughter of my own, having you in my life has more than made up for it. You know that, don't you? I love you like you're my own."

Tears stung my eyelids. "I love you too. You're much more than an aunt to me. I lost my mom, but then I got another one."

"And now you made me a grandma, too." She managed a small grin.

"Now take that beautiful baby and go home. Take a nap and rest. You have to work tonight."

"You think I can work while you're in the hospital?" I demanded incredulously.

She nodded. "You can. You will. Let Denise watch him. Once you tell her what's going on, she'll be happy to help. Don't be stubborn, Presley. This is what friends and neighbors do. Especially since we don't have anyone else."

"But I want to be here with you."

"There's nothing you can do. You can come tomorrow for the surgery, but today I'm truly too exhausted to do anything but sleep. And you need to sleep too."

I was torn but she nodded firmly. "Call Denise and tell her you're going home. Let her watch the baby while you sleep and then she can take him home with her when you go to work."

I hesitated but she was right.

I didn't want to lose another job, and there was no point in watching her sleep.

"Okay, I'll go, but I'm bringing you your phone on my way to work," I said. I'd forgotten in the hurry to get out of the house, and I needed her to be able to reach me.

"Good idea." She squeezed my hand. "Go on. I'll see you tomorrow."

"I love you."

"I love you too."

21

———————

Z *eke*

With everything happening in my life, I hadn't reached out to the band at all, so they had no idea anything was going on. We were supposed to be in the studio tomorrow to start the new album, but I was restless tonight. I needed to talk to someone other than my parents, and for the first time in a while, I sent a message to Carter.

ZEKE: Hey, what are you up to? You want to hang out?

CARTER: It's not like I can go have a drink or anything.

ZEKE: I can come over, we can order pizza, and I can show you the new song I'm working on. Plus I have news.

CARTER: Dude. I'm not drinking or doing drugs. I'm completely sober. You don't have to come babysit me.

ZEKE: Not everything is about you. Did it ever occur to you that I might have something happening in my life?

CARTER: Yeah, right. Give me a break. The band reaches out one at a time, like I can't figure out what you're up to.

That was news to me, but I'd been out of the loop for the last week.

ZEKE: Are you seriously being a dick right now? I legit have something to tell you and you're pouting because your band actually gives a shit about you. Boo fucking hoo.

CARTER: I'm not pouting. Tell me your fucking news.

ZEKE: Oh, nothing big. I just met my kid for the first time, but hey, go ahead and act like a pissy little bitch.

My phone rang a second later, and I smirked as I answered. "Oh, that got your attention."

"Are you fucking with me?" Carter demanded.

"No."

"Christ. Get your ass over here."

"I'm on my way. Order pizza. Large. With sausage and pepperoni."

"Consider it done."

I disconnected and grabbed my favorite acoustic guitar. It was the first one I'd ever bought, and it was the one I almost always used when I was writing music on my own. I was itching to turn lyrics into melodies, and Carter and I always worked well together. Of course, first I had to tell him about Jeremy. And Presley.

"Yo." Carter was leaning against the front door of his Beverly Hills condo as I came down the hall. He looked better than he had in a while, having added a few pounds to his lean frame.

"Hey, man." I clapped him on the shoulder. "You're lookin' healthy."

He shrugged. "I guess."

I stepped inside, surprised to see his condo glaringly immaculate. It was usually a pigsty, so he'd changed more than just his party habits.

"Pizza just got here," he said, leading me to the living room where he'd put it on the coffee table, along with some paper plates and napkins.

"I have soda or water," he said. "You know I don't do milk."

"I don't drink milk either," I said. "Water's good."

We settled on his massive leather sectional and ate in silence for a few minutes.

"So, tell me about the kid." He leaned back after eating only one piece, taking a pull from his water bottle.

"He's pretty fucking cute." I opened my phone to show him pictures, something I seemed to be doing a lot lately.

"Wow. Looks just like you. How old is he? A few months?"

"Four."

"I can't believe Aurora hid this from you."

"And I can't believe you fuckers wouldn't let me fire her," I muttered.

"It's complicated, you know? She's been with us since the beginning. One lapse of judgment shouldn't—"

"Lapse of judgment?" I stared at him. "I missed Presley's entire pregnancy and the first four months of my kid's life. She had no business manipulating me like that."

"You had no business getting in bed with her." He gave me a look, his blue eyes shrewd. "We warned you she was bad news on a personal level."

"I don't want to do business with someone who isn't a good person," I said quietly. "It shouldn't matter how good she is in business."

"We've always been loyal to the people who started with us," he said.

"But she hasn't been loyal," I said. "And I had a long chat with Lexi not that long ago. She pulled some shit with Nobody's Fool, too. Shit we didn't know about."

"Like what?" he asked.

"She lied to them about how much space they could have on the stage, so on the first day of rehearsals they had to totally revamp their set-up. They wouldn't have signed the contract if she'd told the truth."

"Son of a bitch." He made a face. "We told her not to give them too much when they first started with us. I thought she was protecting our interests, not lying about shit."

"Yeah, and it was shady." I was truly frustrated by everyone's devotion to Aurora. She wasn't that big of a deal. We were her first and only big client, so it wasn't like she'd gotten us our deal. Back then, she'd been a brand-new manager. We'd needed someone to take the reins, and she'd needed experience. It had worked out well, but as far as I was concerned, it wasn't working anymore.

"Talk to her," he said quietly. "Maybe work things out. It doesn't do you any good to be pissed off about it."

"I'm not willing to work things out," I said. "She did something unforgiveable, and she did it because we were sleeping together. On and off, but it never occurred to me she was looking for a ring."

Carter chuckled. "Aren't they all?"

Not Presley. Hell, she wasn't even looking for friendship. Something I had to change.

"Yeah, well, that was never going to happen."

"Did she know that?"

"She should have." I wasn't sure if I'd ever used those exact words, but I'd sure as hell told her I wasn't interested in anything serious or long-term. "Anyway, I don't want to talk about her. I've got a new song I want to show you."

"What about the kid? You moving him and the mom to L.A.?"

"Presley doesn't want to move to L.A. She barely even wants to talk to me. Mostly I deal with her aunt. Aunt Meg is cool. You'd like her."

"She hot?" He wiggled his eyebrows.

I laughed. "I mean, if you're into grandma porn, sure. She's in her sixties, I think."

"Hey, older women know their way around a penis."

"Well, she may be down. You'll have to ask her." I couldn't wait to see Carter hit on Aunt Meg. She'd either give him a complete dressing down, or she'd be into it, and I'd potentially catch them in bed together at some point. Christ, that made me cringe. But Carter had a way of charming women of all ages. Even baby girls adored him. There was something enigmatic about him. It was one of many reasons he was so popular with the fans.

"So, the aunt's cool but mom's still pissed about you abandoning her."

"Yeah." I wiped my mouth with a napkin and downed the rest of my water bottle. "I'm trying, though. I need her to forgive me."

"How come?"

"Because we'll be co-parenting a kid, and I don't want him growing up watching us fight and bicker all the time. We're family now."

He arched his brows. "You're actually going to try to be involved in his life?"

"Well, yeah. Why the fuck would you ask me that?"

"How will you make it to T-ball games and PTA meetings when we're touring eleven months of the year?"

"I don't know," I admitted. "We'll have to cut back like we've talked about. Or build in more time off in between, so I can fly home to be with him."

"That'll get old," he said quietly. "Trust me."

"You don't understand," I protested. "It's different once it's your kid. I already miss him, and I've only known him a week. I can't imagine letting months pass without seeing him."

Carter averted his gaze, opening another bottle of water. "I dunno, man. Seems to me once we get back out on the road, we're going to get our groove on, and home will seem far away."

"Maybe because none of us have anything to go home to," I said. "Tommy's divorced, Kellan brings Didi on the road with him when they're not fighting, and the rest of us are perpetually single. I think we'd all feel differently if we had something to go home to."

"Look, I'm the wrong person to ask," he said quietly. "For me, being sober is just never-ending monotony. I don't like golf. I don't give a shit about fast cars or big houses. Couldn't care less about clothes. So far, women bore me after a few hours. The only fun in my life was being high and playing music. I can still play music but being on stage an hour a day leaves twenty-three hours to fill with fucking nothing. I've already heard all the psychology, so don't bother with all that. I know I can still live an exciting, fulfilling life without drugs." He rolled his eyes. "And I'm working on it. But don't expect me to be happy about it."

"I'm sorry, man. I know addiction is hard."

"You don't know," he said, an edge to his voice I'd never heard from him before. "Until you've lived it, you don't know. Anyway, you still got the hots for Presley or you just being nice so you can see your kid?"

"Jury's still out," I admitted. "I don't know her beyond the night we spent together. She's sweet, though."

"If I recall, she was manipulative and ambitious."

"I may have been grumpy when I said that stuff," I admitted.

"So, there's a possibility of the two of you getting together for real?" He eyed me suspiciously. "You know a kid isn't a good reason to be with the mother."

"All I said was that she's sweet," I reached into my pocket and pulled out the folded sheets of paper I'd written the song on. "And she inspired a song."

"She inspired a song." He took the papers all while giving me a look. "Dude. You're acting like a guy who's in love."

"I spent one night with her. Gimme a break."

He wiggled the papers I'd just handed him. "And a year later you wrote a song about her."

I probably didn't want to mention that the idea for the song had been in my head since that night.

Christ, I had a hard-on for my baby mama, and she wasn't even speaking to me.

This wasn't going to end well for me.

Instead of talking, I grabbed my guitar and started to strum. "Stop being a dick and just listen." I hummed along with the melody. "What do you think? Love song? Power ballad? Or full on heavy shit?"

"Play it again." Carter closed his eyes, tapping out a random drumbeat on the table. "Power ballad," he said after a minute. "It has that feel. Lemme look at this." He unfolded the paper and started to read. "Oh, yeah, this is cool… innocent heart, damaging touch… I can hear this in King's voice. If he gets a little gritty with the 'need you so much' part, the ladies'll all get hot and bothered."

I nodded. "That was my thought too."

"This is good, Z." He got up and disappeared down the hall. He came back a minute later with one of his basses and perched on the arm of the sectional. "Play that chorus again."

I went back to it, and he thumped out a bass line that felt heavier than I'd originally been thinking but somehow worked. It was a love song, but rough around the edges, which was our signature sound. We were hard rock, with a little metal, a lot of blues, and a touch of soul from Kingston's voice. This song, that I'd titled "Not Going Away," had emotion, grit, and the potential to be a single. I'd been doing this long enough to know instinctively what did and didn't work.

This was going to work.

I knew it with every fiber of my being.

"The boys are going to like this." Carter was grinning as he played, and the melody just came to me.

"Dude. Your phone is ringing."

I'd been so into what we were doing, I hadn't noticed my phone buzzing on the coffee table. I'd turned off the ringer, but it still vibrated and I reached for it, surprised to see Presley's name on the screen.

"It's Presley. She's never called me before." I answered without waiting for him to respond. "Hello?"

"Zeke!" Her voice was soft but frantic.

"What's wrong?" I asked automatically. "Is it the baby?"

"N-no. Jeremy is fine." She sniffled.

Was she crying?

Oh, fuck.

Dread filled me.

"Aunt Meg?" I hated myself for the relief that shot through me when she'd said Jeremy was okay, but it wasn't because I wanted something to happen to Meg.

"She had a heart attack," she said, her voice breaking. "And now the insurance won't cover the surgery she needs. Zeke, I don't know what to do. Please, you have to help us!"

22

P *resley*

I'D BEEN frantic since the hospital administrator had come to tell me that Aunt Meg's insurance wouldn't cover the procedure Dr. Shanahan wanted to do. Something about her MS and a second opinion and a bunch of other shit I didn't understand. After calling them myself and getting nowhere, I'd broken down and called Zeke. As much as it pained me to do it, I'd swallow every ounce of pride I'd ever had if it would help Aunt Meg.

Twelve hours later, Zeke walked into Aunt Meg's hospital room.

"Hi." I stood up, whispering as I put a finger to my lips. She'd had a rough night and was finally resting, so we walked into the hallway together.

"How are you?" he asked, putting a hand on the side of my shoulder.

"Scared," I admitted, wrapping my arms around myself.

"Tell me who I have to talk to, and I'll guarantee payment so they can operate as soon as possible. We can fight with the insurance afterward."

"Thank you," I whispered, fighting back tears. "I really appreciate this. I know this has nothing to do with Jeremy, so it's not your responsibility, but I didn't know what else to do. She's all I have, Zeke."

"It's okay. I'm glad you called."

Our eyes met and his were filled with warmth. Concern. Tenderness.

Why was he always being so nice? And helpful. And hot. He never stopped being hot, and it pissed me off that I still noticed.

It made it so hard to stay mad at him. Especially after he'd flown all this way at the drop of a hat. I'd called him late last night and he'd managed to get on the first flight out of LAX at six o'clock this morning. It was barely noon, and he was already here. That counted for something. Hell, it counted for a lot.

"Where's the baby?" he asked after a moment.

"With Denise. This is no place for him."

"No, definitely not." He put his hands on both my shoulders. "Find me the person I need to talk to, and let's get Aunt Meg that surgery."

"Okay. Thanks." I pulled the administrator's card out of my pocket and called her, asking her to come down to the room.

"Have you eaten anything today?" Zeke asked as we settled in the visitors' lounge just down the hall from Meg's room.

I shook my head. "I can't. My stomach is in knots."

"As soon as I talk to this woman, we'll get something to eat."

"I don't want to leave Aunt Meg."

"She's sleeping, and you need to keep your strength up."

I wanted to protest but I was too tired. I hadn't slept last night at all, sitting by Aunt Meg's bed until after midnight and then coming back at seven. It was hard to leave Jeremy with Denise again, but she'd been a godsend and I needed to be with Aunt Meg as much as I could.

Zeke spoke to the woman from the accounting department, filled out some paperwork, signed something, and then turned to me. "Ready to go eat?"

"Yeah. I guess." I was shocked that was all it had taken, but money spoke volumes apparently.

I let him lead me out of the hospital and toward what I assumed was a rental car. It was a big SUV of some kind and I climbed into the passenger seat, letting my body relax against the soft leather. It felt so good to sit somewhere comfortable.

God, I was tired.

The last few days had been stressful, so it was nice to let someone else take over for a while. Lately, it felt like I was in charge of everyone and everything: my life, my job, my baby, my aunt. Not to mention the house and everything that went into running it. Adding the situation with Meg's insurance on top of it all had been more than I could handle, so I didn't know how I'd ever thank Zeke for coming like this. Hopefully the doctor would reschedule the procedure quickly now that the hospital had a guarantee for payment, and I could breathe again.

"What do you want to eat and where should we go?" he asked, pulling onto the street.

"There's a place that has breakfast all day not too far from here," I said. "I suddenly feel like pancakes."

"I could eat pancakes," he said. "Just guide me in the right direction."

Ten minutes later we were seated at a small booth in the back of the restaurant, and I had a steaming cup of black coffee in front of me. I took a sip and sighed happily.

"You're a big coffee drinker?" he asked, sipping his own cup.

"It started in college, and I picked it up again after Jeremy was born."

"Long nights, huh?"

I unconsciously yawned before clapping a hand over my mouth. "Yeah, he's still not sleeping great."

"Is that normal? I don't know much about their schedules at this age."

"Well, it's different for all babies. In our case, he's a big, healthy boy, but simply not a great sleeper. The doctor says it'll get better. We'll start him on a little cereal soon and that might help. They think if he's fuller, he'll sleep more."

"You can't start the cereal now?"

"There are a lot of different opinions on when to start them on solid food versus just formula. My pediatrician says we can start when he's five months, but I know people who started at two months. There's research about their stomachs not being able to handle it, stuff like that. I'm just going to listen to our doctor because doing my own research was a very unhelpful rabbit hole."

"Sounds reasonable."

We paused to give the waitress our orders before resuming our conversation.

"So last time I was here, Aunt Meg told me you never got your e-magazine off the ground. I'd like to help with that."

I was startled but then shook my head. "That ship has sailed. I have neither the time nor the energy to take that on. Between work and the baby, I'm way too tired."

"I've been giving some thought to that too. I was thinking you should quit your job and do the magazine full-time. Let me support you while you get it off the ground."

"What? No. I can't let you do that." I stared at him.

"Why not? It would be better for Jeremy if you're home with him, and what's the difference if I pay for full-time daycare so you can go work at a job you may or may not like, or if I give you that money so you can stay home and follow the dream I unintentionally stole from you?"

"There's no guarantee it'll go anywhere," I protested. "Then what?"

"It could give you the chance to retake that final class you failed and get your degree. By the time Jeremy starts school, you could get a regular job if things don't work out with the magazine. But for the next five years or so, stay home and be a mom. I can afford it, Presley, and the truth is, I owe you. It's about more than money, and you know it."

I stared at him, wishing I could say yes but knowing I couldn't.

"Will you think about it?" he continued when I didn't respond right away. "I know you're about to say no, but will you just take a few days to think about it? Please?"

"All right." I was truly too exhausted to argue with him, and I wanted to wait until I knew Aunt Meg was on the mend before I made a huge decision like this. I was tempted, though. How awesome would it be to stay home with Jeremy and work on my e-zine? More like a dream-come-true.

"And a little more food for thought," he said, giving me a devilish smile. "I spoke to Carter. He said he would be willing to talk to you about his struggle with addiction for your first big article."

My eyes widened. This was totally unexpected. "Really?"

"He read a few of the articles you wrote about those local bands and said he likes your style. And of course, he'd do it because I asked him to."

"That's... amazing," I whispered, suddenly overwhelmed with his generosity. "Really. There are no words."

"I also have tons of friends who'll all be willing to do interviews as a favor to me."

"Zeke." I didn't even know what to say. I'd given up on getting my degree, but it had been a bitter pill to swallow. He wasn't just giving me back my dream of starting an online music magazine, he was also giving me the opportunity to finish what I'd started with college.

"Like I said, think about it." He reached across the table and laid one of his big hands on mine. "The first thing we have to do is get Meg through this surgery. Then we can talk about everything else. Okay?"

"Okay." I nodded, wishing the simple touch of his hand didn't affect me the way it did. "And thank you. I mean it."

"I told you, I'm here for you now. No matter what."

Was it weird that I believed him when he looked at me like he was looking at me now? Despite everything that had happened, the moment those gorgeous eyes of his met mine, it was as if we were back at the resort bar, talking and getting to know each other again. I was doing my level best to keep him at arm's length, but I was failing miserably. The fact that he'd jumped on a plane the moment I asked him to, even though it had nothing to do with Jeremy, made me second guess myself.

Of course, Aunt Meg had been right that I still had feelings for him. I'd always heard that your first was special, so I'd chalked it up to nothing more than a romantic fantasy, but my heart told me it was more than that whenever we were in the same room.

Not that I thought he felt what I felt. He appeared to be stepping up to be a good father and to try to make up for everything that had happened between us. That didn't mean he wanted anything more than a peaceful co-existence so we could parent our son. He had the money to make this easy on me, so I had to keep that in mind every time he did something sweet and thoughtful. This wasn't about anything except making the best of an awkward situation. I had to be careful not to mistake kindness and generosity for romantic feelings.

"You look like you're ready to drop," he said as we finished eating.

"I didn't sleep at all last night," I admitted. "I'd love to take a nap."

"How about I take you home, and you can nap while I take care of the baby?"

I frowned. "Are you sure? And what about Aunt Meg?"

"You can call her on the way. Unless they're doing the surgery this afternoon, you need to rest. I'd like to do as much as I can for you while I'm here because I have to leave tomorrow."

"Already?" The word tumbled out before I could stop it.

"We were supposed to start recording the new album today," he said quietly. "I told them I had a family emergency, but I can't miss much time because we're paying for the studio whether we use it or not."

"Oh."

Why was I so disappointed?

"I can stay one, maybe two, more days if you need me," he said, handing the waitress some money.

"You have responsibilities," I said. "It's okay. I understand."

"Presley." He turned to face me once we were outside.

"Yes?" I gazed up at his gorgeous face, mesmerized by his voice.

"If you want me to stay, all you have to do is ask."

23

Z^{eke}

I WAITED, watching the play of emotions flit across Presley's pretty face. She wanted to. Wanted me. But she was scared. Whether she was afraid I would somehow hurt her again, or merely disappoint her, I couldn't be sure, but there was no mistaking the conflict in her eyes.

And I fucking hated it.

"Ask me to stay, Sunny," I whispered, deciding to make a move. I slid a hand around the back of her neck and pulled her closer.

"Wh-what are you doing?" she whispered back, her eyes glued to mine.

"Convincing you to ask me to stay." I lowered my head and ever-so-lightly brushed my lips across hers. "Reminding you I'm not the bad guy."

"Zeke." Her voice was so soft I barely heard it, but it was the only invitation I needed.

I dipped my head again and pulled her the rest of the way against me, so our bodies were touching.

"I'll stay if you need me. Just say it."

"I...need you... to stay." Her mouth parted and as much as I wanted to slide my tongue between her beautiful lips and take everything I'd been thinking about for the last year, I had to be patient. This was too important. If I rushed her, she'd run, and I was finally making progress.

I kept my kisses chaste, gently sucking her lower lip until she made a tiny sound of pleasure. I brushed her hair back from her face, looking down at her. She was beautiful, but there was no mistaking the dark circles beneath her eyes or her sunken cheeks. Whether she'd said the words or not, she absolutely needed me to stick around. The band would be pissed, but there was no help for that. Family came first, and she and Aunt Meg and Jeremy were part of my family now.

"I'll stay for a couple of days," I said, pressing my forehead to hers. "Okay?"

"O-okay."

"Let's go back to the house. You need to rest."

"But Aunt Meg—"

"Call the hospital and find out what's going on. I'll take care of the baby while you take a nap. No arguments."

"You'll wake me if you hear anything?"

"Promise."

She dozed off almost the moment she climbed into the passenger seat, and I carried her into the house when we got there.

"Hey, Denise." I smiled at their elderly neighbor. "Let me get Presley settled in bed and then I'll be down to take care of Jeremy."

"Oh. Hello." She looked flustered to see me, but I just smiled and headed up the stairs.

Presley's room was a mess, the bed unmade and clothes strewn every-where. There were two piles of laundry, one that looked like hers and the other Jeremy's, folded neatly on the dresser, but beyond that her room looked like the space of someone who was busy. And tired.

I made sure she was warm and comfortable in bed and then quietly began gathering up the clothes from the floor. There was a hamper in the hallway, so I put them all in there, even though I wasn't sure they were all dirty. I picked up a couple of empty baby bottles and carried them down-stairs to the kitchen before joining Denise in the living room.

"Thanks again," I told her. "I'm happy to pay you for your time."

She looked affronted. "Absolutely not. Meg and I have been friends for decades. This is the least I can do. I think I'll go over to the hospital to sit with her if the two of you are staying home."

"For a few hours at least. Presley hasn't been sleeping much so I'm trying to help out where I can."

"That's good. Presley takes on too much sometimes." She paused at the door, looking over her shoulder. "Don't hurt her, Mr. Zerkesian. She's a good girl. And she's had enough heartache in her life."

I nodded solemnly. "No plans to hurt her. You have my word."

She smiled. "Let me know if you need anything. I'm happy to watch Jeremy anytime while Meg is in the hospital."

"Thank you. We will." She closed the door behind her, and I pulled Jeremy out of the bouncy seat where he was happily gnawing on some kind of teething ring thing. It was early for teeth, according to the book I was reading about babies, but that didn't mean he couldn't play with it.

With Jeremy distracted and happy in his highchair, I loaded the dishwasher. I wiped down the counters and made a couple of bottles, so we'd have them in case we had to leave for hospital without much warning. The fridge still seemed well-stocked, and I figured I'd make us omelets or something once she woke up. I was too wound up to sit still, and desperate for something to do, I poked around until I found a notebook and a pen.

Then I sat down and, with my son bouncing on my lap, started to write.

PRESLEY SLEPT THROUGH THE AFTERNOON, and I finally went to wake her around five. She needed to rest, but she'd fallen asleep around two, and if I let her sleep much longer, she'd probably be up at midnight. Meg's surgery wasn't until tomorrow, so we had nothing to do tonight but relax. I was going to try my best not to let her go back to the hospital until morning. Meg was being well cared for and Denise was still with her, so she wasn't alone.

This would also give me time to be alone with Presley. Not that I planned to seduce her—not yet anyway—but it was beyond time for us to talk. Spend time together that wasn't rushed or solely focused on the baby. We needed to find out who we were again, even though part of me already knew. There was something about her. That was why I'd never forgotten her. My gut told me we would have found our way back to each other somehow, even without Jeremy.

"What time is it?" she murmured as I perched on the edge of her bed with the baby on my lap.

"Almost five-thirty," I said.

"Oh. Wow." She turned over and blinked, reaching for her glasses. "How's Aunt Meg?"

"Denise is with her and said she's resting. They spent the afternoon watching soaps. Surgery is at eight in the morning. Denise will come over around seven and we can head to the hospital."

"You've been on top of things," she murmured, sitting up and reaching out to press a kiss on Jeremy's head. "Did he nap?"

"Yup. Two hours."

"He's probably hungry."

"Not yet." I smiled. "Why don't you freshen up or whatever you need to do and let's figure out food. How do you feel about breakfast for dinner, even though we had breakfast for lunch?"

"My favorite." She smiled up at me. "I could eat it all day, every day."

"Then let's do it. Do you have a preference of ingredients in your omelet?"

"Anything but broccoli."

I chuckled. "Bacon, cheese, and onions?"

"Perfect. I've got to go to the bathroom, and I'll be right down."

"Okay." I left her alone and went down to the kitchen.

It had been a while since I'd cooked, but I enjoyed puttering in the kitchen on the rare occasions I had the chance to. On the road there were no opportunities, and at home my mother always took over, but I did get in there at breakfast sometimes. Hence my suggestion of breakfast for dinner. I genuinely enjoyed breakfast food, but it was about all I knew how to make. I could grill a mean steak, but we hadn't defrosted anything, and I wanted to keep things simple. I had no idea when or if I'd have another chance to hang out with Presley like this, so I didn't want to spend the whole time cooking and cleaning.

"Bum bum bum!" Jeremy pounded his little fists onto the table of his highchair after I strapped him in.

"Gonna be a drummer?" I asked him.

He pounded some more in agreement.

I laughed, ruffling his soft dark hair. He was the cutest damn kid.

My kid.

My *family*.

This could be my family if I wanted it.

The reality that this might be the real deal, a forever kind of thing, hit me right in the gut.

The only question was whether or not I wanted it.

And, of course, whether or not Presley would be on board.

Technically, we barely knew each other, but it didn't feel that way. I knew a lot about her life with Aunt Meg, the loss of her parents, how hard she worked to make ends meet. I knew she was a good writer and an excellent mother. She cared about her aunt and the people close to her. I also knew what it sounded like when she came. How sensitive her clit was. How easy it was to get her off.

What else did I need? I'd figure out her favorite color and whether or not she liked horror movies as we spent more time together. I just had to talk her into giving me another chance, which was why tonight was so important.

"When was the last time you changed him?" she asked, coming into the kitchen. God, she looked great in a pair of tight faded jeans and a loose sweatshirt that hung off one shoulder. Her feet were bare, and she'd left her hair down, falling in soft waves around her shoulders.

I really wanted to kiss her.

"Like fifteen minutes ago," I replied, turning back to concentrate on the onions I was chopping.

"What can I do to help?" she asked, coming over to stand next to me.

"Nothing. Keep the baby entertained and tell me where things are if I can't find them."

"I'll set the table." She reached over my head to get a couple of plates, exposing a few inches of bare torso and I couldn't take my eyes off of her. Her skin looked soft and creamy, just the way I remembered it, and from what I'd seen so far, she didn't appear to be carrying any residual pregnancy weight. As far as I was concerned, she was perfect.

She hummed as she worked, pulling out forks, knives, and napkins. I didn't recognize the song, so I asked about it.

"Oh, it's my friend Sam's band's song. They don't have any recorded music yet, but they play it live and this one is my favorite. It's called 'Forever Forgotten.' It's about a dog, actually, but the lyrics are vague enough to apply to a person too. I guess it reminds me of me."

"Do you feel forgotten?" I asked, turning to look at her.

"Well." She met my gaze. "I was forgotten. My whole pregnancy. At least that's how it felt."

I slowly put down the knife and walked toward her, taking her chin between my thumb and forefinger. "You were never forgotten, Presley. I didn't know anything about what you were going through, and after the way I behaved that morning, I didn't think you'd want to hear from me anyway. But I never forgot you."

"You...didn't?"

"No." I reached up and took off her glasses. Then, still holding her chin, I lowered my mouth to hers. Our lips met tentatively, and I waited for her to respond. And just like this morning, her mouth opened for me, inviting me in. This time, I didn't hesitate. I pulled her to me and slid my tongue against hers. She was as sweet as I remembered, tasting faintly of toothpaste. I wrapped one arm around her waist, keeping her tight against me as I deepened the kiss, taking pull after pull of her tongue. Her body was warm and soft, molding perfectly against mine, and the memory of her naked beneath me came rushing back.

A soft cry from Jeremy pulled us apart, but I didn't let her go. She felt too good, and it had been too long since I'd held her.

"I should pick him up," she whispered, her eyes a little glassy.

"He's fine," I countered. "You should stay right here so I can look at you."

Her cheeks turned pink, but she didn't look away.

"Why do you hide your beautiful eyes behind glasses?" I asked softly, running my fingers along the curve of her jaw.

"Because I can't afford new contacts, so I save the ones I have by only wearing them for work."

"I'll buy you new ones."

"You don't have to keep buying me things."

"But I want to. Especially if it means I get to look into your pretty eyes. They remind me of honey and sunshine and daisies."

She flushed. "You don't have to say things like that."

"Like what? That I think you're beautiful? That I love the color of your eyes? That my dick is so hard from just kissing you? Sorry. But it's all true."

She finally looked away, pushing gently at my chest and moving to soothe Jeremy, who'd gotten a little fussy.

"We shouldn't, I mean, we're not..." She cleared her throat. "We're not going to sleep together, Zeke. That can't happen. Never again."

24

P *resley*

Instead of being upset, Zeke looked amused. There was a playful smile on his face as he said, "Never ever?"

I made a face. "You weren't the one with nine months of twenty-four-seven morning sickness, swollen feet, and stretch marks. Don't even get me started on childbirth. I'd like to avoid going through that again at all costs."

"Fair enough." He ran a finger along my cheek. "But there's lots of stuff we can do that won't get you pregnant."

I swallowed.

How was he so irresistible?

I was so tempted.

And so, so horny.

I'd been horny when I was pregnant too.

Not that I'd tell him that.

"Don't tell me you weren't turned on just now." He made a trail with his finger, sliding down my throat, along my collarbone, and then stopping at one of my very hard nipples. "Your eyes are glassy. Your nipples are hard. And I'll bet if I touched your pussy, you'd be soaked."

"Zeke!" I glanced at Jeremy, who seemed content again, thumping his little fists on the table in front of him.

Zeke chuckled, a warm, rich sound that turned me on even more. "He doesn't understand. Not yet anyway."

"No, but I still don't think this is a good idea."

"What? Us making love?"

"Look what happened last time. I don't want to ever be in that situation again."

"Pregnant or alone?" he asked softly. "Because while I can't one hundred percent guarantee the first won't ever happen, I absolutely can the second."

"Sex just isn't a good idea," I mumbled, though my eyes followed his finger as it moved to my other breast, rubbing lightly against my taut nipple.

"I think you're wrong. In fact, it's a *great* idea." He used his finger expertly to tease me, making my breath come faster and my heart rate kick up. Even through the fabric of my thin sweatshirt, my breasts ached with need, anxious for more. Why had I thought not wearing a bra was a good idea? I'd assumed the sweatshirt would sufficiently cover my breasts. But I hadn't anticipated this type of direct contact. "I think a few orgasms are exactly what you need to relax. And what we need to reconnect."

"Wh-why would we do that?" I whispered shakily. My resolve was melting away faster than my panties probably would, and there was nothing I could do to stop it.

"Because we have a son," he said, his voice dropping a few octaves as he backed me against the counter. "Because I've thought about that night we spent together more than you'll ever know." He dragged the fingers of one hand through my hair, ending at the back of my neck and squeezing lightly. "Because you want me as much as I want you. All you have to do is admit it."

"I do," I whispered miserably. "But I don't want to get pregnant again. It's almost a phobia. That's how terrifying the thought of having sex again is in that regard."

"You're not on birth control?"

I shook my head. "Why would I be? I was pregnant and then healing and now... who has time for dating with an infant and an elderly aunt?"

"Then we'll get you on whatever type of birth control you're comfortable with, and even once you're convinced it's taken effect, we'll continue using condoms. Will double protection make you feel safer?"

"You'd do that?" I asked in surprise.

"Of course. Sex is no fun for me if you're nervous or afraid." He skimmed his lips across my cheek. "But for now, I'm going to make us dinner. Then we'll put the baby to bed."

"And then?" I was almost afraid to ask, but I did anyway.

"Then I'm going to show you all kinds of ways I can make you come without risking pregnancy."

My eyes fluttered closed as he lightly pressed his lips to mine.

Then he moved away, whistling as he continued chopping onions.

Like he hadn't just gotten me all worked up.

I didn't know what I'd agreed to just now, but he was impossible to refuse.

Ironically, Aunt Meg would be delighted at this turn of events.

I was more pragmatic.

Getting involved with him was dangerous. It would take more than a few days of conversation and generosity for me to trust him, and if I didn't trust him, why was I even considering this?

It was a good question, but one I honestly didn't have the answer to.

All I could do at this point was follow my gut.

DINNER WAS QUICK BUT DELICIOUS. Zeke fed Jeremy while I cleaned up and then we went upstairs so he could help with his bath. By the time we were done, Zeke had almost as much water on him as Jeremy, and my heart melted a bit as I watched them together. Jeremy somehow already knew his father and accepted him into the fold, always laughing and pulling at his hair. Zeke didn't appear to have any issues with fatherhood either, taking to the role like he'd been around the whole time.

Aunt Meg seemed to be willing to give Zeke a second chance, and when we spoke on the phone a little while ago, she said that Denise had told her she thought he was a "fine young man for Presley."

I was the only one harboring doubts and hanging on to the past.

It wasn't so much about forgiveness anymore. It was more about self-preservation. I had almost no experience with relationships and this one had already skipped a bunch of steps because of the pregnancy. There was no option for us to go slow and see what might happen. The biggest thing had essentially already happened, so we were either going to be together or we weren't. There was no in between for us and that was the part that gave me pause.

How did we go back to simply co-parenting Jeremy if we tried to be together and it didn't work out? And if I was honest with myself, what were the chances it would turn into something serious? He was one of the hottest, most successful rockstars in the world. He could have anyone, and I was no prize. Not for a guy like him. I was just a regular girl from the Midwest. Not a model or actress or even a professional. I was a single mom who happened to have had his baby, and I didn't think that was enough for us to start a real relationship.

"He's asleep," Zeke said softly, bringing the baby into the bedroom where I'd been putting away some laundry.

"Just put him in the crib on his back," I whispered, walking over to stand next to him as he laid the baby down.

"He's so perfect," Zeke whispered. "I had no idea babies could be like this. Round and soft and happy most of the time."

"He's pretty awesome," I agreed.

"Let's go downstairs so we don't bother him," he said. He slid his hand around mine and we padded down to the living room. To my surprise, he sank onto the couch and tugged me onto his lap, wrapping his arms around my waist.

I wasn't sure what to do at first but resisting him seemed like so much work when I could just snuggle against his broad, hard chest. So that was what I did. I was still exhausted, and he felt so warm and comfortable. I could fall asleep right here in his arms. That wouldn't be the worst way to relax.

"Tired, Sunny?"

The nickname made me smile and I nodded. "Yeah."

"Comfortable?"

"Very."

"Good." He gently stroked a hand up and down my back. "It's okay if you fall asleep. I'm not going anywhere for a couple of days. We have time. If you need to sleep, let yourself go. I'll keep an ear out for Jeremy."

"Zeke?"

"Yeah?"

"Will you come upstairs and lie down with me?"

"Sure." He lifted to his feet without putting me down and carried me back upstairs.

It occurred to me I needed a shower, but it felt too good to be this close to him.

He was a big guy and there wasn't a hell of a lot of room in my double bed, but he turned onto his side and pulled me up against his front. "Rest," he whispered. "I'll get up with the baby."

"Okay." I let his warmth envelope me and didn't even realize I'd fallen asleep until Jeremy's whimpers woke me.

"I got him," Zeke whispered, stirring beside me. "Go back to sleep."

I turned over but it was hard to sleep knowing Zeke was here. The bed felt strangely empty without him beside me, and I had a feeling I wouldn't be able to settle down until I was in his arms again.

Luckily, Jeremy was pretty good at night, and once you changed him and gave him a bottle, he'd drift off quickly.

Sure enough, Zeke was back fifteen minutes later, putting Jeremy down and then crawling in behind me.

"You're so warm," I murmured, wiggling back against him.

"Keep that up and I can think of at least one body part that isn't going back to sleep," he whispered against my ear. One hand drifted over my hip and slid along the seam of the jeans I'd never taken off.

"Sounds intriguing."

"Yeah? Then you'll be so much more comfortable without these," he murmured.

"Mmhm." No doubt about that. I let him unsnap the button and pull down the zipper, but instead of sliding them down my hips, he ran his hand along my mound. He pushed his fingers down into my jeans, but kept them on the outside of my underwear, cupping me with a firm but gentle grip.

"Feels like I'm going to have to shave you again."

"It itches when it grows back," I protested meekly.

"Then we won't let it grow back. Every morning when you wake up, I'll shave your pussy and then eat it."

I moaned at the thought of doing that every day.

"Oh, you like that, huh?" He rumbled a soft laugh, rubbing his fingers against my sensitive areas. "You wet for me, Sunny?"

"You tell me," I teased, giving in to my need for him and arching into his hand. His fingers slid beneath the edge of my panties, and right down my slit. He put the tip of his finger at my soaked entrance and pressed lightly.

"Very, very wet. I want to put my tongue there, baby."

"I want that too."

"Clothes off," he whispered, sitting up and yanking his T-shirt over his head.

I wasn't sure which of us got undressed faster, but it was only a few seconds before our naked bodies were pressed together. Warm and hot and so, so sensual.

"I promise, no intercourse tonight," he said against my mouth. "But anything else goes?"

"Oh. Yes." I couldn't resist finding his mouth and pushing my tongue between his lips. I needed him. Whatever reservations I had would have to wait for a time when we weren't naked in bed together. When he didn't have his hands all over me. When we weren't frantically kissing and touching and exploring. If the chance of pregnancy was off the table—and he'd promised it was—I was all in.

"You ever done sixty-nine?" he asked, his voice low.

"If you and I didn't do it, I haven't done it," I responded.

He flipped onto his back and patted my backside. "Climb on top of me so your pussy is right above my mouth. Then I want to feel those hot, wet lips around my cock."

I couldn't move fast enough, crawling over his body to get into position.

The first swipe of his tongue made me groan, and when he spread me wide with his fingers, it was all I could do not to cry out. Doing this quietly would prove tricky, especially for me since I recalled being loud when I orgasmed. And I was going to come hard.

"Taste me, baby," he said in a soft growl.

I gripped his massive cock in my hand, running my fingers up and down the length before licking the tip.

This time he was the one who groaned, his hips shifting restlessly.

I nibbled the soft skin for a few more seconds, enjoying the tangy taste of the pre-come leaking from it. It was hard to concentrate, though, because he was doing wicked things with his tongue, stabbing it inside of me with short, rhythmic strokes. He wasn't just licking me, he was fucking me with his tongue, and I momentarily couldn't focus on anything but how good it felt.

A light slap to my backside brought me back to the task at hand, and I managed to wrap my lips around him. I opened my mouth as wide as I could to accommodate his girth and sucked deep. I felt him shudder so I sucked harder, enjoying the fact that I could distract him the same way he was distracting me. I'd read about doing this in books, but the descriptions were nothing compared to how good it felt to experience it.

Zeke slid a finger inside me as he sucked my clit and I clamped my lips around his cock, knowing it wouldn't be long until I got off. I wanted him to come when I did, so I sucked harder, moving a hand up and down his shaft in time to the motion of my mouth. But there was no stopping what was happening to me.

The coiling in my belly didn't build gradually, but ripped through me unexpectedly, and my orgasm was explosive. I practically wailed from the force of it, barely aware of him pumping in and out of my mouth. It wasn't until I choked that I realized he'd come deep in my throat, and I swallowed twice as I caught my breath.

"Holy shit," I breathed. "That was amazing."

"Fuck yeah. I think we should—" He was cut off by the sound of Jeremy crying.

Son of a bitch.

We hadn't been quiet at all.

25

Z*eke*

A YEAR AGO, I would have been annoyed as fuck at the interruption of our post-coital intimacy. Tonight, I chuckled and gently pushed Presley off me so I could grab our son.

"Be right back," I said as I handed him to Presley and then hurried to the bathroom to clean up.

I hated that we'd woken him up, but it made it that much clearer to me that I had to convince Presley to come to California. As soon as we knew Aunt Meg was going to be okay, and hopefully could travel, I would take them back to L.A. with me. I had plenty of empty bedrooms and I'd find the best doctors to take care of Meg. My parents would be over the moon to spend time with the baby, the band would be relieved I was there to work on the album, and I'd make sure Presley had everything she needed.

The only obstacle would be talking Presley into it. She was proud and stubborn, and while I respected that, I couldn't stay in Minneapolis more than a few days. I needed her and my son to be with me, plain and simple. The spark between us burned brighter than ever, and that was all I'd needed to know. Sex wasn't everything but in a case like this, where we didn't have a lot of time or history together, it was indicative of the potential for something more. I'd had lots of good sex. That was easy. Meaningful sex was different, and that's what this had been.

Even after all the pain and heartache I'd caused her, she'd given herself to me without hesitation. Physically, at least, she trusted me, and once we got past this overwhelming fear of pregnancy, things would get even more intense.

She got up when I got back to the bedroom and whispered, "I'm going to the bathroom. He's already half-asleep. Just keep rubbing his tummy and he'll drift off."

"You got it." I paused to quickly press my lips to hers and she smiled as she returned the pressure. Then I got to watch her wiggle her bare ass as she walked out of the room.

"Hey, big guy. You almost cock-blocked me, buddy. You know that?" I spoke in a soft, gentle voice, rubbing my hand on his stomach the way I'd seen Presley do it. Sure enough, his eyes closed and he was asleep before she got back from the bathroom. I quietly put him back in his crib and then reached for Presley.

"I'm cold," she whispered.

I pulled up the blankets and wrapped my arms around her, kissing the top of her head. "Better?"

"Much."

"How'd that orgasm work out for you? Feeling more relaxed?"

She giggled against my chest. "Maybe. How about you?"

"I'm pretty damn relaxed."

"If we keep doing this, there will probably be a lot of interruptions."

"If? Is there still a question mark about what we're doing?"

"Maybe a few."

"Like?"

"What are we doing, Zeke? Sex is fun. It feels good and is relaxing and all of that. But emotionally it's dangerous for me. I'm already dealing with what we'll call undiagnosed postpartum depression, and even if I wasn't, I don't think I'm equipped to handle a friends-with-benefits thing."

"Friends with benefits?" I countered. "What the hell makes you think that's what I'm proposing?"

"What else can it be? We're not dating."

"We could be. Will be. If you'll agree to come to California."

"I can't come to California, especially not now. Aunt Meg needs me. You know that."

"Both of you. All of you, I mean." She was the only woman I'd ever met who could twist me up inside without even doing anything.

"Aunt Meg is probably going to need months to get better. Maybe even rehab or—"

"I know all that, honey." I shifted our positions so I could look into her eyes. "I have room at the house for the three of you. We can put Meg into a rehab facility or have a nurse come to the house. Whatever you need."

"But why?" she whispered. "I don't understand why. This can't be because you're in love with me, and if you're not, then all we're doing is setting one or both of us up for heartbreak."

"I can't call it love," I admitted. "But I can call it desire. And I don't mean sexual. I want to be with you. I like you. I love spending time together."

"We've literally spent two nights together."

"Are you telling me you don't feel it too? The need to see what we could be if we gave this a chance?"

"Yes, but it's different for me. You have very little to lose. You have massive job security, a big family, your band, a home, and really good health insurance. I literally have nothing except Aunt Meg and the baby, both of whom rely on me. If I quit my job and come to California, what happens to my life if you send me packing?"

"That won't happen," I said smoothly. "I'll pay for the upkeep on this house and any bills to go with it. I'll make sure you and Meg have everything you need and I'll deposit money into your account. I was meaning to do it right away, but I was distracted when I left here last time. How much will make you feel secure? A hundred grand?"

Her mouth fell open. "This isn't about money!" she hissed, pushing at my chest. "We have to think about other people too, so this is about doing the right things for the right reasons. And money has very little to do with that."

"What other reasons do we need? I want to be with you. I want to touch you every minute of the day. I enjoy talking to you. Cooking and eating dinner tonight, even with a needy four-month-old in the mix, felt normal. Natural. Good."

"Yes. It feels good now because you have nothing else going on. What happens next week when you're at the studio fourteen hours a day and I'm in a strange house in a strange city, trying to navigate Aunt Meg's doctors or bills or whatever else might come up?"

"I have people to do that stuff," I replied. "You can come to the studio some days to listen and hang out. Bring the baby up to meet my friends, get to know them. And it won't be fourteen hours a day unless we get behind. Typically, we're there six to eight hours every day, like a regular job except with skewed hours sometimes. Noon to six is our sweet spot, though we'll go later if we're in the groove. We're a pretty well-oiled machine once the songs are written. There are exceptions, but that's what they are—exceptions. It's not the norm. So I'll be around a lot more than you think."

"I'm scared," she finally said. "And I don't know what to do about it."

"Trust me. I know I don't have the right to ask that, but can you try? Take a leap of faith, Presley. For me, for you, and for us."

"I'm trying. Really. But I've been taking care of myself for so long, I don't know how to trust anyone beyond Aunt Meg."

"Can I ask you a question?"

"Sure."

"Why did you trust me with your virginity after only knowing me for a few hours?"

"It wasn't really trust," she said thoughtfully. "I was tired of being a virgin, not knowing what sex was all about. And you were..." Her voice trailed as she chewed the inside of her cheek. "I don't know. Hot. Sexy. Famous. You clicked all the boxes when I asked myself why not."

"Okay, but if you were so anxious to get rid of it, why not just sleep with your friend Sam or some other good-looking guy you met?"

"It didn't feel right, I guess."

"Exactly."

"I don't understand."

"It felt right for me too. It just did. There's no way to explain it, you have to feel it. Trust it. Trust *me*." I covered both her hands with mine and brought them to my chest. "I won't hurt you, Presley. If things don't work out, I'm still going to take care of you and our son."

"Money solves a lot of your problems, doesn't it?" she asked after a moment.

"It can. Yes. But that's not what this is. I have the money to make things easier for us, but it won't change our situation or what happened in the past. All it will do is give us the opportunity to move forward." I paused, hating the uncertainty on her face. "I want to make your life better, not worse."

"You're hard to refuse," she whispered.

"Say yes, Presley. You have my word this will be a good thing."

"So, we're going right from barely knowing each other to living together?"

"We don't have to. If you'd rather I find you somewhere else to live, I can do that."

"That's a waste of time and money," she said softly. "And even if I say yes, Aunt Meg has to weigh in."

"Absolutely. And we'll get with her doctors to discuss her recovery. If we have to wait four or five weeks until she's able to travel, we'll make it work until then."

To my surprise, she leaned forward and kissed me. It wasn't chaste, but it wasn't the same as the passion-filled kisses we'd shared a little while ago either. She was promising me something, but it wasn't as cut and dried as a simple yes or no. She was giving me a gift, but I knew instinctively it was one I would have to unwrap slowly. This wasn't sex or romance or even love; this was a type of soul baring. Something I was sure neither of us had ever experienced before. Her trust was her most prized possession.

And she was going to make me work for it.

The light, promise-filled kisses turned to something more and before I knew it, she was straddling me, her mouth hungrily demanding my attention.

"Baby, I promised you no intercourse," I moaned as she ground against my steely erection. "But this isn't fair."

"Consider it payback for nine months of morning sickness," she whispered, sliding her tongue back into my mouth.

Oh, fuck.

There was no way I would be able to control myself if we kept this up, in this position. But I had another idea. I playfully pushed her off me and then got off the bed. I tugged her toward me by her feet, and she clapped a hand over her mouth to cover her squeal.

"What are you doing?" she hissed as I picked her up and tossed her over my shoulder.

"It's morning."

"So?"

"Time for a shave and then breakfast."

"What?"

I carried her into the bathroom and set her on her feet. "Hop up on the counter, baby, and spread those beautiful thighs."

Her eyes widened and her mouth formed a little "O."

"Are you..." She gazed up at me.

"Sure am." I grinned, wiggling my eyebrows. "I told you we'd start every day this way and since the alarm will go off soon anyway, we start now." I looked around. "You got a razor?"

"Zeke, we can't—"

"We can. We are. Now tell me where the razor is and get up on the counter. Don't make me spank that pretty ass."

Her cheeks turned red, but she quickly got up on the counter. "There's a new razor in the cabinet. Second shelf."

I got what I needed, along with a washcloth and soap from the shower and turned to find her spread out like a fucking feast. God damn, she was perfect. I didn't even care about her damn pubes—I'd eat that pussy any chance I got, no matter how much hair there was—I just enjoyed being able to do something so intimate with her. It also reminded me of that first night together.

The first of many, I hoped as I dropped to my knees in front of her.

26

———————

P *resley*

I'D NEVER BEEN to California.

Hell, I'd never even been on a plane.

Yet two weeks after Aunt Meg's stent surgery, we were here.

Zeke had sent a car service to pick us up, saying he would be waiting at the house. He'd found a rehab facility where Aunt Meg would stay for the next two weeks, but we were going to his house first so we could meet his family. She was doing incredibly well since the surgery, so I was beginning to feel comfortable with this new development in my life. All of our lives.

As I'd predicted, Aunt Meg thought it was a great idea. She was excited to visit California, meet Zeke's family, and have what she was jokingly calling her mid-life adventure, instead of a mid-life crisis.

Personally, I was a nervous wreck. Flying for the first time had been harrowing, Jeremy had cried for much of the flight, and no matter how many times Zeke promised me his parents were going to love me, I was still worried. If I were in their shoes, I would wonder about this woman who'd slept with my son once and was now moving into his house and his life. Especially since I came with baggage. Not that I'd ever call Aunt Meg or Jeremy baggage, but to people who didn't know or love them? It wasn't just me Zeke would be supporting, but two extra people.

Of course, the flip side of that was that I certainly wouldn't be here if not for Jeremy, and if Aunt Meg wasn't welcome then I wouldn't stay either.

"Stop worrying," Aunt Meg said, patting my leg. "It's going to be fine."

"You don't know that," I muttered.

"I thought things with you and Zeke were good," she said.

"They are. He's not who I'm worried about."

"Why wouldn't his parents like you?"

"You know why."

"That's old-fashioned and ridiculous," she said. "And if they're upset about something as archaic as premarital sex, they should be upset with their son. You didn't get pregnant by yourself."

"It's not just his parents," I said. "His band. Their girlfriends or whoever. I mean, the woman who supposedly didn't tell him when I called is *still* the band's manager. Imagine how that meeting is going to go."

"Hopefully with her apologizing." Aunt Meg's eyes glittered with amusement. "Stop worrying, would you? Look at me. I'm bright-eyed, bushy-tailed, and ready for an adventure. Are you sure I'm the old lady of the two of us?"

I laughed. "I don't think anyone would ever call you an old lady."

"Damn straight." She reached out to play with Jeremy's bare toes. He'd been miserable until we'd undressed him and since it was warm here in Los Angeles, I'd left him in nothing but his diaper and a onesie. The adorable little jumper I'd had him in to start the day was now stuffed in one of my carryon bags, along with his socks, shoes, and baby-sized baseball cap.

"I'm so tired of being scared," I admitted softly, staring out at the non-stop rows of palm trees.

"Then don't be."

"How can I not? There's a lot more at stake here than me getting my heart broken by a rockstar. This could impact Jeremy's future. Mine. *Yours.*"

"I'll be fine." She waved a hand. "I shouldn't be part of the equation in that sense at all. I'm going to rehab for a few weeks to get strong again, and then I plan to go right back to recording my Eye-Lights videos and trying to build that up. I'll be the sweetest, oldest makeup influencer out there!"

I grinned at her enthusiasm.

If only it were contagious.

"It'll be fine. You'll see." She squeezed my hand and then went back to playing with Jeremy, who was strapped into a car seat the service had provided.

Zeke had told me to leave the big stuff at home. He'd bought duplicates of everything I would need for the baby in the last week or so. Well, he'd bought new and better versions of all the things I had for him in

Minneapolis. He'd found the best quality and safest items on the market and then sent me links so I could approve them.

The amount of money he'd spent was mind-boggling to me, but it probably was nothing more than a drop in the bucket for him. I had to admit, he made everything feel easy. He'd done everything imaginable to make this move happen with as little effort as possible on my part. The hardest things I'd had to do were pack and clean out the fridge. Beyond that, he'd had people coming to oversee the new roof installation, to clean, and he'd opened a new bank account for me with more money than I'd ever seen in my life.

In fact, it was so much I was going to have to mention it to him once we were alone. I didn't need that kind of money, especially not when he was paying for everything Jeremy needed. He'd said he wanted me to feel secure, but that kind of money just made me feel weird. Like I was some kind of high-class prostitute or something. It wasn't accurate, and Zeke hadn't said anything of the sort, but I was nothing if not insecure.

"Holy shit," Aunt Meg breathed as we pulled through a tall, wrought iron gate. "Is this his house?"

Zeke had refused to send me pictures ahead of time, assuring me it would make me uncomfortable. And boy, was he right.

This wasn't a house.

This was a massive estate.

From where I was sitting, I could see the house, which was huge, but also a bunch of outbuildings. One of them looked like a garage, but I couldn't figure out what the others were. Guest houses? Fancy sheds? It was interesting. Then there was the big fountain, the Maserati, and the gorgeous, lush lawn. I'd never seen anything like it.

But the best thing I'd seen in two weeks had just strode outside.

Zeke had on shorts and a T-shirt, with his long hair pulled back in a ponytail. He looked relaxed, comfortable and at-home here, which made sense, but he was also watching the approaching car with interest. The moment it stopped he opened one of the doors.

"Hey, Meg." He smiled at her but leaned over and kissed me without hesitation. And it was a real kiss too. Firm and lingering, with a promise for more, as he smiled and helped me out.

"Hi," I whispered, feeling somewhat breathless.

"I'm so glad you're here." He hugged me to his chest.

"Me too." And I meant it. I was nervous, but once I'd made the decision to come to California, I couldn't keep an emotional distance between us. That served no purpose. If he broke my heart, well, there was no help for that now. We'd decided to be together, so that was what I was going to do.

"Let me take care of Jeremy," he whispered. "And introduce you to everyone. Then we'll talk."

"Okay." I went to give Aunt Meg a hand, though she seemed comfortable with her cane.

"There's Daddy's boy. What happened to your clothes, huh? You puke on whatever cute outfit Mommy had you in?"

I chuckled, amused that he'd guessed exactly what had happened.

"We didn't want to wear much of anything today," I told him. "Much less the cute outfit or shoes."

"Well, that's okay. We don't wear a lot of clothes here in L.A. either." He winked.

"I think I'm going to like it here," Aunt Meg said, grinning.

I rolled my eyes at her, taking her arm as we approached the front door.

Just as we got onto the front porch a middle-aged woman practically came skidding through the door, her eyes wide.

"William Zerkesian! You didn't tell me they were here," she yelled.

I stifled a laugh as Zeke tossed Jeremy in the air, making the woman who was undoubtedly his mother gasp.

"Zeke! Stop that."

"Ma, would you relax?" He shook his head as he approached her. "I'd like you to meet Margaret Forrester and Presley Figueroa."

"Hello."

"These are my parents, Armand and Fatima Zerkesian."

"It's very nice to meet you," I said politely, shaking their hands.

"Please pardon me if I don't shake," Aunt Meg said. "We don't need me falling over."

"Over course, of course. Let's go inside." Fatima let us walk in ahead of her, and I tried not to be overwhelmed by the massive foyer. A chandelier hung above us that was bigger than our living room in Minneapolis, and the floors were what looked like expensive hardwood.

"And this is Jeremy," Zeke said once he'd closed the door behind us.

"Oh, my goodness." Fatima's eyes filled with tears as she touched his bare foot, taking care not to startle him. "Hello, little one. I'm your Grandma Fatima." She turned to me. "What can he call me?"

"Anything except Mom or Auntie Meg," I said, smiling.

She smiled back before turning to him. "Can you say Grandma? Probably not yet." She held out her arms, and Jeremy frowned. He turned, burying his head in Zeke's shoulder.

"Not yet," Armand said, lightly ruffling Jeremy's hair. "He'll get used to us."

"Please, let's sit." Fatima ushered us into a brightly lit sunroom that overlooked a beautiful pool and deck area. There was a table set for six by a set of sliding glass doors. "I made lunch. I hope you're hungry."

"Starving," Aunt Meg said, sitting in a chair at the table.

"I'll have Lois bring everything in. I thought we'd eat in here."

"Lois is my housekeeper," Zeke whispered to me, as if he was anticipating the question.

"Thank you," I whispered back with a smile.

"Go on and sit," he said. "I'll keep Jeremy on my lap so you can relax some."

But Jeremy wasn't having it. He wiggled and fussed, eventually all but launching himself in my direction. He was normally even-tempered and easy-going with change, but I figured between the early morning, the flight, and now a whole new place, he was out of sorts.

"It's okay, Mommy's here." I got up and bounced him as I walked.

"Let's take him upstairs," Zeke said. "I'll show you what I have set up for him, and we can change it if you don't like it."

"Okay." I followed him, hoping Jeremy would settle down after a nap.

"So this is my room." Zeke opened a set of double doors and my jaw fell open once again. His room was massive, with sliding glass doors that led out to a balcony, a gorgeous three-sided gas fireplace, and a bed set on a platform that was three steps up from the rest of the bedroom.

"Seriously?" I demanded, bursting out laughing.

He grinned too. "Yeah, kinda. I'm a big guy. I need space. And comfort. And I work hard when I'm on the road. I deserve to relax in style."

"You do. But this is..." I bit my lip.

"Over the top? Fine. And we'll see how over-the-top you think it is when I fuck you on that bed."

"You do realize that in a few months he's going to start imitating sounds and saying things like Mama and Dada, so there will be no more cursing in front of him?"

"Yeah, yeah." He walked around the fireplace to what was a sitting room. "I considered setting up a nursery in here but decided against it. You and I need quiet time at night too. So I had it set up here." He walked to the far end of the room and through a door I hadn't noticed at first. It led into a bathroom, but as we walked through it, we came out in what was now Jeremy's nursery.

And it was beautiful.

The crib was made of carved oak, and the room was done in soft shades of yellow, green, and purple. There was a rocking chair by the window, and a changing table and dresser on one wall.

"This is awesome," I whispered, looking around. Someone had lined the wall above the crib with a string of tiny twinkling lights, and I spotted a state-of-the-art video monitor on the dresser. "How did you manage it so quickly?"

"I put my mom in charge," he said. "It made her feel included and saved me a lot of time."

"It was very thoughtful."

"We'll be able to see and hear him from our room," he said. "And I have two units, one for each side of the bed, so we'll both be able to see and hear him even if the other one of us gets up."

"It's perfect. Thank you." I looked around. "Did you bring up the diaper bag? I have a bottle in there."

"Yeah, I think everything's in my closet. Hang on, let me get it."

I sank into the rocking chair, letting Jeremy settle against my chest. His eyes closed almost immediately, and he started to drift off. It seemed like he was already at home, and when Zeke came back in with the bag and the bottle, I motioned for him to be quiet.

I carefully laid Jeremy in the crib, and he didn't move.

Zeke put the bag down, threaded his fingers through mine, and tugged me back to our room.

27

Z*eke*

"Shouldn't we go back downstairs?" she asked as I pulled her toward the bed.

"Nope." I climbed up the three steps of the pedestal, scooped her up, and tossed her onto the bed before I joined her.

"There is zero chance of any funny business in the middle of the day while your parents and my aunt are downstairs having lunch." She was attempting to sound stern, but her lips twitched with mirth.

"There's going to be funny business at all hours of the day and night now that you're here," I said, leaning back lazily. "But right this minute I want to talk."

"Um, okay. What's up?" She eyed me curiously.

"First, are you okay with the set-up for Jeremy?"

"It's perfect," she whispered, leaning over to kiss me. "Thank you for thinking of everything."

"I may not have thought of everything, but I tried." I toyed with a lock of her hair, really wishing we could get naked. Sometimes being an adult with responsibilities was a pain in the ass.

"I appreciate it."

"After lunch, my thought was we leave Jeremy here with my parents while we go get Meg settled. I know it's not ideal since he doesn't know them yet, but I promise he'll be fine with them. I honestly think it would just be a lot of chaos to take him to the rehab center with us while we check Meg in and make her comfortable."

"I agree," she said. "I was wondering what I would do with him if your mother couldn't watch him. I need to make sure Meg is okay before I leave her anywhere."

"Okay, perfect. We'll come back afterward, have dinner, get Jeremy settled for the night, and then we both need to get a good night's sleep. I have a long day tomorrow because we're behind schedule. That being said, I don't want you to feel like I abandoned you with two people you don't even know yet, so I've got options for you."

She chuckled. "I know you have to work. My plan was to take Jeremy to go see Aunt Meg tomorrow morning. Then come home so he can nap and I can try to unpack some of our stuff."

"That's a good plan, but my mother is going to go into full-on grand-mother mode the minute we allow it, which means you'll have more time on your hands than you think."

"So, what are my options then?" she asked.

"Well, option one is you can come to the studio and listen for a while, maybe around lunchtime? We usually take a break around one, and I'd like you to meet the guys. It'll also give you a chance to talk to Carter, so you can set up a time for your interview."

"I hadn't even thought about that," she said. "It's been a crazy couple of weeks."

"I know, but this is your chance to get the magazine updated and ready for a re-launch. I mentioned it to my publicist, and she said she'd be happy to put the word out about a new rock mag. Her name is Dorian and I'll intro-duce you to her too."

"Zeke, you don't have to do all this," she said softly. "I'm not here because of what you can do for me. This is about Jeremy. And us."

Hearing her say that felt good, but I still felt like I owed her. If she decided not to pursue her e-zine, or if she wanted to be a stay-at-home mom until Jeremy was older, that was okay too. I just had to make sure it wasn't because I hadn't done what I'd promised her. She hadn't asked for anything, but I'd told her I would make it happen, and I wouldn't go back on my word. If for no other reason than to assuage my guilt. I'd been such a dick to her last year.

"I want you to go back and finish your degree," I said after a moment. "If you decide the magazine isn't something you want to pursue after that, it doesn't matter to me one way or the other. But I inadvertently kept you from graduating and that's not fair."

"I have other priorities right now," she said, moving closer to me and winding her arms around my neck. "You and Aunt Meg and the baby are all I need. I finished college. The only thing missing is that piece of paper, and I don't know how important it is."

"If it's important to you, then it's important to me." I lifted her chin so she would look at me.

"It was."

"Then you should go back and make it happen. Find out what you have to do to re-take that final class or whatever it was, and let's get it done."

She smiled. "You're being awfully sweet for a guy who isn't getting laid."

I laughed. "Oral sex is still sex."

"If you say so." She reached out and ran a hand back and forth over my crotch, watching as I hardened at her touch.

"You're playing with fire, sweetheart."

"Uh huh. I know." She squeezed lightly and I had to take a deep breath to stay in control.

"There are condoms in the bathroom," I growled. "Say the word and I'll fuck you long and hard."

"Not now," she whispered, sucking on my earlobe. "Maybe later."

"You know what happens to bad girls who tease me?"

She arched her brows. "Nope."

"They get tied to the bed and fucked hard."

"Once I'm on birth control, you can do anything you want to me."

Sweet Jesus.

I didn't think she had any idea what she'd just set herself up for.

Now that I had Presley and Jeremy in L.A., it was easier to concentrate on music. For some reason knowing they'd be there when I got home grounded me, and I was in a good mood when I got to the studio. Unfortunately, it wasn't long-lived because Kingston was out in the parking lot waiting for me.

"What's up?" I asked, pushing my Ray Ban's up on my head.

"Fucking Carter."

My heart sank. "Not again."

"Not H, but he's wasted. Apparently, he stayed here late last night and invited some friends to play music. They wound up getting drunk. Far as I can tell, it's just alcohol, but what the fuck?" He threw up his hands. "I don't know what to do anymore."

"Fuck." I followed him inside where Tommy and Kellan appeared to be force-feeding Carter coffee.

"Z, man, get these fuckers off me," Carter mumbled to me.

"Why'd you fall off the wagon?" I demanded. "You were doing so damn good."

"It was just a few drinks. I've been stone cold sober for so long it didn't take much for me to get fucked up. It was like three shots of Jack. That's it."

I gritted my teeth in frustration. Did he truly not understand that he was an addict? That one sip was all it took sometimes. God, this was hard. I wasn't his parent or his lover. It shouldn't have been my job to babysit him, but we ran a multi-million-dollar business together. If he couldn't play today, we'd fall even further behind schedule. If he couldn't play on tour, we'd lose millions. Literally. This was a lot more complicated than simply washing my hands of him, and that took out the fact that I cared about him.

"I need you to grow the fuck up," I said in a steely voice. "We have an extremely lucrative business with Onyx Knight. This isn't some half-assed garage band anymore. We have bills, employees, and families that count on us. Not to mention the fans. Are you really going to throw it away over Jack Daniels?"

"I'm not throwing anything away!" He stood up so fast he almost toppled over but managed to right himself. "I'm here. I'm ready to play. Why are you fuckers up my ass all the time? You're driving me nuts. What do you care if I'm an addict? Why do you care if I enjoy getting high? It's none of your business as long as I do my shit, and I. Am. Here. What more do you want?" He stalked down the hall, disappearing into the bathroom.

"That was fun." Kellan sank into a chair, shaking his head.

"We could hire one of those sobriety coaches or whatever they're called," Kingston said, "but we'd have to handle the cost because he won't pay for it."

"I don't know, man." Tommy sat on the arm of the couch, a look of frustration on his face. "He's been miserable since he got sober. Maybe it's not our place to tell him how to live his life."

"And when he can't record or misses performances on tour? Then what?" I asked.

"Then he gets fined. We make him sign something to that effect." Kingston shrugged. "We tell him either he signs it or he goes back to rehab. Every time he misses something, it's twenty-five grand."

Kellan whistled. "That's steep."

"It's fair," I said. "Maybe it'll make him think twice."

"I'll talk to Aurora about it," Kingston said, pulling out his phone. "I'll be back in a few." He went toward the exit just as Carter came out of the bathroom. It looked like he'd washed his face and freshened up a little, so he didn't seem as hungover anymore.

"Let's do this," he said, walking toward the studio.

"Kingston's making a call," I said, following him. Since he got defensive about his sobriety, or lack thereof, I changed the subject. "Hey. Presley is here, and I promised her that interview. You up for it?"

"Yeah." He nodded. "I told you I would. Just tell me when.

"I was thinking she could come up to the studio and when we're done for the day, I'd order food and you two could talk."

"You want to do it here?" he asked.

"Now that we have a full house, including the baby, it's quieter here," I said. "We could go to your place, but why go somewhere else when we could just hang here? It's quiet, private, and convenient."

He chuckled. "Yeah, okay. Anytime you want."

"I'll find out what she's got planned. She's trying to get settled at the house and make sure her aunt is doing good at the rehab center."

"They call it rehab for drug addicts *and* for heart attack survivors?" He made a face.

"Apparently." I hadn't thought about that until he'd said it, and it was kind of weird. "I guess it's all about the fact that you're rehabilitating something that's broken?"

"That seems wrong somehow." He scratched his head. "But maybe I'll go visit auntie and get a different kind of rehab. Think it'll help?"

I grinned. "It can't hurt to try, buddy."

We looked at each other until he finally glanced away, picking up his bass. "I'm sorry about last night. It was a moment of weakness. But I swear it was just a few shots. I hadn't eaten anything all day so it hit me harder than it should have. I'm not using any drugs, though, and I'll keep the alcohol to a minimum. Is that fair?"

"You're a grown man, Carter. I just don't want to see you throw away everything we've worked for."

"I'm good." He hit a few notes on his bass. "You know Imma make that visit to Auntie Meg happen, right?"

All I could do was laugh because I had a feeling he and Aunt Meg would get along great.

"Do what you gotta do, man. Do what you gotta do."

28

———

P*resley*

WE'D BEEN in California a week before I felt ready to meet Zeke's bandmates. For the most part, I'd spent my days getting Jeremy settled into a new routine, making myself at home in Zeke's room, and getting to know his parents. His mother came across as a little overbearing, but she was incredible with Jeremy, and it had only taken him a day or so to warm up to her. Armand was a bit more standoffish; friendly when we saw each other but not overly chatty. He was good with Jeremy, though, and they had coffee together in the morning.

As soon as I got downstairs with him, Armand would take him and read him the sports pages as he drank coffee and Jeremy had a bottle. It was cute to watch, and it gave me time to enjoy my own breakfast before getting into the day. I went to see Aunt Meg almost every day, and she was doing great. The doctors said she would be ready to come home in another ten days, which was good news. Zeke planned to set her up in what he called a casita, which was one of the little guest houses on the property. Apparently, there were two, along with a shed and a pool house.

His grandmother lived in the bigger one, though she was in New Jersey for the next few months, visiting family. The smaller one was basically a studio apartment, with a kitchenette, a full bath, and one big room for sleeping and living. It would give her privacy along with enough independence to not feel like a burden, which was something I knew she wouldn't like. On the other hand, she was only a few steps away from the main house, so she would never be completely alone.

Zeke had it professionally cleaned, and I'd been slowly putting Aunt Meg's things away so it would feel like home once she arrived. Since we planned to be here for an extended period of time, we'd shipped things we hadn't been able to bring on the plane, like some of our craft supplies and favorite kitchen gadgets. Those hadn't arrived yet, so I'd take care of them when they did.

In the meantime, I was starting to feel settled. It was odd, because I'd only lived in two places my entire life. The apartment I shared with my mother until her death, and Aunt Meg's house. Yet Zeke's house was already home. There were moments of discomfiture, like when his mother was busy in the kitchen and I wanted to scramble myself a couple of eggs. It wasn't that she wouldn't let me, but I wasn't used to someone doing things like that for me. And she seemed determined to mother me.

Today I was heading up to the studio to listen to some of the new music and do my interview with Carter. I'd spent several hours this week researching everything I could find about him ahead of time, and his life was both fascinating and sad. He'd been born to a drug addict mother and a deadbeat dad who'd left when he was a baby. He had no siblings, had never been married, and had been on his own since his mother's death when he was sixteen.

He'd been to rehab half a dozen times, arrested twice for minor infractions like disturbing the peace, and owned over forty cars. I didn't know what to make of that last piece of information but planned to ask him about it. Honestly, I felt bad for him. He had to be one of the loneliest, most messed up celebrities in the world.

Zeke's father dropped me off at the studio since Zeke would bring me home, and I took a moment to steady my nerves. I was comfortable around Zeke, but the rest of the band was something else. I'd been a fan since high school and knew the words to every one of their songs. When Zeke and I were together, he was someone else to me. The father of my son. My boyfriend? We hadn't given our relationship a label yet, but that seemed to fit. He was many things, but not the world-famous lead guitarist for Onyx Knight. He was just Zeke.

In this setting, however, he was Big Z, and that was someone I didn't know. Not really.

"Hey, babe." Zeke was waiting for me and immediately came over to kiss me.

"Hi." My heart seemed to skip a beat every time he touched me, and this was no exception.

"How's J?" He'd begun calling Jeremy by the first initial of his name, and it was starting to stick.

"Completely spoiled by his grandma," I said dryly. "She went shopping."

Zeke rolled his eyes. "Good grief. There goes my credit card bill."

"You must be Presley." Carter came over to us and to my surprise, pulled me into a big hug. "I'm Carter. Z talks about you *all* the time. It's nice to finally meet you."

I wasn't sure what I'd been expecting, but a tall, lanky platinum-blond with a playful grin and long-lashed dark eyes wasn't it. I'd seen pictures, of course, but he was larger than life in person. He didn't seem high or drunk or anything, and his voice was warm and friendly, immediately making me feel comfortable. I had a feeling he was an old pro at interviews, so he knew exactly what to do.

"It's nice to meet you too," I said. "I've been a fan for a long time."

"Favorite song?" he asked, squinting a little as if my answer was important to him.

"Judgement Call," I replied automatically.

"Oh, fuck yeah!" He immediately held up his hand for a high five. "She's old school, Z!"

"Well, yeah." Zeke put his arm around my waist.

"Okay, stop hogging Z's new girlfriend," Kellan said, coming over to us. "I'm Kellan. Nice to meet you."

I met Kingston and Tommy next, and they were all friendly and laid-back. I wasn't sure what I'd been expecting in general, but this was almost as casual as when I'd met Zeke's parents. They seemed down-to-earth and, for lack of a better word, normal. They all wore jeans or shorts and T-shirts. Though Kingston was known for wearing eye liner and mascara, and dying his hair a different color every tour, his face was clean today and his hair was a dirty blond color that appeared natural to me, since I didn't see any roots growing out. Other than an overabundance of tattoos and earrings, they could have been anyone, instead of world-class musicians who'd sold nearly forty million albums to date.

"Ready to hear some new music?" Zeke asked me after we'd all talked for a few minutes.

"Sure." I nodded.

"Let's do 'Not Goin' Away' for her," Carter said.

Zeke looked hesitant for a moment, but then nodded. "Sure. You can stay in here," he said to me. "It's too loud if you come inside the room."

"Okay." I nodded, excited about hearing music that no one else beyond the band's team had heard.

The song started with a soft, haunting melody played by Zeke. Maybe four seconds of his beautiful finger work before the rest of the band came in, adding layers of depth and harmony. But while the tune was catchy, it was the lyrics that hit me right between the eyes.

> *Innocent heart*
> *Damaging touch*
> *I need to hold you*
> *Too damn much*
> *You're not the one*
> *Who stole my heart*
> *But something's been there*
> *Right from the start.*

THEY SPOKE to me as if they'd been written just for me, and I didn't understand when or why or how. Had he just written this recently? Was it about me or was it a coincidence? Song lyrics could mean anything or be about almost anyone. That was done by design. But Carter had specifically suggested this song, and Zeke had been hesitant. That had to mean something.

I wanted to write out the feelings it evoked in me, but I was too enthralled watching and listening to risk missing anything. I'd seen Zeke play online dozens of times, but being this close was enchanting. Knowing him the way I did now changed everything about the way I looked at him. Millions of fans all over the world lusted over him, but very few knew him intimately. The man behind Big Z the guitar player was so much more complex than his professional persona.

And it was beautiful to be able to mesh the two. The huge star and the simple man beneath. The self-assured musician and the tender, patient father. The friend and the lover. It was only now that I recognized just how multi-faceted he was, and in how many directions he was pulled on a daily basis. When we were together, though it had technically been just a few weeks total, it was easy to forget he was a rockstar. Not just any rockstar, but one of the biggest in the world.

Watching him now took my breath away.

No wonder women threw themselves at musicians.

If he wasn't already my boyfriend, I would've had to consider trying to seduce him. It was that simple.

They played two more songs, both of which had me moving to the beat. They were so freakin' talented, and the new album was going to be huge. I didn't need to know anything about the inner workings of the industry to know that. It was instinctive; you knew a hit when you heard it and they'd just played a couple of them.

"What do you think?" Carter asked when they were done.

"It's amazing," I said. "Seriously some of your best stuff to date. 'Destiny and Dust' is going to be the single, right?"

They all looked at each other and burst out laughing.

"She's got our number," Kingston said. "And yeah, that was our thought, though we've still got two more songs to record."

"We done for the day?" Kellan asked. "It's date night, and Didi's gonna be pissed if I'm late."

"See you tomorrow!" Kingston told him.

"Nice to meet you, Presley!" Kellan waved and within a few minutes, everyone was gone except Zeke, Carter, and me.

"Chinese or Italian?" Zeke asked me.

"I don't care. You guys worked hard today, so you pick."

"Chinese," Carter said.

"Italian," Zeke said at the same time.

They both looked at me and in unison said, "Tie breaker."

We all laughed.

"Fine. Let's do Chinese."

Zeke placed the order while Carter and I settled on two chairs in the lounge.

"How do you want to do this?" Carter asked me. "You have a list of questions?"

"I have notes on my phone, but let's make it a conversation," I said. "It's more comfortable that way."

"Sure. Fire away."

"Let's start with easy stuff. Tell me about the new album."

"Oh, hell." He grinned. "I can talk music for hours."

"That's okay. Me too."

"Man, the new album is gonna blow people's minds," he said, leaning back. "It's raw, gritty, heartfelt. It's still got our signature heavy riffs, but the songwriting on this one has been rock solid. We always have a few hundred songs in reserve. From the beginning. Some that just weren't ready. Some we didn't feel fit with the rest of the album when we wrote it. Always some reason they didn't make the cut, but we keep them and revisit them every time we start a new album. Then we add new stuff that we all contribute. Z wrote 'Not Goin' Away' on his own, but when he brought it to me a few weeks ago, I polished it up some. Then we took it King and he added harmonies, updated some lyrics, and bam. Done."

"So all five of you don't work on every song?" I asked curiously.

"Sometimes we do, sometimes we don't, but all songs, no matter who wrote most of it, are split five ways. Tom and Kell both bring different things to the songwriting table. Tom isn't big on lyrics, but he creates riffs and solos —even guitar and bass solos—like nobody's business. And Kellan, man, he's a master at harmonizing…" Carter talked for another twenty minutes about the album, the music, and each individual song.

I wouldn't be able to use it all, but it was too fascinating to stop him.

"Food's here," Zeke called out.

"You want to talk while we eat?" Carter asked me.

"Sure, as long as you don't mind if Zeke listens in."

"Nah. Z's my bro. I don't have secrets from him."

29

Z*eke*

I'D BEEN PLANNING to give Carter and Presley some privacy, more for Carter's sake than hers, but when he said he didn't have secrets from me, I decided to stay. I also wanted to eat, but I could've taken my General Tso's chicken into another room. I had to admit I was curious, both about how Presley handled her interviews and how Carter would react to specific questions about his addiction. He'd said it was okay, but I wondered if he would gloss over it the way he did most things he didn't like talking about.

Presley was a natural reporter, in my opinion. Working in entertainment was tricky because while you wanted to touch on the important topics, journalists also had to be careful not to get too personal. A lot of celebrities I knew got prickly when you asked about family issues, trouble with the law, anything that could make them look bad or divulge something they didn't want out there.

Carter didn't seem to have any qualms, because when Presley guided the conversation to his recent stint in rehab, he didn't even hesitate.

"Look, addiction sucks," he said. "I wish I understood why my brain is wired this way. I wish it was easier to say no when the opportunity to get high presents itself. Even after all the therapists, counseling, and the multitude of programs I've been in, it all boils down to one thing: I *like* being high. That's the long and short of it. Is it wrong? Probably. But I can't help that part. So, when I talk to the shrinks or whatever, there's nothing they can say to me to change what I enjoy. Do I enjoy other things? Sure. It's just not the same."

"Do you ever think about the example you set for your fans? Especially the young ones?" Presley's voice was soft and neutral, merely asking the question without any obvious judgment.

Carter sighed. "You know, that's the kicker. I *do* worry about that. I don't want the kids out there, or anyone for that matter, to do what I do. I'm a mess. I was born addicted. Most people don't know that, but my mom was using all through her pregnancy, so it seems inevitable for me to be that way too. But to all the kids out there, don't do it. Don't be like me. If it runs in your family, stay the hell away from drugs and alcohol. Sex is way better for you."

We all chuckled at that, and I noticed that Presley's cheeks turned pink even though she didn't comment.

"What about your own future family?" she asked instead. "Do you worry about that?"

"I don't know that a family's in the cards for me," he said quietly. "My genetics are way too fucked up. Maybe I'd foster a kid someday, if I meet the right woman and she's down, you know? Maybe make a difference in someone else's life. But a biological kid? Not in my plans."

"How long have you been sober this time?" she asked.

He glanced over at me, and our eyes met.

Ah, hell. He didn't know whether to be honest about last night or not, and I didn't know what to tell him. I didn't want him to lie to Presley, but it would probably be embarrassing to admit he'd already fallen off the wagon.

"As far as drugs go," he said after a moment, "I've been sober for four months. I've had a few drinks since I got out, but my issues have never been with alcohol. I understand that it doesn't matter when you're an addict, but for me there's a distinct difference. Drugs take me down hard and fast, especially heroin. A shot of Jack Daniels loosens me up and helps me feel better, play better, do everything better."

"Do you think there's more temptation on tour or when you're at home?"

"Both are pretty equal. At home, I'm so bored I go looking for it. On tour, it finds me no matter what."

"How do you plan to combat this on the upcoming tour?"

"I don't know. Probably with some kind of sobriety coach the band wants to hire. You know, a glorified babysitter."

"It might not be a bad thing, though."

"Here's the thing. When and if the time comes that I can't fight the demons off anymore, I'm going to find a way. That's all there is to it. No matter who's watching or how much they fine me or how many people are rooting for me, I'm going to do what an addict does."

"So you have no hope of remaining sober?"

"Short-term, absolutely. Long-term, I don't think it's possible. I don't do drugs because I can't help myself. I do them because I want to. And I don't think that desire will ever go away. It's like somebody telling me I can't have sex ever again. How long do you think I can go before it's too much?"

Jesus.

This was some deep shit, and I almost felt dirty sitting here.

He was baring his soul to Presley because I'd asked him to, and I suddenly worried whether or not the emotional toll would be too high. The whole world could potentially read this article and the things he was saying scared me. They would inevitably freak out our management company and everyone else close to us. And he wasn't done yet either.

"I have one more question for you," Presley said.

"Hit me." Carter took a bite of his pork fried rice.

"Where do you see yourself in ten years?"

"That's easy," he said without hesitation. "Dead."

PRESLEY WAS quiet on the drive home, and I wasn't sure which one of us had been more impacted by Carter's interview.

"You okay?" I asked her, reaching for her hand.

"I'm fine. Just kind of sad. Carter is so sweet and funny. I hate seeing what he's going through."

"Trust me, I know the feeling."

"It must be a hundred times harder on you, watching someone who's like a brother to you struggle. I just met him, and my heart is broken. You must be... *devastated.*"

"It's even harder because I have to find a balance between being the friend who cares about him and just wants to help, and the business partner who needs him to get his head out of his ass. We have money, contracts, commitments. There's a lot at stake. Hearing him say he doesn't think he'll be around in a decade makes me believe we have to be tougher on him, and that's going to suck."

"You don't think he was saying it just for shock value?"

"That's not his style. He's straight up honest. Sometimes to a fault."

"He needs a woman," she said quietly. "And maybe a kid. Someone to live for. Something beyond music that will make him want to get out of bed every day without wanting to get high."

"You know anyone interested in a sweet but broken addict who needs to be saved?"

She laughed. "Not off the top of my head, but we can work on it."

"He seems anxious to meet Aunt Meg. Maybe she can help."

"That's a good idea." She grinned. "Can you imagine them together?"

"I totally can. Making trouble for everyone."

"For sure. Maybe we can take him to the rehab center. She loves company."

"Yeah, let's set it up. Maybe Sunday?"

"I'll ask her, but it's not like she's going anywhere yet."

"So, uh, are you planning to put that in the article? The part about him being dead in ten years."

She hesitated, staring straight ahead thoughtfully. "I don't know. I think it's impactful and important. Something that people need to hear, so to speak. A warning, if you will. But I won't do it if you think it'll impact the band or portray you guys in a negative light."

"I can't ask you not to use what he gave you. The band will have to deal with it. I'm just hoping you can find a way to soften it."

"I'll let you read it before I publish anything."

"You don't have to."

"I know. But I want to."

"I appreciate it." We were quiet for a bit before I said, "I've been thinking about something. I don't believe I've ever taken you out on a proper date."

"A date?" She turned to stare at me.

"Yeah. You know, dinner and a movie? Disneyland, if that's your jam. Maybe see a band on the Strip. What do you like to do on dates?"

She didn't respond for far too long and I squeezed her hand. "Hey, what's wrong?"

"I've never gone out on a date as an adult. I did in high school, but that was movies and skating and dances, usually in a group. I went out with friends in college, but never an actual date. So I guess I don't know."

How was this possible? I didn't understand how guys weren't interested in her. If nothing else, didn't they want to try and get in her pants, like normal guys that age? She was tall with long legs and perky little tits. She had sweet lips and a pretty face, even with those big, oversized glasses she wore. I truly didn't get it.

"Well, then, I guess we'll have to try a bunch of different things and figure out your favorite."

"Can you… go out on regular dates?" she asked slowly. "Don't you get recognized?"

"If we go to a club on the Strip? Yes, I'll get recognized. But if we went to dinner and a movie in, say, Brentwood? Nah. And if someone did recognize me, they'd just smile and leave me alone. It's not like I'm George Clooney or anything."

"You're way hotter than George Clooney," she said, laughing.

"Thanks. He probably wouldn't be happy to hear that, but it makes my day."

"Well, if nothing else, he's older than my father would have been, so you know… not really my thing."

"Good to know." I was already mentally planning our date.

Dinner and a movie sounded so simple, but if she'd never done it, that would probably be fun for her. Sometimes I forgot just how innocent and naïve she was. She truly hadn't lived at all, and I'd knocked her up before she had a chance.

I needed to rectify that.

"By the way," she said, interrupting the turn my thoughts had taken. "I started on birth control last night."

"Oh, really." My dick was incredibly happy about this information. "How long does it take to be effective?"

"The gynecologist I saw said seven days to be safe."

"So we're starting a countdown."

"I guess we are."

"Do you remember what it felt like when I was inside of you?"

"I do. When I was pregnant…" She paused, biting her lip. "I was so horny all the time. I would masturbate thinking about… that."

"That? Or me?"

"Both. You being inside of me. Doing all the things we did that night."

"Did thinking about the way I fucked you get you off?"

"Yes." Her voice was barely a whisper.

"Are you embarrassed?" I asked, glancing over at her.

"And turned on."

"Welcome to my world. Having you in bed beside me every night and not being able to do the things I want to do is torture."

"A few more days," she said. "Then we can do it all."

Her extreme nervousness about pregnancy made me nuts, but since I hadn't ever been pregnant, it wasn't my place to tell her it was ridiculous. All I could do was be supportive and hope the next seven days went by quickly.

30

———————

P *resley*

AUNT MEG WAS RELEASED from the rehab facility the following week on Saturday, so Zeke and I planned a small welcome home party for her. Just us and his parents, along with the band. Kellan was bringing Didi and Tommy had been dating someone named Jasmine, so it was small and fairly intimate. Aunt Meg was feeling good, walking every day and relying on her cane less and less. They'd tried a new cocktail of medications for her MS that seemed to be working, so she was healthier than I'd seen her in a long time.

Fatima had been cooking all day, no matter how many times Zeke tried to tell her he wanted to order food, so he'd given in and left her to it. It seemed to make her happy, though I wondered if there would ever be an occasion for me to cook for him since she seemed to hold the monopoly on anything to do with the kitchen.

"Is my mom driving you nuts yet?" he asked after I put Jeremy down for his nap. Aunt Meg had wanted to shower and change the moment she got home, so we had a little quiet time before everyone arrived.

"She's been nothing but lovely to me," I said.

"Uh huh. But?"

I laughed. "There's no but. My only complaint is that I'd like to cook you dinner sometime, but she always does it before I can do anything. I asked her one day, and she told me I was busy enough with the baby."

"She has a point, you know," he said, reaching for me and pulling me close. "You have an infant who keeps you busy. Plus, the magazine you're trying to start up again. You don't need to cook."

"But I want to cook for *you*," I said softly, wrapping my arms around his neck.

"I'll send them away for a few days," he whispered, lowering his mouth to mine.

We'd done a lot of fooling around the last two weeks. We were intimately acquainted with each other's bodies, and I'd never known a person could come so many times just from a man's mouth and fingers. Last night he'd fingered my ass and that had been another level of ecstasy that shocked me. I'd been even more startled when he'd asked me to do it to him.

It felt like I still had so much to learn in the bedroom, but Zeke never rushed or pushed me beyond what I was comfortable with. He always asked if I wanted to try something new, as if I might say no. My fear of getting pregnant was starting to diminish, overshadowed by my desire to please him the way he pleased me. I knew he enjoyed the things we were doing, but it wasn't the same as intercourse, and I was suddenly anxious to do it again.

"You're driving me wild, baby," he murmured against my mouth. "But we don't have a lot of time."

"Would we have time if I told you I was ready?" I stepped back and pulled my top over my head, standing there in nothing but low-slung shorts.

"Ready..." His eyes burned into mine. "You sure? I don't want you in a panic about pregnancy."

"You have condoms, right?"

"A whole fucking box."

I stepped out of my shorts, leaving myself bare save for a tiny black thong.

Zeke licked his lips. "Will you turn around for me? Do a little spin?"

I smiled, pulling my hair over one shoulder and walking in a small, slow circle. When I was facing him again, I tossed my hair back and cupped my breasts, squeezing lightly as I pulled my lower lip through my teeth. All cliché but it had the desired effect because he yanked off his shorts and boxers in one swift movement.

"Bed," he growled. "Now."

I smiled, sashaying in that direction, but taking my sweet time since I knew he was watching me walk.

He brushed past me and reached into his nightstand, pulling out a handful of foil packages and dumping them on the bed. Then he pounced, pinning me beneath him as he kissed me.

"The first time might be quick," he whispered softly. "It's been a while for me."

"How long?" I asked, running my fingers through his hair. "I won't be mad. I just want us to start with a clean slate and no secrets."

"A couple of months. Since just before I found out about Jeremy," he said. "I don't remember exactly, but no one since you came back into my life."

That made me stupidly happy for some reason, and I leaned into his kisses. Despite his need for me, he wasn't rushing, and I fell a little more in love with him every time he did something so thoughtful and considerate. Hell, I fell more in love with him every single day. It would have been embarrassing considering the condensed timeline of our relationship, but I didn't care anymore.

He was good to me, wonderful to our son, and practically a hero in her eyes since Aunt Meg's heart attack, so what else was there? I could waste time worrying about how fast things were moving, how difficult it was for me to trust him, and all the issues we might have moving forward, but what did that get me other than anxiety? Why not just enjoy everything he was offering? If he was going to hurt me, that would happen whether I worried about it now or not.

Our kisses grew heated and fervent, each of us vying for dominance, but with me ultimately giving in and letting him take over. It was hard to think when he was touching me like this, and despite my nervousness, I had vivid memories of what it felt like when he'd been inside of me.

"I can't wait to feel you inside me again," I whispered against his ear.

"Same, baby." He moved on top of me, devouring my mouth as he dug his fingers into my hair. It was glorious to be together like this, naked bodies pressed together, legs tangled, mouths fused.

I arched my hips and let my legs fall open in an obvious invitation, anxious for more of him. All of him.

"Ah, baby, you're so beautiful." He let his forehead hit mine, reaching down to line up his cock at my slick entrance. Before I had a chance to react, he started to press into me, inch by glorious inch.

Somehow, he was bigger than I remembered, and my body strained to adjust to such a magnificent intrusion.

"Easy," he whispered when I gasped.

"I need a second," I panted.

"Just tell me when." He softly touched his lips to mine. "You like how it feels when I put my cock inside your pretty little pussy?"

I shifted, wrapping my legs around his waist and taking him deeper.

"God damn, I'm not going to last long at all if you keep doing that."

"It feels so intense." I squeezed around him as the sensation of him filling me started to feel good.

"Can I fuck you now?" he whispered, his voice rugged and husky.

"Yes, fuck yes." My eyes rolled back in my head as he began to stroke in and out of me. It was slow and methodical at first, each thrust a little deeper than the last, until he bottomed out and we both moaned.

His soulful eyes met mine as he picked up speed, keeping us connected in a way I'd never felt before. A hurricane-strength wave of pleasure rocked through me, taking me to a whole new level of pleasure. I was coiled tight, aching for release, desperate for him to push me over the edge. He'd made me come dozens of times since that night in Minneapolis, but this was different.

"Tell me how much you can take," he said, "because I'm so fucking close."

"All of it. All of you. I need you, Zeke."

He crashed his mouth to mine and punched into me so hard I saw stars. Each thrust was more punishing than the last, and when he reached down to push my knees back against my chest, the new angle sent me over the edge. My world splintered and my mouth opened in a silent scream. Each surge of my orgasm rolled over the last, until it was nothing but one continuous tidal wave of ecstasy.

Zeke's growl of release was the most animalistic thing I'd ever heard, and it sent another round of aftershocks shooting through me. I was breathless, boneless, completely overwhelmed, and yet, more content than I'd ever been in my life. We were covered in a light sheen of sweat, but Zeke didn't move, resting the side of his face against mine. It was like he sensed how important this moment was and was as unwilling as I was to let it go.

"Watching you come like that is the sweetest thing I've ever seen," he murmured, sucking on the side of my neck.

"Watching you make love to me is the sexiest thing I've ever seen," I countered.

"Then I guess we have to do it as often as possible."

I wrapped my arms around his neck. "Okay."

"Did I hurt you?"

"God, no. It was a little intense at first, since it's been so long, but once I adjusted it was... so, so good."

"I'm glad." He kissed the tip of my nose and lifted his head. "Should we shower? Our guests will be arriving any minute now."

I tugged him back down so our torsos were touching again. "Just a little longer," I whispered. "I love how it feels, when we're connected like this."

"Me too."

We didn't move for a long time, until finally the noise coming from downstairs told us our magic moment had to end.

"Tonight," he whispered. "When everyone is gone, we'll be just like this again."

"But it won't be the second *first time*." I met his gaze, silently imploring him to understand because it was a little embarrassing to express all the emotions I'd been experiencing lately.

"Ah." He nodded solemnly. "A new beginning for us."

"Yes."

"Okay. Then they can wait." He paused. "Am I heavy?"

"I like it. I'm not sure what it is, but in addition to how sexy it is, I feel safe like this with you."

"I like that you feel safe. I hope I can always make you feel safe."

"I'd like that. It's been a long time since I felt that way. Most of my life has been filled with uncertainty and different levels of fear. Not the horrible kind of fear from abuse or anything like that, but when you don't know how you'll pay the bills, it's a constant, subconscious fear. Adding a baby to the mix, I can't explain how terrifying it is to worry about making sure your child will have everything he needs."

"You will never, ever have to worry about that again," he said softly.

"Being with you comes with a whole new set of worries," I admitted. "Totally different, and some are kind of selfish, but if we're being honest, I have to mention them."

"Tell me."

"What happens when you go back out on tour? I can't always go with you. Jeremy can't grow up on tour. He'll have to go to school and have some semblance of a normal life. If you're touring for two years straight, what happens with our family?"

"I don't have specific answers for you, but we're not doing that anymore. After the last tour ended, we had a conversation about building in breaks. We have to, for everyone's sanity. Now that I have a family, I'm going to be strict about it. Yes, we'll be apart some when we tour, but we'll do the fun places, like Europe, in the summer, so you and Jeremy can come with me. I'll make sure I can fly home for a week or two at a time every couple of months. It won't be easy, but we can make it work if you're willing to try."

"I'm here, aren't I?"

"You are."

"Zeke?" Fatima's voice filtered through the door. "Are you still in the shower? Your guests are arriving!"

"A few more minutes, Ma!" he yelled.

Our eyes met, and we stifled our laughter.

"I guess cuddle time is over," I said.

"Later," he whispered. "We'll continue this later."

31

Z *eke*

IT TOOK us a little while to get downstairs. Maybe more than just a little while. Between showering, where another couple of orgasms had been involved, Presley needing to dry her hair and put on makeup, and then Jeremy waking up, we were very, very late. The only person who seemed to notice was Meg, though, because her eyes twinkled as she called out to us. Or maybe that was because she was on Carter's lap.

I had no idea what had happened for the two of them to already be besties—or God forbid, something else—but it was kind of funny. The look on Presley's face was a ridiculous combination of humor and horror, and she blinked a few times before looking up at me.

"I warned you they would be trouble."

"You don't think..." Her voice trailed, as if she couldn't quite bring herself to say the words.

"If you think it hasn't at least crossed his mind, you're delusional."

"Great." She shook her head. "Nope. La la la la. Not going there." She took Jeremy from me and marched over to them. I followed since I was kind of entertained by the whole idea of Carter and Meg together. He loved older women, but somehow, knowing she'd only recently gotten over a major health scare and surgery, I had a feeling he was more interested in being her friend. I hoped so anyway.

"There's my boy." Meg got up and held out her arms, taking Jeremy from Presley and hugging him tightly. Jeremy wrapped his little arms around her as much as he could, cuddling against her neck. "Did you miss Auntie Meg?"

Jeremy babbled at her, and they both laughed.

"Hey, when do I get to hold the little guy?" Carter asked, scowling at her.

Meg just smiled and gently set Jeremy in his lap.

"Hey, buddy." Carter wrapped one hand around his middle and used the other to gently poke his tummy. "What's goin' on, little dude? You have a good nap?"

Jeremy kicked his feet and gurgled.

"Close enough." Carter ran a tender hand over his head. "He's beautiful, Z. Really fucking beautiful. You're a lucky man."

"Thanks." For some reason, seeing Carter getting emotional about my kid made me a little emotional too. Kids, family time, all the things I was currently experiencing had never been on our radar as a band. Even married, Tommy had been a party animal. Hell, he and his wife had partied harder than a lot of single people I knew. It was no surprise to me they'd gotten divorced, though I knew he'd been devastated when she left. The life we led wasn't easy, no matter what people thought. Money was nice but it truly didn't fix everything.

"Never thought I'd see the day," Carter said quietly. "You all settled down, with a kid, having family cookouts and shit."

"Is it weird?" I asked curiously.

"No way. It's fucking cool. It's different, but that's what makes it cool, you know?"

"For sure." Meg had been listening in and she put a gentle hand on Carter's arm. "Different is what makes the world go round. We all need changes in our lives sometimes."

Her words had a lot more meaning than what they sounded like on the surface. I could only hope Carter understood that on some level. You never knew with him.

"I hope everyone is hungry!" Mom called out. "There's a lot of food."

"I can take him," I told Carter.

"Nah." He shook his head. "I'm good hanging with the little guy. He's cute."

"He's probably going to need a new diaper soon," Meg told him.

"You think I never changed a diaper?" Carter asked, quirking his brow at her.

"How would I know?" she asked, laughing.

"You want me to get you a plate, Aunt Meg?" Presley asked her.

"Yes. Thank you. I'll sit here with Carter and Jeremy."

Presley went toward the buffet my mother had set up in the sunroom and I sat across from Carter and Meg.

"Meg wants to come hear some of the new music," Carter told me. "Once she's gotten more of her energy back."

"Anytime," I told her.

"Carter said I should ask Kingston to do one of my makeup tutorials with me," Meg said, grinning.

I laughed, shaking my head. "Hey, King! Come 'ere!"

Kingston ambled in our direction, a plate piled high with food in his hand.

"Yo. What up?" He cocked his head.

"Meg wants you to do a makeup tutorial with her on her InstaPixel channel," Carter told him.

Kingston grinned. "Sure. Maybe just before the next tour. We can frame it like a stage makeup thing. For guys, of course."

"Of course." Meg beamed.

She looked a decade younger today, her eyes twinkling and a perpetual smile on her face. It was amazing what the proper medical care and good friends could do for you. I couldn't help but wonder how long she'd been dealing with heart issues she hadn't wanted to deal with because of money. I really hoped I could make sure that never happened again.

There were some things money could fix, and that was one of them.

CARTER HUNG out long after everyone else had left. He spent most of his time with Meg, but a good amount with Jeremy too. Presley seemed intent on memorializing the whole day in pictures, using both her phone and a fancier camera I'd never seen before. I wasn't sure what it was about today that was so special, but I liked the idea that she wanted to get photographs of everyone. She was partial to Jeremy, of course, but also to me. Her favorite thing seemed to be pictures of Jeremy and me together, which made sense, but she took pictures of everyone who held him. She'd even made Kellan, Kingston, and Tommy hold him for photos.

"You doing okay?" I asked her as it got later in the day. Carter was walking Meg to her casita so she could lie down for a while, but it had been thirty minutes and he hadn't come back.

"I'm wonderful," she said, leaning against me.

My father was playing with Jeremy, so we had a little quiet time, which was nice after such a busy day.

"You think—" She'd just started to ask me a question when Meg and Carter came back in.

"Couldn't sleep," Meg said with a smile. "But Carter was busy making me laugh so that might have something to do with it." She playfully elbowed him, and he pretended it hurt.

"Ow! Damn, woman. Take it easy on me. I'm not that strong, you know."

"Well, you'll need to toughen up if you're going to hang out with me. There is no wuss in my game."

They breezed past us, laughing and cracking jokes, heading for the kitchen.

"What is happening there?" Presley whispered.

"I honestly don't know, babe. But whatever it is, she looks happy and he looks healthy. Something they both need. If them being friends can produce results like that in one afternoon, we need to leave it alone."

"You have a point." She stared after them. "It's always been easy for her to make friends. Much easier than it's ever been for me."

"Why do you think that is?" I asked curiously. "You and I hit it off right away."

"We did, but..." She paused, chewing the inside of her cheek the way she tended to do when she was thinking about something. "Do you think it was because you were exhausted from touring and needed a distraction?"

I shrugged. "Maybe? But at the end of the day, I could have gotten a distraction in the form of a woman almost anywhere. What I got from you went way beyond a distraction. Why do you think I was so angry when I heard you on the phone? You were more than a simple distraction. I was planning to get your number, maybe fly you out to a show. I wanted to see you again."

"You did?"

How had we never talked about this before?

"I did. That's why I blew up. It hurt to think you were like everyone else."

"I'm sorry," she whispered, leaning against me, her eyes filled with tears.

"No. Hell no. Don't cry." I wrapped my arms around her. "Babe, we both screwed up and now we're past all that. And I never, ever want to make you cry. Please don't. We started fresh, remember? We're not going back to that. Okay?"

She nodded. "Okay."

"You and me, babe, we're good."

"I know."

I kissed the top of her head, hoping she did know.

If there was any doubt, I was going to have to work a lot harder to prove it to her.

32

———

Z eke

WE FINISHED the album in almost record time. Despite a little drinking, Carter was healthy and on time every day, Kellan and Didi weren't fighting as much as usual, Kingston was banging some supermodel that was going to star in the first video for this album, and I was happier than I'd been in years. Tommy always went with the flow, doing whatever had to be done no matter what, so we were set for post-production.

To celebrate, we were attending a red-carpet movie premiere tonight. We'd written a song for the film, so it was a big deal. We'd rented a limo and it would be here to pick us up in a few minutes. My house was the last stop, so they were running a little late, but that was probably a good thing because Presley was a nervous wreck.

She looked stunning in a form-fitting red dress I'd bought her from a designer Dorian had recommended. It was long with a slit up one thigh and low-cut in the back. It had spaghetti straps that showed off plenty of skin and cleavage, so I'd bought her a ruby necklace that matched the dress and shoes. She'd had her hair and makeup professionally done, and as far as I was concerned, she was going to be the most beautiful woman in attendance tonight.

"You sure this is okay?" she asked for the tenth time.

"Woman, would you relax?" I asked, pulling her against me. She finally put her heels on after Kingston had texted that they were ten minutes out, but that had been about eight minutes ago. "They'll be here any minute."

"Ugh. I don't think I can do this."

"I'll be by your side all night," I promised. "Everything is going to be fine."

This was our first real public outing as a couple, so there would undoubtedly be some questions from the press, but I wasn't worried about it. My personal life had never been of much interest to anyone, so I didn't think about attending these types of events. Of course, it had been years since I'd had a steady girlfriend, and they would be digging into every detail of Presley's life. I hadn't told her that, of course, because she was nervous enough, but I'd given Dorian a head's up. She would be there tonight as well, so she would be close by if I needed her to run interference.

I probably should have mentioned it to Presley, but she was a worrier, and it wouldn't serve any purpose for her to be stressed about something we couldn't control. If we were going to be together, she'd have to get used to the scrutiny. I'd protect her as much as I could, but there were limits. I was in the public eye, and she would be too whenever we were out in public. Hopefully, they'd get bored with us once we'd been together for a while, but for now it was new enough to garner interest.

We walked down the stairs hand in hand and found my parents playing cards with Aunt Meg. Jeremy was already in bed, and they were deep into a game of gin rummy. Aunt Meg paused when we came down the stairs, a bright smile on her face.

"I have to say, you guys are two of the most beautiful people I know," she said.

"That dress is stunning, Presley," Mom said. "Red is your color."

"Thank you." She blushed, though there was a big smile on her face.

"I think your limo is here," Dad called out.

"Have a wonderful time," Aunt Meg said. "Take pictures!"

Presley held my hand tightly as we walked out to the limo and the driver got out to open the door for us. Presley got in first and I followed, startled to see Aurora in the car. I was going to kill someone, and I shot Kingston a dirty look.

"Over here, Z," Aurora said in a sugary voice. She patted the space beside her, and I quickly glanced around.

Presley was sitting next to Tommy, who hadn't brought a date, and I gave him a hard stare. "Go sit with Aurora so I can sit next to Presley," I told him.

He hesitated but then nodded, moving over and letting me sit in his place.

Presley wasn't stupid, so she knew something was up, but I'd never mentioned the fact that Aurora and I had been fuck buddies on and off over the years, which now seemed like a mistake. One I would have to rectify sooner rather than later.

"Presley, I love your dress!" Didi said, smiling. They'd met a few times now and seemed to get along, which I was grateful for.

"Thank you. Yours is pretty too. I love pink."

"It's my favorite."

"You look like a piece of bubblegum," Aurora said to Didi, scowling.

Didi was nonplussed. She and Kellan had been dating on and off for something like four years, so she could hold her own. "Bubblegum is fun," she responded. "Better than boring old black."

Aurora, of course, was wearing black.

"Color is good at an event like this." Cheyenne Wilder, Kingston's date, spoke with a light Australian accent. "You'll stand out, Didi."

"Thanks."

I introduced Presley to Aurora, who looked her up and down with a critical eye. "That's an Alexis Humboldt, isn't it?" she asked.

"It is." Presley lifted her chin a notch, as if steeling herself for an insult.

"It was a good choice for you. Did Zeke pick it out?"

"Bloody hell, Aurora, put the claws away." Cheyenne gave her a look. "Can't we just have a nice time? You're giving me a headache."

I dipped my head to hide my laughter and noted that Presley's lips twitched too.

"Hey, Presley, I read the article last night," Carter said to her. "I just want to say it was awesome. Thank you. You made me look human instead of like some addict rocker who can't get his shit together."

"I'm glad you liked it," Presley said softly.

"What article?" Cheyenne asked.

"Presley has a little e-zine she's been trying to get off the ground for a few years," Aurora said, smirking.

Fuck, I was going to smack the shit out of Kingston for not giving me any warning.

"It's not—" I began, but Cheyenne cut me off.

"I love e-zines!" she said enthusiastically. "So much more convenient than buying a physical magazine. I love being able to just go online and read on my phone or tablet. What's it called? Can I subscribe?"

"Right now, there's no subscription fee," Presley said, her cheeks pink. "I'm still trying to get it off the ground. It started out as a college project, but it was hard to keep it going without access to interesting people to interview."

"You can interview me if you like," she said with a grin. "I love doing interviews."

"It's a music magazine. The next issue will feature the article about Carter and one about a band back in Minneapolis who just got their first record deal."

"Oh, lovely." Cheyenne smiled. "You'll text me the name later, okay? I can't wait to read it."

Aurora rolled her eyes, but we'd just arrived at the event, so there was no time to say anything else.

I had a feeling it was going to be a long night.

"WHAT THE HELL is wrong with you?" I hissed under my breath to Kingston the first chance I had. "What made you think inviting Aurora was a good idea?"

He sighed. "She's our manager, and she wanted to come. What was I supposed to say? No, you can't ride in the limo with us because Zeke is grumpy about the way you treated his girlfriend?"

"You could have given me some warning," I snapped. "So I could prepare Presley. This is all new to her."

"She and Cheyenne are already like two peas in a pod," he said, motioning to where the two of them were heading toward the ladies' room together. "She's fine."

"For now. Aurora was being snarky in the limo, and I'm sure she has a lot more where that came from."

"You don't have to sit near her during the movie. Just chill, man."

"Are you purposely trying to piss me off?"

Kingston shook his head. "Come on. You know me better than that."

"I thought I did, but this was a dick move."

"Look, I'm sorry, but you and Aurora need to get past this. She's our manager and damn good at what she does."

"We don't need her or anyone else at this point in our career. We manage our own shit for the most part, she just handles the details."

He looked away.

"What aren't you telling me?" I demanded. "She have something on you?"

"Not on me, no." It wasn't like Kingston to be cagey like this, and it was starting to worry me.

"Then who?" I demanded.

He met my gaze almost guiltily. "Carter."

"What can she have on *him*? He's a hot mess, but essentially an open book. He doesn't give a shit what anyone knows."

"I don't know the details, but I overheard them arguing. She was threatening to go to the press about something, and he called her a cunt. After that their voices were too low for me to hear much."

"Seriously?" Carter was a wild child, but also a gentle, sometimes overly sensitive soul who adored women and didn't like to argue with anyone. I couldn't imagine what he was hiding.

"She said he better hope we don't fire her because the whole world would find out. I tried talking to him, but he told me to mind my own business, he had it under control."

"You don't believe that, though."

"No. He was spooked when they were arguing."

"Fuck." I tapped my foot. "You have any idea what it could be?"

"Something that could impact the band?"

"Then we need to make him tell us."

"Good luck. You've been distracted so I've been trying to pry it out of him, but he won't budge with any info."

"Which means we're stuck with Aurora forever?" I groaned. "That's bullshit. I'll talk to him."

"We could get him high, then he'll tell us anything we want to know, but that's kind of counter-productive," he said dryly.

"I want her gone," I said in a steely voice, meeting his gaze. "I don't care what he did. If our manager, who's supposed to be on our side, is blackmailing him, she's not someone I want as part of the team."

"I agree, but he's just out of rehab and already teetering on the edge of sobriety. Do we really want to risk whatever this is getting out until we've had a chance to do damage control? And what if it's something really bad?"

"Like he killed someone?" I wrinkled my nose. "You think Carter's capable of that?"

"Maliciously? Of course not. But what about vehicular homicide? Him driving under the influence?"

"I think we would've noticed."

"I don't know. And to be honest, Kellan and Tom and are so far up Aurora's ass, I don't know how we'll ever get them on board."

"Irony here is that when I wanted to fire her a few months back, Carter was the only one on my side. How come?"

He didn't hesitate to meet my angry glare. "Because this is a business, and there's a lot of money on the table. The band is already on the outs. We're not close like we used to be, and it's starting to show."

"Starting to show? To whom?" I demanded.

"You think we wrapped up this album in record time because we're that good?" he asked quietly. "Or because we just wanted to be done, so we could get the hell out of there?"

I stared at him.

He stared back.

"Is that what this is?"

"You've been distracted, and rightfully so. I get it. If I had a kid, I'd want to be there for everything too. But you've missed a lot the last few months. Other than a few events we were committed to for the band, we didn't hang out once while Carter was in rehab. When was the last time we went three or four months without hanging?"

"We just spent two years on the road together twenty-four-seven," I protested.

He spread his hands, palms up.

"Is this my fault?" I asked, starting to get an uncomfortable feeling in my gut.

"It's not one's *fault*. It's our current reality. It's happening, regardless of who or why or what. And if we start fucking around with the foundation— namely the people who helped get us where we are—I think it's going to make it worse."

"Did it ever occur to you making some changes might make it better?"

"Sure. But is it a risk we want to take? We're on top and changing things could impact everything we've built. Especially if Aurora is the vindictive bitch she's showing herself to be."

I didn't have an answer to that.

Not yet anyway.

But I was going to figure one out.

33

———————

P *resley*

I'D NEVER BEEN on a red carpet before, and I would've been lying if I said it wasn't exciting. Even with the weird vibe happening with Aurora, I was having a blast. Cheyenne and Didi were both nice, especially Cheyenne. She was one of the top supermodels in the world, but very down to earth and easy to talk to. Didi was a lot more reserved. Zeke had told me she and Kellan broke up and got back together regularly so she tended to keep her distance from the band and anything they were involved with.

Cheyenne had no such qualms, even admitting to me that things with Kingston weren't serious.

"Oh, it's just sex," she said, dabbing gloss on her lips. "Don't get me wrong, he's lovely. Handsome, good in bed, rich, generous. He ticks all the boxes. But he's thirty and I'm only twenty-two. I'm at the height of my career and nowhere near ready to settle down."

"Is *he* ready to settle down?" I asked curiously.

She laughed. "These guys all want that. They're just not comfortable admitting it, as if needing some stability to go with the chaos of rock and roll is something to be ashamed of. It's bloody ridiculous."

"Zeke seems ready," I said thoughtfully.

"Oh, please." Aurora came out of one of the stalls, shaking her head.

"You had his kid, honey. That's the only thing he's interested in. Once the band goes back out on tour, he's going to forget all about you."

"I live in his house," I said, refusing to let her intimidate me. "So I doubt he's going to forget me."

She looked momentarily surprised but then shrugged as she washed her hands. "It's convenient. He doesn't want to schlep back and forth to Minnesota or even to some little house he sets you up in, in the Valley. Plus, he has a very high libido." She smirked at me. "Keeping you close is advantageous. He gets to see his kid whenever he wants, *and* he gets to fuck the pretty little thing that's already in his bed. Who wouldn't like that kind of arrangement short-term?"

"What would you know about his libido?" I snapped, irritated at her insinuation that it was nothing but sex between Zeke and me.

She paused, cocking her head. "Honey, I was sleeping with Big Z while you were still in middle school. I'm guessing he didn't mention that."

I was too shocked to respond, so I was grateful Cheyenne had my back.

"Past tense, eh?" She cocked her head. "It's always a bitch when you're replaced with someone half your age."

Aurora narrowed her eyes. "I'd be nicer to me if I were you. The women in the boys' lives come and go, but you know who's been here through all of them? Me. And I have no plans to go anywhere."

Cheyenne wasn't even a little bit put off. "I could have every one of those boys eating out of the palm of my hand with a snap of my fingers." She glanced at me. "No offense." Then she looked back at Aurora. "If I wanted you gone, you'd be gone."

"Don't flatter yourself. You're nothing but Kingston's flavor of the month. Like you said a few minutes ago—it's nothing but sex."

"You're the one flattering yourself if you think someone like Zeke is going to marry a woman almost as old as his mother." This time Cheyenne was the one who smirked.

"Go to hell." Aurora tossed her dark hair back over her shoulder. "Pretty little things like you are a dime a dozen. They like fucking you but when it comes time for something with a little more depth, they come to me. And don't kid yourself—if I wanted you gone, I can make it happen just. Like. This." She snapped her fingers like Cheyenne had.

Cheyenne laughed. "Careful, Aurora. Your fangs are showing." She reached for my arm. "Come on, Presley. Let's go find our *dates.*" She said the last word as an obvious insult since Aurora had come alone, and I grimaced as we stepped into the hall.

"Thanks for sticking up for me," I told her, "but she's their manager and I really don't want to cause trouble for Zeke or the band."

"Looks to me like there's already trouble," she said, her gaze traveling down the hall to where Zeke and Kingston looked to be in a heated discussion.

They immediately stopped talking when we approached, and Zeke took my hand. "Ready to go in?"

"In a moment." Cheyenne looked at Kingston. "I don't appreciate being threatened or spoken down to. I don't care who Aurora is to you, but she's a fucking cunt and I'm not riding back in the limo with her. So, you can go home with her or go home with me. You decide."

"She threatened you?" Kingston looked surprised and annoyed.

"She also had some fun information for Presley," she said, glancing at me.

"It was nothing," I said quickly. "I'm fine."

"Don't do that." Cheyenne shook her head. "That's how trouble starts. Don't try to protect him—he's not the one who needs it. Trust me on this." She slid her arm through Kingston's. "Let's go."

"What did she say to you?" Zeke asked me as they headed into the theater ahead of us.

I didn't look at him, feeling both frustrated and embarrassed, even though I hadn't done anything wrong. "She told me about the two of you."

"Fuck." He pulled me close. "You know that's all in the past, right?"

"Yes, but why didn't you tell me? I thought we'd agreed on honesty and a clean slate."

"It didn't seem important, to be honest, because we kept talking about starting fresh, you know? What was the point of bringing up the past? It was only going to make you uncomfortable."

"Probably less uncomfortable than I was finding out from *her* in the ladies' room."

He sighed. "I'm sorry, babe. Really. I had no idea she was attending tonight. If I'd known, I would have hired our own car to bring us here. Can you forgive me?"

"Do you promise not to keep things from me anymore?"

"I promise."

"Then you're forgiven."

He smiled. "Shall we go find our seats?"

~

THE MOVIE WAS an action-adventure type thing, with lots of explosions and car chases. Everyone in the audience seemed to enjoy it, and we all cheered when Onyx Knight's song played in the background. What I hadn't realized was that Cheyenne had a small part in it, playing herself in a scene with the hero. It was only two lines, where he hits on her and she shoots him down, but I reached over and squeezed her arm.

"Congrats!" I whispered.

"Thank you."

I liked Cheyenne a lot, but Didi and Aurora made me uneasy. They seemed to have formed an alliance, with Aurora sitting next to her and the two of them whispering the whole time. I wasn't sure what was going on but there was an odd tension amongst the band. They smiled and waved as we left the building when the movie was over, but they didn't look at or talk to each other. For guys who'd been friends for so long, something was off with them.

We went to a party at the home of the movie's director after the premiere. He lived in an opulent mansion in Bel-Air, and there were so many famous people here I had to stop myself from staring.

"Overwhelming?" Zeke whispered in my ear, one arm around my waist.

"A little."

"We can leave whenever you want. I thought we'd make an appearance, maybe have a drink or two, and then we can take off."

"I'm fine. I just never imagined being in the same room with some of these people."

"Me either." Our eyes met and we smiled.

"I'm going to hit the head—will you be okay for a few minutes?"

"I'm fine." I nodded.

He disappeared around a corner, and I wandered out to the pool area. There were people everywhere, talking, drinking, eating, and even dancing. Big name movie stars, musicians, models, influencers. It was heady to be here among them.

"Well, hello." Someone came up behind me and I recognized him from a popular television show.

"H-hi."

"I don't think we've met. I'm Greg."

Gregory Mink.

I knew who he was all too well.

"Presley."

"Like Elvis?"

I smiled. "My parents were big fans."

"Now I'm a big fan." He leaned forward. "What do you do—no, wait. Let me guess." He squeezed his eyes shut as if thinking. Then snapped his fingers and pointed at me. "You're very tall... model?"

I laughed. "Nope."

"Aspiring actress?"

"Not even close."

"Hmm. I'm stumped. Do you sing?"

"Only in the shower."

"I'd like to see that."

"I don't think—"

"Knock it off, Greg." Carter came over and put his arm around my shoulders. "This is Z's girl. Presley, this is Greg Mink. He's a pain in the ass, but mostly harmless."

"Man, you never let me have any fun." Greg flashed a million-dollar smile before shaking Carter's hand. "It's good to see you, Carter. Heard you were back in rehab."

Carter nodded. "Yeah, you know how it is. People worry, they do an intervention, I wind up in rehab."

"I'm familiar."

The two locked eyes for a second but then Greg turned back to me. "Well, Ms. Presley. Big Z's a lucky man. Have a good night." He wandered back inside, and I looked at Carter.

"You didn't have to step in."

"He's a good guy but I've seen him get handsy when he's had too much to drink, and Z would lose his mind if he came out here and found someone with his hands on you. I was just heading off trouble at the pass."

"I appreciate it."

"You doing okay?" he asked quietly. "Aurora was a real bitch, and I'm sorry about that."

"Don't worry about me. I'm learning to navigate these unfamiliar waters I've been treading the last month or so." I paused. "What about you? Is it hard to be at a party like this? Being sober, I mean?"

He hesitated. "Not really? At least at a party like this there's stuff to do, people to talk to, damsels in distress to rescue—" He paused, pretending to give me the stink eye, and we both laughed. Abruptly, he sobered. "Being home alone is the most dangerous time for me. There's nothing to do and no one to do it with."

"How come you don't have a girlfriend?" I asked. "You're hot, rich, and successful. They must be banging down the doors for you."

He shrugged. "The ones I usually like don't want to be with someone on the road for two years at a time. The ones that want me don't want the real me, they just want Carter Ambrose the rockstar. And the one I love, well, she belonged to someone else."

"Belonged?"

"It's complicated."

"Zeke and I are almost always around if you ever just want to hang out. You know? If you're alone and you think you're going to do something you shouldn't. Just reach out."

"Carter, there you are." Aurora came over and slid her arm through his elbow. "There are people I want you to meet. Come on."

"I'll find you in a minute," he said, his tone snippy. "Presley and I are in the middle of a conversation."

"For fuck's sake, Carter, I said—"

"And I said no. Give me five."

"Fine." She turned in a huff and Carter exhaled sharply.

"You okay?" I asked him, watching him follow her retreating figure with his eyes.

"Do yourself a favor and stay far, far away from Aurora," he said softly.

"Hey, there you are." Zeke joined us. "I was looking all over for you."

"Sorry," I said. "I came outside to get some air and then Greg Mink was hitting on me and Carter came to the rescue."

"I see." Zeke smiled. "Thanks, man."

Carter nodded. "Anytime. Now, I have to go see what the she-devil wants."

"She-devil?" Zeke asked as he walked away.

"Aurora."

Zeke stared after him. "You want to go home? I have a feeling she's going to do everything in her power to cause trouble."

"Same." I hesitated. "But should we leave Carter alone?"

"I'll make sure Kingston keeps an eye on him."

"Okay."

We walked back into the house.

34

Z*eke*

WITH MY MOTHER in the house, we were able to sleep most mornings. She would get Jeremy up and ready for the day, so Presley and I didn't have to. More than once, we'd both told her she didn't have to, but she seemed to be making up for lost time with him much the way I was. Presley worried it was too much, but it turned out to be a nice break for us since one of us was still getting up once in the middle of the night with him. He couldn't seem to get past that three a.m. feeding time, and Presley had said she was going to start adding cereal to his formula this week.

It was noon before we got up the day after the movie premiere. I couldn't remember the last time I'd just lounged around in bed with a woman, and I was enjoying the hell out of it. We'd made love, cuddled, and she'd just picked up her phone a few minutes ago. She appeared to be scrolling social media when she gasped.

"Zeke!"

"What's wrong?" I leaned over to see what had startled her.

"This is me!" Her eyes were as round as saucers as she stared at a picture of us on the red carpet.

"It is." I took her phone from her and grinned. "You looked fucking amazing last night."

"Oh my god. They're calling me Big Z's Big Squeeze," she said, making a face.

"Well, you are. Aren't you?"

"I guess." She looked up at me. "Am I? I mean, you moved us here and we live together, but that was because of the baby. Now that it's been a few weeks, we should probably have a conversation about the future."

"I thought we already did that," I said, pulling her astride me so she was straddling my hips. I rested my hands on the sides of her thighs. "If this was just about Jeremy, I could have bought you a house or condo nearby. I could see my son regularly and move on with my life. But that's not what I want."

"What do you want?" she whispered. Her eyes were clouded with doubt, and I wondered what Aurora had said to put that there. She'd been fine until now.

"You know what I want," I said patiently. "You. Me. Us. Our family."

"For how long?"

"Come on, baby." I ran my hands up her sides until I got to her shoulders. Then I clamped down on them, pulling her torso down so we were eye to eye. "I've told you this. You want to head to Vegas and get married this afternoon? Will that convince you I'm in this for the long haul?"

"M-married?" Her eyes rounded all over again.

"If you want to. If that's what it'll take to convince you I'm serious."

"Zeke, I don't want to manipulate you or guilt you into anything. Marriage is a serious commitment and—"

I yanked her against me and kissed her, long and hard and deep. "I'm good with serious. I'm good with commitment. And whatever bullshit Aurora put in your head, forget about it. She's jealous. I'm sorry I didn't tell you she and I had a thing, but it was never serious, and she knew it. I never lied to her or any woman I've ever been involved with, and I don't intend to start now. If I didn't want you here, do you really think I'd have you and Aunt Meg living in my house, immersed in my family, sleeping in my bed? Babe, you've been mine since the first time I saw you."

She cocked her head. "At the bar?"

"No. At the venue, when none of us wanted to give you an interview. I only caught a glimpse of you, standing there looking so hopeful and nervous, and whatever it was I felt, it hit me in the gut. I've never, not in the decade I've been doing this, felt guilty about blowing off a reporter. But I did that night. Obviously, it was fleeting and not enough to make me turn around, but fate brought us together again. The fact that you gifted me your virginity was special, and I think even then, I was subconsciously freaking out because I knew you were different. That's a big part of the reason I reacted the way I did when I heard you on the phone. I was scared, Sunny."

"I was so hurt," she whispered, dropping down so her head now rested on my chest and her long, lean body was sprawled across my bigger one.

"I know." I wrapped my arms around her. "But that's in the past, and I want us to look toward the future. If you want to drive to Vegas today to get married, let's do it. It's probably not the big wedding you've always dreamed of, but we can do that later. I want you to be part of me. Officially."

"Aunt Meg would kill me," she said, laughing.

"No one has to know. We can do it secretly and come back from Vegas engaged. Then we'll plan the wedding."

She lifted her head and stared at me. "I want to say that's crazy. It *is* crazy." She paused. "So why doesn't it feel crazy?"

"Because we're meant to be."

"How far is it to Vegas?" she asked, sitting up and rolling to the side.

"About three-and-a-half hours, depending on traffic. I can make it in three if traffic cooperates. We'll take the Maserati."

"What about Jeremy?"

"Sweetheart, if I'm going to make you my wife today, the baby is staying here with Grandma, Grandpa, and Auntie Meg. We are *not* getting up with him on our wedding night."

We stared at each other for a long time.

"What about a prenup?" she asked quietly. "I'm not in this for the money, and I don't want anyone to say I am. In fact, I'd feel better if we had one."

I sighed. "Fine. I'll call my lawyer and have him draw something up. He can email it to me, I'll print it, and we'll find a notary in Vegas who can witness us signing. But let's be clear, I'm not putting anything stupid in there, like you get a million dollars for every year we're married or shit like that. I'll stipulate something that protects the band's interests, and any holdings I have with my parents, but beyond that, I'm not playing games here, Presley."

"I know. Thank you."

It felt like I needed to tell her I loved her, but the words stuck in my throat. Not because I didn't feel it, but because the timing felt off. I wasn't sure why, but this wasn't the right time or place. Maybe once we got to Vegas? First, I had to find a full-service place where we could get the license and have a small ceremony. Then I had to make a few calls because she needed a ring.

"Hey." An idea came to me as I followed her into the bathroom. "I know we said no one should be there, but I need a best man. What if we asked Carter to go?"

She turned. "I'd love that. But then I'd need someone to stand up for me or it would feel weird. I'd call Cheyenne, but then we'd have to tell Kingston."

"And then we'd have to tell the other guys."

Shit.

Somehow, I wanted Carter to be there. He was more my brother than my actual brother, but if the whole band came, then things would get complicated.

And now I felt bad that she didn't have any friends here. That had to be lonely, especially when I was working. Taking care of Jeremy and spending time with her elderly aunt wasn't the same as having friends. I liked that she'd gotten along with Cheyenne, but she wasn't the type of friend who'd be available for shopping and lunch dates. She barely had time for Kingston.

"We could bring Aunt Meg," I said finally.

"And leave her in Carter's care?" she asked, dissolving into laughter.

"They might take care of each other," I said thoughtfully. "She'll keep him mostly out of trouble, and he'll make sure she doesn't fall or anything. Despite his addiction issues, he's a good guy. And he seems to adore her."

"They've met twice!" she said, stepping into the shower.

"I know, but he's like that. And they text every day according to him."

"All right. Call him or whatever. I'll talk to Aunt Meg after I shower."

"Can she keep a secret? Because if my parents get wind of this, it will be chaos. And my mother absolutely cannot keep a secret. I mean, if someone was sick or in real trouble, she would, but something like this? It would explode out of her in diamond- and butterfly-laden vomit."

She'd just lathered up her hair and snorted so hard shampoo went flying.

"I don't know if I'm disgusted or intrigued," she said, rinsing her eyes.

"Sorry." I decided not to join her in the shower since I needed to call a jeweler without her hearing me.

There was a lot to do.

~

Two hours later we were speeding down the highway in my Maserati. Meg was with Carter in his Lamborghini, and we got to Vegas in just under three hours. The traffic and cop gods were apparently on board with this impromptu trip, so we pulled up to the valet at the Bellagio just after five.

With Carter involved, I'd gotten a lot done in a short amount of time. I didn't know what kind of ring Presley might want, so we'd chosen simple wedding rings online, and they were being delivered to the hotel. Tomorrow, we'd shop together for an engagement ring because I needed her to not just like it, but love it, because I hoped she'd be wearing it forever.

There was a chapel off the strip that would handle both the legalities and the formalities, and we had a seven o'clock appointment. Carter had made dinner reservations for eight o'clock at one of my favorite restaurants. It was almost comical how good he was at taking care of details. I'd never seen him do anything this organized for the band, yet he was planning my wedding like a fucking boss. I'd have to give him shit about at some point. Just not today.

"I packed two different things to wear," Presley was saying as we got to our suite. "Which do you like better?"

"Neither," I said. "A local shop is arriving any minute now with a bunch of dresses for you to try on. A bride should have something new, even if she's eloping."

"They're bringing dresses here for me to try on?" she asked.

"Yup." I leaned over and kissed her cheek. "Welcome to my life, baby. And get used to it. I plan to spoil you as much as I can."

"Zeke." Her eyes filled with tears, and she threw herself against me. "You make me so happy."

"Then why are you crying?"

"Because I'm happy. Duh."

I chuckled. "That's a girl thing, right?"

"Maybe." She sniffled.

There was a knock on the door, and I grinned. "That'll be the dresses. I'm heading over to Carter and Meg's suite so you can choose and surprise me."

"Send Aunt Meg over?" she asked.

"Sure thing."

Carter and Meg were sharing a two-bedroom suite for safety reasons, just in case she needed anything. Carter had promised me he'd look after her and be on his best behavior, which was just as scary as when he was high because Carter was the consummate ladies' man. I'd seen him sleep with women three times his age when he was younger, so I didn't put it past him to make a move on Meg.

I chuckled to myself just thinking about it and must've had a humorous look on my face when Carter opened the door.

"Hey. Presley's looking at dresses and wants Meg to join her."

"On my way." Meg still used her cane, but she looked flushed and happy today, making me wonder about her and Carter yet again. I just couldn't bring myself to ask.

"She has thirty minutes," I called after her. "We have shit to do."

She just laughed.

"Tell me you're not the reason she looks flushed," I said to Carter when we shut the door.

He rolled his eyes. "We've been up here like twelve minutes, and while I'm good, she's not some twenty-year-old. I'd have to put some time into it with a woman like Meg."

"Please don't." I shook my head.

He just laughed. "Did love turn you into a prude? Consenting adults, man. If she was down and the situation arose, I enjoy my way around an older woman's body."

I groaned. "Thanks, bro. Way to ruin my wedding day."

"*Marriage* day. It's not really a wedding."

I scratched my chin. "You think this is a bad idea?"

"I think Presley deserves the whole wedding experience and this—" He motioned around us with his hand. "Is a shortcut. What made you decide to do it today?"

"After last night, I think Aurora is going to cause trouble for us. Not me and Presley specifically, but all of us." I gave him a look. "And it's because of you, right?"

He blew out a frustrated breath. "I'm telling you—leave it alone. Some secrets are kept that way for a reason."

"You have to tell me so I can help," I said quietly. "Let me help you, man. Let's get her out of our lives."

"It's not just about me. There are innocent people involved and blowing up their lives, in addition to the band, isn't worth it. I'll handle Aurora."

"But you're not. And what could be so bad that you can't tell me?"

"Listen to me. If anything ever happens to me, there are instructions in my will. You'll take care of my wishes, right?"

I threw up my hands. "Dude, I don't know what *it* is. And don't talk like that. Fuck."

"It's just a precaution. As long as I'm alive, I've got it under control. Trust me, okay?"

As frustrated as I was, this wasn't the time, so I would have to trust him whether I wanted to or not.

35

———————

P *resley*

"By the powers vested in me by the State of Nevada, I pronounce you man and wife. You may kiss your bride."

Zeke bent his head and our lips touched.

And just like that, I was married.

Mrs. William Zerkesian.

Holy shit.

Myriad emotions whipped through me as he gently cupped the side of my face and a tiny flicker of doubt hit my subconscious.

What had I just agreed to?

What were we doing?

Marriage was supposed to be a lifetime commitment, but he hadn't even told me he loved me. It felt like we'd rushed into a monumental decision, yet deep down, it still felt like I'd made the right one. As he'd said this morning, there had been a connection from the start. There weren't words to accurately describe the intensity of our feelings, so maybe that was why we hadn't articulated them with the words 'I love you."

I did love him, though.

Maybe I was being a romantic fool, but how could I not? It hadn't been love at first sight but pretty damn close. Now I was his wife. And he was my husband.

"Congratulations." Aunt Meg's eyes were filled with tears as she hugged me. "I'm so happy for you."

"Thank you." I hugged her tightly.

"Let's go eat," Carter said after he'd hugged me and shook Zeke's hand.

"Let's do it." Zeke wrapped his hand around mine and we walked out toward the waiting limo.

We were immediately assaulted by camera flashes and a mob of reporters.

"Oh, fuck." Zeke pulled me closer to his side.

"Big Z! Did you get married?"

"Who's your wife, Z?"

"Carter, were you the best man?"

"Is she pregnant?"

"About a year too late for that," I murmured under my breath.

Zeke chuckled. "Come on, guys. Don't crowd us like this. You want a statement, I need you to respect a little personal space. You see my aunt has a cane. If she falls, someone's going to jail."

To my surprise, they immediately backed up a few feet.

Zeke seemed to command respect and he looked every ounce the strong, confident celebrity he was as he slid an arm around my waist. "Yes, we got married. This is my wife, Presley. And you better be nice to her going forward."

"How long have you been dating?" someone called out.

"On and off for a little over a year."

That was a lie, but how would anyone know?

"Is it true you have a son together?"

"Yes." I felt Zeke stiffen, but his smile didn't waver, and he answered a handful of other questions before lifting a hand. "Listen, we got married in Vegas to avoid this kind of fanfare. Now we've got dinner reservations, so we have to go. Thanks, guys." He guided me closer to the limo and the waiting driver, who quickly opened the door. Zeke pushed me inside, while Carter helped Aunt Meg, and finally, the doors locked behind us.

"Well, that was exciting," Aunt Meg said breathlessly as the long sleek car pulled into traffic.

"You know tomorrow they're going to say we're dating," Carter said to her.

She grinned. "Well, it might suck for you, but that'll be the coolest thing to ever happen to me."

She and Carter cracked up, as if they had some kind of inside joke.

"How the fuck did they find out?" Zeke glared at Carter. "Who did you tell, man? I asked you not to say anything. This was important to me."

"Hey, don't look at me. I didn't tell a soul!" He held up his hands. "Not even when King interrogated me about why I was going out of town."

"Babe?" He turned his gaze to me. "It's okay if you told someone, but I need to get in front of this. Dorian is going to have my ass for not giving her the chance to do a press release."

"I swear," I said. "The only person I told was Aunt Meg."

"It was me." Aunt Meg hung her head. "I'm so sorry. I never dreamed my Eye-Lights followers would put two and two together. I edited a few seconds of video of Presley trying on those dresses... I figured people would speculate, and since the plan was to be *engaged* when you get home, I honestly assumed they would think she was dress shopping for a future wedding, not actually getting married on the spot."

"Ah, hell, Meg." Zeke shook his head, clearly exasperated.

"You have a lot of followers, Meg-let," Carter said to her.

"Meg-let?" I mouthed to Zeke. His eyes crinkled as he gave me a little shrug.

"Well, what's done is done." Zeke was all business. "I have to call Dorian because this will be news very quickly."

"But how did they find out where we were going to be?" I asked, though it was mostly rhetorical.

"The press lives for this shit," Zeke told me. "They're like super spies when it comes to finding us if they have even an inkling of a newsworthy story."

"I guess it's water under the bridge," I said. "Now we have to focus on what we'll tell people."

"We have to lie," Carter said thoughtfully. "To the band and everyone else. We decided to bring Meg to Vegas to celebrate getting a clean bill of health from her doctors. Then we pretend this was a spur-of-the-moment thing. Otherwise, the guys will be hurt and—"

"Not to mention my mother," Zeke said. "She's going to have a fit."

"We have to pinkie swear," Aunt Meg said, holding out one of hers. "This wasn't planned. It happened organically."

Zeke looked at her like she was offering him something disgusting, but Carter didn't hesitate to wrap his pinkie around hers, so I nudged Zeke.

"Come on. Pinkie swear and get it over with."

"Fine." The four of us linked pinkies just as Zeke's phone rang.

"Aurora," I said, reading the name on the screen. "Well, that didn't take long."

"Here we go." He put his phone to his ear. "Hey, Aurora."

~

INSTEAD OF A QUIET, romantic post-wedding dinner, it turned into a circus. The press followed the limo, so even though the restaurant wouldn't allow them inside, they knew where we were. Once some of the guests inside the restaurant recognized Zeke and Carter, it became a free-for-all. Eventually, the restaurant manager had to get involved because fans and curious onlookers wouldn't let us eat.

"Christ, I'm sorry," Zeke whispered to me.

"It's okay." It wasn't, but what choice did I have?

"Did you bring your laptop with you?" Carter asked as we got back into the limo.

I nodded. "Yes. Why?"

"Upload the article."

"What? I was going to do it on the fifteenth."

"I know, but if you upload it now, people will mostly forget about the wedding and it'll bring the focus back to me."

"You don't need that kind of negative attention," Aunt Meg said to him, putting a gentle hand on his arm.

He shrugged. "I'm used to it. And my addiction isn't a secret. The things you're going to publish are my exact words, so there's nothing to hide. I'm fine with it. If I hadn't been, I wouldn't have said them."

"Carter." Zeke gave him a look. "You don't have to throw yourself under any fucking bus for me. We didn't do anything wrong. We got married. Big deal. We don't owe anyone explanations about timing or anything else, beyond soothing my mother's ruffled feathers. She'll be a little hurt, but if we let her do some of the wedding planning, she'll get over it."

"Yeah, but the timing is right to give the band some attention," Carter said. "Once our name is front and center again—and a Vegas wedding won't provide that—everyone will start asking about the new album. It's the perfect time to start promoting it."

"It's not coming out for months," Zeke protested.

"So we move up the timeline. Who's in charge here, us or them?"

"Who's them?" Aunt Meg asked.

"The corporate machine that runs our organization," Carter replied glibly. "The man. The band's equivalent of the government. And Aurora, I guess."

"Fuck Aurora," Zeke muttered.

"No thanks." Carter made a face.

"It's going to put Presley's life into a tailspin," Zeke said after a moment.

"That's why we were waiting until later in the month. To give her time to prepare."

"No time like the present," Aunt Meg said thoughtfully. "You weren't planning on going on a honeymoon, so what else does she have to do?" She was mostly joking, but she had a point and I nodded.

"If this is what you want, Carter, I can certainly ride the momentum. Meg talked to Lexi Rousseau the other day and she's going to be my next story, talking about the difficulties she's faced as a woman in the music business."

"Is your business model going to be one big story a month?" Carter asked.

I nodded. "That's the plan. One big story a month, along with some album reviews for new music and small, fluff pieces about rockstar birthdays and such."

"Oh, so for the June issue you'll find guys who have birthdays in June?"

"Or ladies," Aunt Meg said, nudging him.

"Zeke said he'll help me reach out to a few people who have birthdays each month, if they're willing to tell me their plans. That leaves me with relatively small amounts of content to curate, but hopefully all with big impact."

"This is cool," Carter said with a grin. "Can I help you curate content?"

"Sure."

"You guys want to have dinner in our room?" Zeke asked, lifting his phone. "I'll call ahead, see if I can have room service delivered."

"You two should have a little privacy," Aunt Meg said. "Carter can take me to dinner in the hotel."

"The press will have a field day with you two," I told her, laughing.

She laughed. "Come on, when was the last time I had any excitement in my almost sixty-one-year-old life? Maybe a little adventure will keep me younger. God knows, between my heart and MS I'm not getting any healthier."

"It'll be okay, Meg." Carter patted her hand. "I'll keep you young. We'll raise some hell tonight."

"Not too much hell," Zeke said to him pointedly.

Carter just grinned. "I'm good, man."

He looked down as his phone started to ring.

"Aurora's a pain in the ass," Aunt Meg said, glancing at the screen.

"I'll call her back later," Carter said, sliding an arm around Aunt Meg's shoulders. "I've got a date tonight. Aurora's going to have to wait." He stuffed his phone back in his pocket just as we pulled up to the hotel.

36

———

Z*eke*

PRESLEY and I had been up late, talking and making love and enjoying our first night as a married couple. Despite the chaos surrounding the press finding out so quickly, it had been a good day. Today we were going ring shopping and while we had temporary wedding bands, I planned to buy her a fantastic wedding band/engagement ring set that matched. I liked the simple titanium band we'd chosen for me, but she needed something unique and extraordinary because *she* was unique and extraordinary.

I'd only slept about five hours, but for some reason I was wide awake at nine on the dot. Like I had a day job waiting for me somewhere. I glanced down at where Presley was sprawled on her stomach, long dark hair fanning around her, her bare back enticing me to touch the creamy skin I'd been lucky enough to caress for most of the night. My wife was beautiful. Sweet. Perfect.

My only fear was that the insanity of Onyx Knight would touch her, or somehow change her. For whatever reason, I didn't relish the idea of meshing my two worlds or exposing her to the rock and roll lifestyle. I loved it, craved it even, but keeping her and our son out of it would have been my preference.

Except that wasn't reality.

I couldn't just keep her locked away at home while I toured the world and played music. She had to be there with me at least part of the time, whether I wanted her to be or not. We'd go back to flying from city to city on the next tour, which would make things easier, and for now, Jeremy was easily transportable. We'd have to revisit the conversation in a few years, but I was slowly formulating a plan.

We already had a tour in the works beginning in September to go along with the September release of our next album, but it was possible to move the album release up a little if we needed to. It wouldn't change anything to do with the tour, but it would get a buzz going. It was almost June now, which meant the next phase of the band's success was right around the corner.

Obviously, I'd never been married during a release before, so everything would be different this time, but I didn't mind that. I just wanted Presley to be prepared. I hated the way she'd found out about Aurora and me, and there were a lot of women I'd slept with out there for her to potentially run into. Some of them had standing backstage access in different cities, and it was hard to remember all of them. I could and would tell my crew that all backstage passes I'd previously approved needed to be revoked, but a lot of the ladies had other connections. Hell, some of them even worked in the industry.

It would be a hard road to navigate, so Presley and I were going to have to talk about those things.

There were so many damn things we had to talk about.

If I was honest, we still didn't know each other that well. I felt like we knew the important things, the big things, but the minutiae of my life would come crashing down on us hard. And I wanted to avoid that as much as possible. Allowing my sweet young wife to be hurt wasn't in the plans.

I'd just rolled over, planning to wake her up with an orgasm, when my phone buzzed. I had every intention of ignoring it but then her phone started to ring, and she hadn't turned off her ringer since we'd left L.A., in case my parents needed to reach us about the baby.

Presley immediately rolled over, her maternal instincts overruling her fatigue and she groaned as she looked at the screen.

"It's Meg," she mumbled, putting the phone back down.

"We can call them back," I said, reaching for her.

"That sounds like a lovely idea." She melted into my arms.

Then her phone started to ring again.

"You think she's okay?" she asked, hesitantly reaching for her phone.

I sighed. "Answer it. Hopefully, she and Carter aren't in jail."

She snickered. "I hope not—good morning." She stiffened as she put the phone to her ear. "Wait, Meg, stop crying, I can't understand you." Her eyes flew to mine as she pulled away and sat up. "What are you talking about... oh my god. Zeke, get dressed." She was already on her feet, practically vaulting across the room to where her suitcase was open.

"What's going on?" I asked, springing into action and reaching for my boxers.

"Aunt Meg, we're coming. Breathe. Two minutes." She disconnected and turned to me, her eyes wide and filled with tears.

"Honey, what is it? Is it the baby?" I asked, my heart squeezing painfully.

"No." She swallowed. Hard. Tears started to trickle down her cheeks.

"Presley, you're scaring me. What is it?"

"It's... Carter." She covered her mouth with her hand. "He's dead."

THE NEXT FEW hours were surreal. It was like living a nightmare in slow motion, with no hope of waking up. We'd rushed to Carter and Meg's suite, where paramedics had arrived moments before we did. There was no hope, though. Carter was a strange, bluish color, a needle on the floor next to his very still body. He was curled on his side, a few hotel envelopes with his handwriting on them on the coffee table.

Meg was inconsolable, Presley was paler than I'd ever seen her, and my own stomach churned with horror, grief, and guilt. Had I somehow caused this, by bringing him into the shitstorm of my impromptu wedding? Aurora had been on a tear yesterday after the wedding, more furious than the situation warranted, but I'd assumed she would calm down once she got past her jealousy or whatever was driving her reaction.

Right now, I was too shaken to think rationally, but my wife and Aunt Meg needed me to man up. There were cops and hotel staff and medical personnel everywhere, and I had to reach out to the band before the press leaked the news. The easiest thing would be to call Dorian, and I excused myself into the hallway to do it.

"Hey, Z. Thinking about another woman on the morning after your wedding night?" she teased.

My voice cracked. "Dorian... we've got... a problem."

"Z?" Her voice instantly changed, as if on alert. She knew me well, so if I was rattled, she knew there was a serious problem. "What is it? What do you need?"

"It's Carter." Fuck, I was going to break down if I wasn't careful.

"Oh, no. Another relapse?"

"He's gone, Dorian." Yup, I was done. Saying the words out loud brought tears to my eyes and I let my chin hit my chest. Fuck, I didn't want to cry anywhere people could see me.

"Oh, fuck, Z. No." Her voice caught.

We all adored Carter. His playful smile and mischievous antics always had us laughing, having a good time. The drug use was annoying and obviously dangerous, but Carter rarely let it impact his relationships with the band or anyone involved in our organization. The idea that he was gone and would never drive us crazy again was almost too much.

How the hell was I going to move forward?

"I need you, to, uh…" Yeah, tears sucked. I pulled in a deep, shuddery breath, trying to keep my composure until I was alone. "Please. I need you to let the band and Aurora know. I don't know any details, but I'm pretty sure he overdosed."

"Oh, no no no." Dorian was crying now too, not even trying to hide it.

"I'm sorry to put this on you, but I just can't," I whispered. Presley had just come into the hallway and was now burrowed against my chest, holding on to me tightly.

"I'll take care of it," Dorian said. "I just need a few minutes."

She disconnected, and I wrapped my arms around Presley, letting her sob against my chest.

"I don't understand," she cried. "He was fine last night… he and Meg were having so much fun. She was posting on InstaPixel until at least two in the morning, with pictures of the two of them at that club. I don't understand…"

"I don't know that there's any way to explain the mind of an addict," I said gruffly. "Like he told you, it wasn't about a physical need, it was mental. He liked it. Craved it. Ah, fuck, Carter, what did you do?" I couldn't stop the tears that slipped down my cheeks, and as unmanly as it was, the man who'd loved Carter like a brother was devastated.

"Aunt Meg needs us," she said after a while. "She's a mess, but they wouldn't let me stay with her while the police asked her questions."

"We're not going anywhere," I said.

"You think we need to call her a lawyer?"

"I don't think so," I said. "But we will if we have to."

My phone had been ringing nonstop, and though I ignored Aurora's call, I answered Kingston's.

"What's going on?" he asked. "Where are you? Is it true?"

"It's true." I shivered despite the fact it wasn't cold. "We're here with the police and the paramedics. I don't have any news, other than it looked to me like suicide."

Kingston let out a string of curses. "God dammit, Carter. God damn him to hell!" He disconnected.

I knew he wasn't mad at me. He would deal with his grief privately, like I wished I could, and then call me back when he was ready. It wasn't like I had any answers.

"Oh, wow, Cheyenne is here in Vegas," Presley murmured. "She just texted me, asking if we need anything. So the news is already out."

"Great." I leaned against the wall, keeping her close to me.

"What do we do?" she whispered. "I feel helpless."

"Short-term, we wait. In the next couple of days, there'll probably be a shitstorm. We need to get home to L.A. so we can hole up at the house, away from the media."

"What's going to happen?" she asked. "I don't know what to do next."

"I don't have any answers, babe."

There was nothing for us to do but wait and try to process the information.

Carter was gone.

My sweet, big-hearted, goofy best friend was gone.

And there wasn't a damn thing I could do about it.

37

P *resley*

I WAS no stranger to death, but Carter's was difficult to take in. I hadn't known him for very long, and honestly didn't even know him as well as Aunt Meg did, but it hit us all hard. I'd grown up knowing the stories of the car accident that had caused my father's untimely death and how Uncle Jeremy had been a war hero, killed during Desert Storm. My mother had been diagnosed with lung cancer on a sunny day in June, and she was gone by the end of August. At the time, I'd wished for more time with her, but in retrospect, watching her wither away and suffer probably would have been more traumatic to my teenage psyche.

Those had been unavoidable, the kind of bad luck that nothing could have prevented. Carter's death had officially been ruled a suicide, and we were struggling to wrap our heads around that. Zeke was taking it particularly hard, blaming himself and holing up in his den. It had been three days and there was a black cloud over our lives that was hard to vanquish. Taking care of Jeremy kept me grounded, but Zeke had even retreated from the baby.

I understood his pain and was trying to give him space, but last night he hadn't come to bed at all, and I was worried about him. I was also worried about Aunt Meg. She was devastated, also blaming herself, saying she should have been paying better attention. It was all so senseless and heart-breaking.

I hadn't seen Zeke all day and now that Jeremy was in bed, I wandered down to check on him.

"Hi." I knocked lightly on the open door.

Zeke was sitting in a chair by the window, staring out at nothing from what I could tell.

"Hey."

"Are you hungry? You skipped dinner."

"I'm fine." His voice sounded hollow. Gruff. Distant.

"Can I do anything for you?" I asked, walking over and standing behind him, putting my hands on his shoulders.

"No. I'm good."

My eyes strayed to the envelope in his lap. Once the police had made the determination Carter's death had been accidental, they'd released the envelopes that had been on the table. One for Zeke, one for Aunt Meg, one for "Onyx Knight," and a fourth one for someone whose name I didn't know.

"Have you read it yet?" I asked gently.

"No."

"It might give you some closure."

"Nothing will give me closure," he snapped. "He's fucking gone."

"I know, babe." I wrapped my arms around his neck and pressed the side of my face against his. "And I know you're hurting but punishing yourself won't bring him back."

"Leave it alone, Presley." He shrugged off my touch and got up, stuffing the envelope in the pocket of his jeans.

Part of me wanted to remind him that we were married now, and he was supposed to be hanging on to me for strength and support, not pushing me away, but I wanted to give him time. Aunt Meg had been distant too. Personally, I needed my family closer than ever, but it appeared that not everyone grieved the way I did.

"Where are you going?" I called after him, wishing he wasn't shutting me out.

"I don't know." He disappeared down the hall, and I followed more slowly.

We were so new together I wasn't sure how to handle this. Was I supposed to continue giving him space or try being more forceful? Would forcing him to talk to me accomplish anything?

I doubted it, so I wandered into the kitchen, looking for a snack, and found my mother-in-law seemingly doing the same thing. She was staring into the refrigerator as if waiting for something to strike her fancy.

"Hungry?" I asked, walking over to stand next to her.

"No." She shook her head. "Bored, maybe. Frustrated. Sad."

"Same." I sank onto a stool at the island. "And Zeke won't talk to me."

"He's brooding," she said, coming over to lean on the island across from me.

"What do I do about it?" I asked. "He didn't even come to bed last night."

"Don't let him get away with it," she said firmly. "He's strong and stubborn, much like me. That's why we butt heads so much. But as his wife, you need to be firm with him. Stand up to him. Remind him that you're his partner now, not some one-night stand or sexual conquest. The two of you made a commitment and he doesn't get to decide when you're there for each other. You need him now too. Strength and support go both ways."

The thought of confronting Zeke intimidated me a little, but she was right. I couldn't let him continue to be the one who was always in charge, always in control. Sometimes, he had to relinquish some of that to me. Otherwise, it would be a very lopsided relationship moving forward and an unhealthy one at that.

"I'll give him a little time," I said after a moment. "Just until the funeral. If he's still acting like this, then we'll talk."

"Don't let it go on too long," she said. "Trust me. I've experienced it first-hand. Once he gets in a mood, it can take him forever to snap out of it. And your relationship is too new to weather that kind of storm."

"Tell me about it." I rested my chin on my palm.

"Are you sure you're not hungry? I could whip up some quesadillas for us."

I started to say no but changed my mind. "You know what? That sounds good." I hadn't been eating well and it seemed like she needed something to do.

"Great." She moved to the fridge, pulling out some ingredients, and I went to the pantry looking for the mango-peach salsa I'd picked up last week before our lives went to hell.

"Are you cooking something?" Aunt Meg wandered in looking tired but interested.

"Quesadillas," I told her. "You hungry?"

"I suppose I could eat."

"Did someone say quesadillas?" Armand came in a second later. "I was just thinking it's been a while since we had Mexican."

Fatima laughed. "Everyone sit and I'll whip up a batch."

Armand and Aunt Meg settled around the island, talking as Fatima cooked and I got out plates, napkins, cutlery, and sour cream. It was a brief but necessary respite from the haze of grief that had permeated the house, and I was grateful for it.

If only Zeke had wanted to join us.

THE FUNERAL FELL on a beautiful Southern California day, with the sun shining, low humidity, and a clear blue sky. It was hard to enjoy it, considering what was on the agenda. Today's service was for close friends only, since Carter didn't have any family. There would be something public for fans sometime next month, but this one was private and would be a relatively small, intimate affair.

I wore a simple sleeveless black sheath dress, with low-heeled black pumps. Zeke looked handsome in a black suit with a white shirt and black tie, his long hair tied back in a ponytail at the nape of his neck. The baby was staying home with Zeke's housekeeper, Valerie, so his parents were coming with us in the limo to the funeral home.

"I don't think I'm ready for this." Aunt Meg sniffed.

"There's no way to be ready for something like this," Fatima said sadly. "So young. So unnecessary."

"He had demons," Aunt Meg whispered. "The kind you don't get over. The more we got to know each other, the more I worried. But I didn't think he would do it on purpose. They ruled it an accident but him leaving those letters tells me something else."

"He knew he was going to die," I said quietly. "He pretty much told me so during our interview. I asked him where he saw himself in ten years and he said, 'dead.' At the time I thought he was being dramatic, but he knew. Dammit. That was always the plan. He hated being sober and didn't want to live that way."

"That breaks my heart," Aunt Meg said, dabbing at her eyes.

"Are you still going to publish the interview?" Fatima asked.

"I don't know," I admitted. "He wanted me to do it the night we eloped, but I never had a chance. Now I don't know what to do."

"Publish it," Zeke said in a gruff monotone. "That's what he wanted. We should honor his wishes."

"The time doesn't seem right," I protested.

"It's never going to be right," Fatima said. "But if he wanted you to put it out there, then you should."

I didn't say anything, torn between wanting to do the last thing Carter had asked of me and letting the hoopla surrounding his death die down first. By publishing now, it would seem like I was taking advantage of the current media frenzy. "I don't want it to come across as opportunistic," I said.

"You can't help what other people think," Aunt Meg said. "But Carter was your friend, and he asked you to publish it. He said it would help explain not just him specifically, but addiction in general. His story, his struggle, the things he opened up about, were important to him."

No one responded because the limo had pulled up to the funeral home and slowed to a stop.

"I don't see any press," Fatima murmured, looking around.

"They kept the location top secret," Zeke said. "Hopefully no one at the funeral parlor leaked it."

He got out first and held out a hand to help me, Aunt Meg, and his mother. Then the five of us filed inside.

The first thing I saw was Aurora talking heatedly to a woman I didn't recognize, her face contorted as she waved her arms around.

"Is that Harley?" Fatima whispered to Zeke.

He nodded, watching the exchange intently.

"Who's Harley?" I asked.

"Tommy's ex-wife." Zeke broke away from us and approached Aurora and Harley. I couldn't hear what he said, but Aurora's face turned red, and she stalked off in the other direction in a huff. Harley turned to Zeke and hugged him. They exchanged a few words, she nodded, and then followed in the direction Aurora had gone.

"Were she and Carter friends?" I asked him when he rejoined us.

"Yeah. We were all tight. I wonder if Tommy knows she's here. She said he's not here yet."

Right on cue, Tommy came through the front doors of the funeral parlor. And he didn't look good. His suit was rumpled, his hair was sticking straight up, and his eyes were bloodshot and glassy. He'd obviously been suffering in his own way, just like the rest of us.

"Oh, hell." Zeke made a face.

"Hey, man." Tommy stuffed his hands in his pockets. "Am I late?"

"No. You okay?"

"No way in hell was I doing this sober." He looked around. "Fuck, is it packed in there?"

"We haven't gone in yet, but I think so."

"Are we sitting together?"

"The email Aurora sent this morning said the first two rows were reserved for the band."

"Right. Let's go."

"Hold up." Zeke grabbed his arm, hesitating a moment before continuing. "You should know. Harley's here."

Tommy froze, his eyes widened. "*Harley?* My Harley?"

"Your ex-wife, yes."

"Why?" he demanded. "Who invited her? What the fuck?"

"I don't know. She and Aurora were going at it, but they clammed up when I walked over to them. I told Aurora this wasn't the time or the place for her shit, and she took off like her ass was on fire."

"She's always pissed about something lately," Tommy muttered.

"It sounds like it's starting," I said quietly. "We should go in."

"Let's get this over with, man. I fucking hate funerals." Tommy walked ahead of us, and I slid my arm through Zeke's elbow.

"I'll be so ready for a drink when this is over," Armand said.

"I'm going to need a lot of drinks tonight," Aunt Meg agreed. "And I don't drink very often."

"There are certain events in life that require alcohol to survive," Zeke said. "This definitely qualifies."

I wasn't much of a drinker either, but I had to agree.

It was going to be a very long, sad afternoon.

38

―――――――

Z*eke*

THE THING about tears was that they served no real purpose. I didn't like to cry as a general rule, but not showing how much losing Carter had impacted me felt wrong too. For whatever reason, letting my new bride see me cry was unacceptable, which was partly why I'd been avoiding her the last few days, but there was no escape during the funeral. She nestled into my side, supporting me even though I'd been a douche canoe to her lately.

God, I loved her.

I'd pulled her into this fucked-up shit show of a life of mine, and she never hesitated to be there for me.

I had so much to make up for with my new bride, but I was hanging on by a thread. The tightness in my chest was so painful I couldn't breathe sometimes. The only time I got any relief was when I was holding my son. Late at night, when everyone else was asleep, I'd sit in his room and watch him until he got restless. Then I'd pick him up, feed him, and hold him close, drinking in his warmth. His innocence. The unconditional love I'd never felt before. The love of a child was unlike anything else, and right now it was one of the only things I had to hold on to.

Well, him and my wife. Whom I'd been treating like shit.

I promised myself I'd fix it.

Soon.

As soon as I could inhale without feeling like my soul was going to shatter into a million pieces.

There were just so many things to sort out.

We could grieve and take time to process what had happened, but at the end of the day, we ran a multi-million-dollar company that was now missing an integral part. We had a new album coming out and a tour in the works. We had a lot of hard decisions to make, and I didn't even know where to start. No one had said anything, but now that we were together, it felt like the right time.

Except Aurora beat me to it.

"Did you see Aurora's email?" Kingston asked me as we filed out of the funeral parlor.

"No." I met his gaze. "What'd she say?"

"Carter's lawyer needs us all there when he reads the will, and then we need to have a band meeting."

"Without her," I said quietly. "We meet without her first. I don't give a shit who's loyal to her. The band's first loyalty should be to each other."

"Absolutely." Kingston looked around. "Can we do it now? Come with me in my limo? Just the four of us. Didi can ride with your family since we're all going to your house anyway?"

My mother had arranged a casual brunch and almost everyone in attendance at the service had been invited.

"All right. Let me just tell Presley."

I told her the plan, and five minutes later the four of us were in Kingston's limo.

"Has anyone read the letter?" I asked as soon as the doors closed behind us.

Kingston slowly pulled it out of the pocket of his jacket, shaking his head. "The cops read it, to verify what it was, but I haven't yet."

"Maybe it's time," I suggested.

"Yeah." Tommy nodded warily. "Let's get it over with."

"Fuck." Kellan let out a huff.

"All right. Here goes." Kingston blew out a breath and slowly unfolded the piece of hotel stationery Carter had written on. "My dudes. How's it hangin'? I'll bet you're all pissed at me, and I'm sorry about that. But don't look at it that way. I did what I needed to do. Being sober was too hard. In case you've forgotten, my mom was on crack during her pregnancy, so I was born addicted. I never had a chance to beat this, and frankly, after thirty years, I'm tired.

"I'm about to go score and go out on top. Professionally and personally, believe it or not. Aunt Meg became the mom I never had and no, you crass motherfuckers—I wasn't doing her. Jesus. I know that's what you all thought, and Meg and I laughed about it a lot, but that wasn't it at all. I fell a little in love with her because she represented the one thing I never had. A mom. So get your heads out of the gutter.

"Okay, now I need to be serious for a minute. I know I've left you in a mess with the band. I get it. But this isn't the end. That's not what I want, and it's not what our fans want. You need to replace me. Find someone who's going to rock with you like I did. Maybe even better. Take the summer to find the right fit and hit the road hard this fall. Promote the fuck out of the album. I have one final request for that. Would you mind titling it, 'Love, Carter'? Some of the songs on this one were my favorites, and since it's my last, I'd like that. Please.

"It's getting late, and I have a few more letters to write, so here are the last few things I want to leave you with. First, I don't want you fuckers to be mad or sad for too long. Okay? Promise? I'm in a better place. Any place where I'm no longer an addict, jonesing for my next fix, is a better place. I would've spent the rest of my life hating myself every time I gave in to the pull. I want to be done. I am done.

"Second, I need you to fire the fuck out of Aurora. You'll find out all my secrets when my attorney reads the will. I just want to say I'm sorry, because she's been holding shit over my head. I was trying to protect the innocent. Mostly Tommy—but the threesome was your idea, man. That's all I'm going to say about that."

"Jesus fuck," Tommy muttered, looking like someone had just punched him in the head.

"Should I keep reading?" Kingston asked.

"Finish it," I said.

"Finally, I need you guys to take care of River. My son. He's innocent in all this and without me around, you guys need to step up. Tommy, don't blame Harley. This is between you and me. I was in love with her, but she was in love with you. In the end, she left us both. The baby was an accident. But he's going to need a dad. Four uncles would be okay too. If you can't forgive me, please forgive her. She put us, the brotherhood of the band, before herself. I took care of them financially, and now I need you guys to step up and do the rest. River needs a father figure so he doesn't grow up as fucked up as I did.

"Okay, that's it. I love you guys. Don't stay mad at me too long, all right? Even if you don't agree, I'm doing what was right for me. Carter. P.S. I saw a bass player not that long ago on the Strip who blew me away. If you're going to hold auditions, make sure you invite Devyn Cates."

WE SAT THERE for a long time, digesting the contents of Carter's final message. It didn't seem like there was much we could say. We'd somehow missed that Carter had a death wish, and I wasn't even going to try and dissect the whole love triangle thing with him, Tommy, and Harley. That was between them. And frankly, at this point, what difference did it make?

"We should take a day to think about things," Kingston said as we pulled into the big circular driveway in front of my house.

"I don't want to talk band business tonight," I said. "Tonight is about remembering Carter. But tomorrow, before we meet with Aurora, we need to have made a decision. Are we firing her? Because I'll be honest—I'm out if we're not."

There was only a short silence before Kingston said, "I'm done with her. She fucked you over and she was actively trying to manipulate Carter. We don't need that kind of aggravation."

"Agreed." Kellan nodded.

"Yeah." Tommy scratched his head. "I thought loyalty was important, but she's not really loyal to us. She's only loyal to the cut she takes from all our money."

"I'll call Rodney tomorrow," Kingston said, referring to our attorney. "Get him to deal with the contractual parts of this."

"I don't give a shit about the money. If she wants residuals from this album, give them to her. I just want her gone." I rested my hand on the car door. "But we don't say anything tonight."

"Agreed."

We walked into the house as a group, and it took me a while to greet the handful of guests who'd gotten here before us. I needed to find Presley, though, so I went upstairs to our room. She wasn't there, but I heard voices in Jeremy's room.

"He's so beautiful," Cheyenne's familiar voice was saying. "Look at those eyes!"

"I know. Fatima showed me some of Zeke's baby pictures and they're practically identical at this age."

"I can't imagine being a mum," Cheyenne said, "but I think I could get used to playing with the wee one."

"Anytime."

I paused outside the door, wondering if I should interrupt. Presley hadn't spent time with any friends since we'd been together, so it was nice to see that she'd found one in Cheyenne. I needed to talk to her, but it could wait a few minutes.

"Are you doing all right, Presley?" Cheyenne's voice dropped slightly. "I'm sure this has been a lot for you to handle, with you and Zeke still being pretty new."

"It's been…" Presley's voice trailed and there were a few seconds before she finished her thought. "Lonely. Zeke and Aunt Meg really took Carter's death hard, which is totally understandable, and while I'm a little sad too, I barely knew him. We only talked a handful of times, you know? And I don't have any friends here, so I've been alone more than anything."

"Well, you have my number. If I'm in town, I'm happy to go shopping or meet you for lunch or just come play with the baby. Anytime, Presley."

"Thank you. I appreciate that."

Damn, I really felt like a jerk after hearing that.

I'd promised her she'd never be alone again, yet it was happening right under my nose.

Well, that ended now.

"Hey." I walked into the bedroom, smiling at the two ladies. Cheyenne was in the rocking chair with Jeremy on her lap, and Presley was sitting on the floor with her legs tucked under her. "Getting your baby fix?" I asked Cheyenne.

She laughed. "Yep. Then I give him back and go on my way. I'm in no way ready for one of my own!" She got up and handed me my son. "I'm going to go find something to eat. I'll see you two downstairs."

"Bye." Presley smiled after her.

"Hey, beautiful." I sank down on the floor next to her, bouncing Jeremy on my knee.

"Hi." Her eyes searched my face. "Everything okay?"

"That's what I should be asking you."

"I'm fine."

"You're not. You just told Cheyenne how lonely you are."

She dipped her head. "A little. But I'm not upset. I know you're grieving."

"I'm mad," I said softly. "At myself. I let you down, even though it wasn't intentional."

"These were extenuating circumstances," she said.

"Yes, but I promised to take care of you, and I haven't been doing a very good job of it. We just got married and instead of making sure you were adjusting okay, I pushed you away. That's not fair, no matter what else is going on." I reached for one of her hands. "We're married. You need to be able to count on me even when bad shit happens. And vice versa. I love you, Presley, and I want to make sure you feel that every single day for the rest of our lives."

39

P*resley*

Tears stung my eyelids.

I'd been keeping a tight rein on my emotions since our impromptu nuptials because deep down I'd been afraid this was nothing more than a marriage of convenience. I hadn't allowed myself to believe he could ever love me the way I loved him. I'd subconsciously convinced myself that I could be happy even if he wasn't in love with me. That I could and would make this work for Jeremy. Because walking away was no longer an option.

Hearing him say that he loved me opened a floodgate of tears that I'd been holding back for months.

"Oh, baby, I'm sorry." With Jeremy in the crook of his left arm, he used his right to pull me close. "Please don't cry."

I sobbed against his chest, a torrent of emotion escaping me as I let go of all the things I'd been keeping bottled up. From the fallout I'd dealt with after the first time we'd slept together to Aunt Meg's heart attack to Carter's death, I hadn't realized just how tightly wound I'd been. How much I'd been burying to keep from falling apart.

"Shh. I'm here." Zeke pressed soft kisses to the top of my head, holding me against him. "God, I'm sorry. I never want to be the reason you cry."

"I...thought...you...never...would," I choked out between sobs.

"Never would what?" he asked.

"I…thought…" I hiccoughed. "I thought you'd never…love me too."

"Ah, shit, I hate that you felt that way. I'm sorry for giving you reasons to doubt me, Sunny. I've handled everything so badly. I was trying to protect you and protect myself and all kinds of other dumb shit. Please forgive me."

"Will you… say it again?"

He leaned over to gently but firmly kiss my lips. "I love you. More than anything. You're my sunshine. The light in my darkness. The only thing that's worthwhile in my life anymore is our family. You and Jeremy. Aunt Meg and my parents. What we've found together and the future we're going to build."

"I didn't think you wanted… *this*. I thought maybe I was just convenient."

"Fuck no." His eyes darkened. "You think I'd marry you for convenience? We never even got the pre-nup notarized."

I grimaced. I'd honestly forgotten all about it. "Oh, no. I'm sorry! We should have—"

"Don't you see?" He interrupted me with a fierce look on his face. "I don't care about that. I don't give a shit about the money. Take it all. Go shopping tomorrow and spend every dime. I couldn't care less."

"I love you," I whispered. They might have been the scariest words I'd ever uttered, but Zeke's face softened.

"I fucking love hearing that."

I'd smeared makeup on his shirt and Jeremy was starting to fuss, so I sat up, trying to get my emotions back under control. This was too much and just the right amount, at the same time.

"I was waiting for the perfect time to say the words the first time," he said after a moment. "But then Carter…" He sighed, looking away. "I still can't believe he's gone."

"I know." I rested a hand on his thigh, smiling as he held Jeremy up over his head and made silly faces at him to get him to stop fussing.

"Let's go away," he said after a moment.

"Now?" I asked. "Where?"

"Tomorrow is busy. We have to be at the reading of Carter's will and then we have a meeting with Aurora. She doesn't know it yet, but we're going to fire her."

"The band agreed?" I asked in surprise.

"Yup. So, while I'm out, you should pack and book everything for us. I'll leave you my credit card. Anywhere in the world you want to go."

"Without Jeremy?" I asked slowly.

"You and I need time alone together. He has two grandparents and a great-aunt who adore him and need a distraction after the last few days. And we need a mini-honeymoon before we take the real one."

"The real one?" I asked, arching a brow.

"After the real wedding." He smiled. "How does August sound?"

I frowned. "*This* August?"

"You want to wait until next August?"

"No, but... can we plan a wedding in two months or so?"

"Money talks, sunshine. So yeah, we can."

"Okay."

"How about Hawaii? Find a bungalow or something on Maui where we can just be. You and me, with nowhere to go, nothing to do but be together, and fall in love all over again."

"Okay." I nodded, fighting off another wave of emotion. "Yes. That sounds perfect."

"We have a house full of guests. You ready to go downstairs?"

"I think I need to wash my face first, but I'll meet you down there in a few."

"All right."

We both got to our feet, and he put Jeremy in his crib before pulling me against him. "I love you, Presley. Don't ever let me get away with not showing you how I feel. Never again."

"You can count on it." I leaned against him and closed my eyes. For the first time in my life, I felt complete. At peace. Loved. And it was glorious.

Zeke was gone a long time the next day. He'd left just after nine and now it was almost five and he wasn't home yet. I'd booked us five days in Hawaii, leaving first thing in the morning, so I hoped it was okay because I hadn't heard from him. We were packed, Fatima had helped me book a car to take us to the airport, and we'd even gone shopping for a few hours. I had a couple of pretty new dresses and a bathing suit, and I'd written out pages of instructions for them regarding Jeremy. The only thing left was for Zeke to get home so I could tell him the plan.

He walked in just after six looking exhausted.

"Hi." I met him in the foyer, bouncing Jeremy on my hip.

"Hey, beautiful."

Jeremy immediately held out his arms to his father and Zeke took him from me, pausing to quickly press his lips to mine as we walked deeper into the house.

"Are you hungry? I saved you a plate of Aunt Meg's meatloaf and home-made mashed potatoes."

"Sounds good. You mind if I go upstairs and change?" he asked me. "I'll be right down."

"Sure. Go ahead." I took Jeremy from him and went into the kitchen to warm up the plate I'd saved for him. I had a million questions but didn't say anything until he was sitting at the island and had taken a bite.

"Damn, this is good," he said, chewing.

"Beer?" I asked, pulling a bottle of Guinness out of the fridge.

"Thanks." He smiled. "Reminds me of the night we met."

I laughed. "Me too."

"I have so much to tell you," he said between bites.

"Take your time."

"Well, we fired Aurora."

"Good."

"Yeah. But the less good news is that we'll be retiring Onyx Knight."

"What?" I stared at him.

"We don't have any kind of plan going forward, other than releasing the next album, so we're calling it quits."

"Babe." I stared at him. "You must be devastated."

"I don't know what I am," he admitted. "The good news is I've got money in trust for Jeremy so he'll be set for life. This house is paid for, along with my house in Atlanta and—"

"You have a house in Atlanta?"

"Yeah. My parents decided they wanted to live there. Until they didn't. So it's big and empty. We might sell it, unless you'd rather live there than here."

"I can't imagine why we'd want to move. Except the cost of living in Georgia is probably a lot less expensive than here."

"It is, but I don't know that I want to be so far away from my friends and a lot of the music industry. That's all here."

"Then we can stay. Let's sell the house in Atlanta and re-invest the money in something more practical, like a retirement account or whatever."

"That was my thought too. But not now." He put down his fork. "I just want to be... me. Us. For a while. You know? Husband and father. Not Big Z the rockstar. His life is fucking exhausting."

"Then don't be him. You've been battling two worlds for so long, it's no wonder you're tired of it."

"Yeah." His eyes met mine. "You going to be happy here, Sunny? I have plenty of money, so we don't have to worry about that, and I have a feeling the new album will sell well. I'll be getting royalties for the rest of my life, in case you're wondering about the future."

"I'm not," I said softly. "As long as I have you and Jeremy and Aunt Meg, I don't need anything else."

"I love you, Mrs. Zerkesian."

"I love you too, Mr. Zerkesian."

We smiled at each other.

Life was so fucking good.

EPILOGUE

Z^{eke}

Presley's article about Carter came out at the end of June. Her website had so many hits it crashed, and I had to hire a software specialist to help us get it back up. The fallout, for lack of a better word, was incredible. As we'd expected, there was quite a bit of speculation about my wife being the one to publish Carter's last official interview, but there was even more love and support. For her writing, the way she'd portrayed Carter and his struggles, and her ability to bring the man beneath the rockstar to life.

It was pretty cool to watch her flourish and essentially come into her own, right before my eyes. I loved her regardless, but seeing her succeed felt good. I'd given her an opportunity, but then she'd taken it and run. Not only was she working on the next issue, but she'd also contacted her old advisor and he'd arranged for her to re-take her final class. The one she needed to graduate. It had gotten to a point where I was pretty sure it was more important to me than it was to her, but that was okay. I wanted her to have everything.

We were planning a formal wedding and reception that we'd have right here in the yard, and I was enjoying her excitement even though it wasn't that big of a deal to me. She and Aunt Meg and my mother giggled a lot—a whole lot—and that made me smile every single time I saw it happen.

Mom and I were getting along a thousand times better these days. After Carter's death she'd apologized to me for all the spending and insanity that had been going on. She'd admitted to a feeling of entitlement but also one of loss. Despite living in my house and seeing me in the media, she'd said she had never felt more distance between us. The more she spent, the more she felt a connection to me. It was a little twisted, but I understood it a lot more now and worked hard to make time for family. Not just Presley and Jeremy —who were always my priority—but also my parents and grandmother and siblings.

And it felt right.

The band had also moved up the release date of the album, and it had gone live at midnight last night. It was selling like crazy and number one on all the charts we had access to. It was a double-edged sword because the excitement somehow felt hollow without Carter, especially when the words 'Love, Carter' were all over the media. The band was coming over for dinner in a little while because we'd decided we were stronger together, but it was hard to think about being with the guys without Carter.

"Kingston is here," Presley said, sticking her head in the door of my den. I spent a lot of time in here lately, though she was often with me. I didn't want to shut her out again, and she wasn't going to allow it anyway.

"I'll be right out," I told her.

"What's that?" she asked, noting the folded papers in my hand.

"Carter's letter."

"You read it." She came over to me and sat on my lap. "Are you okay?"

I nodded.

"I hate that he had to die, but I kind of get it now. He was so unhappy, Presley." I shook my head. "But you know what's cool?"

"What?"

"You and Meg and Jeremy made him happy towards the end."

Her eyes puddled with tears. "Oh, hell, Zeke." She swiped at her eyes.

"I know. I'm sorry."

"Will you let me read it?"

"I'm going to read it to the band."

"Oh, okay. That's nice. As long as it's not too personal."

"Nah. Carter knew I would read it to them."

"There's the doorbell," she said softly, pressing a light kiss on my lips. "I'll go answer it while you get yourself together."

She already knew me so well.

Our mini-honeymoon had been exactly what we'd needed. Five quiet days in Hawaii, getting to know each other on a deeper level than anything we'd done before. There was sex—dear god, the sex... but that was another story—but there had been bonding. Talking and loving and laughing. Telling each other things that I knew I'd never imagined telling anyone.

But Presley wasn't just anyone.

She was my wife.

The love of my life.

Abruptly, I got up and stuffed Carter's letter in my back pocket. We had company, and I needed to be present. Not just physically but emotionally.

"Hey." I nodded at Kingston and Tommy, who were having a beer at the island in the kitchen. Kellan had said he would be a few minutes late, so we talked until he arrived.

"Sorry I'm late," Kellan said as he walked in. "It was a long day."

"Yeah?" I eyed him. "Everything okay?"

"Didi and I broke up."

I snorted. "Is that news? Come on, man. You guys break up every other week."

He slowly shook his head. "It's different this time. It's for good."

I squinted. "How come?"

"She's been telling Aurora everything we've talked about since we fired her."

It had been about a month, and while there hadn't been any earth-shattering conversations, that kind of betrayal was potentially serious. At least it was to me. We hadn't made any firm decisions about the future yet, but I was hoping we were going to soon. That was part of the reason I'd invited everyone over tonight.

"Do you mean it?" I asked him. "Because you two have a history of this kind of thing."

"Like I said, this is different," he said quietly. "Losing Carter made me re-evaluate a lot of things in my life. Including Didi. The fact of the matter is, I was never going to marry her or give her the life she wanted. She was easy. Convenient. Comfortable. But I was never in love with her. And believe me, I tried. I finally started to realize we both deserved better. But now that she showed her true colors, I guess my reluctance to make things permanent between us makes sense. There was always something missing. Now I kind of know what it was."

"Good riddance to bad rubbish," I muttered, taking a pull from my bottle of beer and then holding it out in a mock salute.

"You can say that again," Kingston agreed, touching his bottle to mine.

"You guys are number one on iTunes and Spotify," Presley said, coming into the room looking at something on her phone.

"Sales are the best we've had in a long time," Kingston agreed. "Maybe ever. We don't have numbers yet, but I've had Dorian on top of it all day and we're getting a lot of love on satellite radio too."

"All the reviews I've seen have been amazing," Presley said.

"Good news all around," Kellan said.

"Which is why I think it's time for me to talk to you about Carter's letter," I said after a moment. "This was separate from the one he left for the band."

"What's it say?" Tommy asked quietly. He hadn't said much about the situation with Carter, Harley, and River, and there was a lot about that in the letter. I figured it was time to share parts of it.

I didn't know for sure that Carter would have wanted me to, but he wasn't here to guide me, and my heart told me this was something we needed. Even if we decided not to keep the band together, we needed to repair our friendship. It had been important to Carter and after reading his letter, I realized just how important it was to me.

"He talked a lot about our early friendship, mine and his, high school and stuff," I said after a moment. "But mostly he talked about the band. The five of us. What we'd accomplished not just as musicians, but as friends. The friendship was the most important thing to him. So important that he kept his son hidden from the world, even though he loved him more than anything."

"Aw, fuck. Is this gonna make me cry again?" Kellan muttered.

"Maybe." I paused, looking around the room and settling on Tommy. "He didn't tell me what went on between the three of you—you, him, and Harley—but he did say he wanted to make it right. He'd been trying to work up the nerve to talk to you, to get you and Harley in the same room together. But he realized he wasn't going to have the chance, so he left that to me."

"Fuck." Tommy was staring out at nothing, the look on his face inscrutable.

"As you already know, he left everything to River, with money in trust for Harley too. And I'm the administrator of that trust, to make sure she always has what she needs to take care of him."

"Good." Tommy still wasn't looking at us.

"Beyond that, the thing he wanted most was for us to continue with music. He said that in his letter to the band and he went on and on about it in the letter to me. And that's why we're here tonight. To vote and make a decision. He knew we would take the easy way out and disband, but he was determined that we don't."

"He was a lot more astute than we gave him credit for," Kingston said. "And I really fucking miss him."

"Same." I leaned against the island, watching Tommy. "Tom? You okay?"

"I don't know what to say," he said. "This is a lot to work through. Not just losing him but finding out that he's the reason Harley left me. Finding out they had a kid together. Knowing they were keeping something so huge from me. It fucking hurts."

"And that's why they never told you."

"But he's gone now," Kellan said quietly.

"This could be a fresh start for us," Kingston added. "New band member, new management, new music."

"New almost everything," I added. "Except our brand. That stays the same."

"Let's vote," Tommy said.

"It has to be unanimous." I finally got him to look me in the eye. "This doesn't work if all four of us aren't on board."

"It's a yes from me," Kingston said.

"Yes from me," I said, looking at Kellan.

He looked from me to Kingston to Tommy before slowly nodding. "Abso-fucking-lutely."

Tommy sighed.

A few seconds ticked by as he stared out at nothing again.

"I love this band," he said finally. "The music, the fans, all of it. Including you guys." He cleared his throat. "Including Carter."

Kingston looked like he was going to say something, but I gave a quick shake of my head, indicating he needed to let Tommy talk this out.

"Something had started to break with the inner workings of the band," he continued. "It started after my divorce. It got worse every time Carter went to rehab. In retrospect, I know Aurora fed that, keeping us at odds so she could control Carter with his secrets and Kellan to a degree through Didi." He lifted his head and looked around. "That ends now. Onyx Knight was built on our sweat and tears. Our music. And more than that, our friendship. It's time to go back to our roots."

"So... yes?" Kingston asked quietly.

"Yes. Fuck yes." Tommy nodded. "Let's do this."

We all grinned and lifted our beer bottles, moving close enough to clink them together. "To Onyx Knight!"

"To Carter," I said softly.

"To Carter!"

We touched glasses again and then each took a drink.

"I just have one question," Tommy said after a moment.

I arched a brow.

"Who the hell is Devyn Cates?"

Thanks so much for reading Rock Bottom! I hope you loved Zeke and Presley as much I did. Next up is ROCK GOD, Kingston and Devyn's story. For more info, turn the page!

ROCK GOD (ROCK HARDER BOOK TWO)

They call me The Rock God. As lead singer of the multi-platinum selling rock band Onyx Knight, I have a life most people can't even dream of... until it all becomes a nightmare.

Our bass player dies.

Now we're tasked with the impossible job of replacing him or hanging it up for good.

On top of the world just shy of my thirtieth birthday, I can't imagine walking away. Not now. Not from the money, the fame or the women. Half the music industry might be vying for the job, but no one feels right.

Until Devon Cates walks in and blows us away. Especially me.

We all have secrets, and Devon is no exception. I'm determined to find out what hers are, without getting too close. But I can't seem to stay away.

When the truth comes out, it could be another death spiral for the band... one I'm not sure we can come back from.

Get Rock God here!

ALSO BY KAT MIZERA

Las Vegas Sidewinders:

Dominic

Cody's Christmas Surprise

Drake

Karl

Anatoli

Zakk

Toli & Tessa

Brock

Vladimir

Royce

Nate

Sidewinders: Ever After

Jared

Dmitri's Christmas Angel

Ian

Dax *(A Royal Protectors/Sidewinders crossover novel)*

Suze's Diary (A Sidewinders Companion Novella)

Sidewinders: Generations:

Zaan

Tore

Anton

Van

Decker

Alaska Blizzard:

Defending Dani

Holding Hailey

Winning Whitney

Losing Laurel

Saving Sara

Chasing Charli

A Very Blizzard Christmas

Tending Tara

Calling Cassie

Playing Peyton

Catching Lana (An Alaska Blizzard Companion Novel)

St. Louis Mavericks (with Brenda Rothert)

Hard Fall

Hard Limit

Hard Pass

Hard Luck

Hard Hit

Lauderdale Knights:

Knight Before Christmas (A Garland Grove/Lauderdale Knights holiday prequel novel)

Slap Shot

Big Shot

Long Shot

Hot Shot

Sure Shot

Rough Shot

Rock Hard:

Play

Pause

Rewind

Fast Forward

Rock Harder:

Rock Bottom

Rock God

The Royal Trilogy:

Nowhere Left to Fall

Nowhere Left to Run

Nowhere Left to Hide

Royal Protectors:

Sandor

Cocky Protector (book 1.5, part of the Cocky Heroes Club series)

Xander

Axel

Dax *(A Royal Protectors/Sidewinders crossover novel)*

Inferno:

Salvation's Inferno

Temptation's Inferno

Redemption's Inferno

Tropical Inferno (formerly "Tropical Ice")

Romancing Europe:

Adonis in Athens

Smitten in Santorini

Lucky in Lugano

View Kat's entire collection of books at www.KatMizera.com

ABOUT THE AUTHOR

USA Today Bestselling author Kat Mizera was born in Miami Beach with a healthy dose of wanderlust. She's lived from coast to coast, and everywhere in between, but home is wherever her family is.

A devoted mom and wife to her wonderful and supportive husband (Kevin) and two amazing boys (Nick and Max), Kat loves to travel the globe with her adventurous, hockey loving family. Greece is at the top of that list. She hopes to one day retire there, spending her days writing books on the beach.

Kat is former freelance sports writer who now writes steamy hockey romance about her favorite fictional teams, the Las Vegas Sidewinders and the Alaska Blizzard. The library of novels she's penned also include sexy contemporary stories about baseball stars, alpha sex club owners, special forces heroes, rock stars and royalty. Regardless of genre, her books about bad boys with hearts of gold will steal your breath, rock your world and melt your heart.

WHERE TO FOLLOW KAT:

WEBSITE
FACEBOOK
TWITTER
INSTAGRAM
BOOKBUB
KAT'S PRIVATE FACEBOOK GROUP